NIGHT AS CLEAR AS DAY

Thirty-Five Short Stories

PAUL O'DONNELL

PAGE PUBLISHING, INC.
New York, NY

First originally published by Page Publishing, Inc. 2017

These short stories are works of fiction. Any resemblance to actual characters or events is entirely coincidental and unintentional.

ISBN 978-1-64082-971-8 (Paperback)
ISBN 978-1-64082-972-5 (Digital)

Printed in the United States of America

To Mother Maureen McCabe, OCSO

Even the darkness is not dark to Thee,
And the night is as clear as day.

—Psalm 139

Contents

The Farthest Thunder

The mob grew in size as it rushed down the street. Stopping to throw rocks into store windows and at passing cars, they felt rage push them on. Kim Jung Lee watched them coming, seeing them loot and then set fire to the liquor store two blocks up. Now they all were drinking heavily, adding fuel to the flames. And they were heading straight for his little market. His wife and daughter had gone home just minutes before, even though the sixteen-year-old Sung spoke English and might reason with these . . . what were they? Hadn't he seen them years before—back home in Korea during the war? It was when the Americans pushed the Communist forces back over the thirty-ninth parallel that a horde of Chinese red guards pushed back and overran his country, inundating his village. Then, he had seen them coming too. But now, more disturbing still, he could hear them like the roll of distant thunder, threatening a dreadful downpour. At that time, so long ago, there had been no way to run away. It was the same now. Things hadn't changed so much in forty years. The past, sooner or later, always caught up to the present. His newly adopted country was still not far enough away from the madness. Curses heralded the approaching mob. Gunshots echoed, and carried by the wind, reported like different languages from the past—first Chinese, followed by anguished Korean, but now Spanish and broken English.

That neighborhood, forty-seven blocks south of downtown Los Angeles, was comprised mostly of African Americans and Latinos. The former were being gradually displaced by the constant influx of the latter. Since the Watts riots of the 1960s, blacks had gained some economic ground, with many moving to far-flung middle-class neighborhoods. Only an hour before, a court ruling let four white police officers go free, the very ones who had beaten the black Rodney King in front of a video camera. The whole lurid scene had been replayed *ad infinitem* on the evening news for months. Blacks, hearing of the verdict, were outraged at the travesty of justice while many Latinos, not knowing much English, didn't really seem to understand what was happening. Mr. Kim surmised that both ethnic groups just wanted to wreak some kind of revenge. They both were somehow second-class citizens, seething in a country of equals. This particular mob, however, consisted not of African Americans but of young Spanglish-speaking gang members, both men and women.

Kim strongly suspected they were not interested in justice or the lack thereof. No, despite their parents' travails as new immigrants in America, many of them were simply jumping on the bandwagon in their lust to loot. He himself had come as an immigrant to this nation of immigrants and settled in Korea-town over on Vermont. Borrowing money from his wife's rich uncle—with a high interest rate to be paid monthly—he managed to set up a small minimarket in South Central, where Caucasian businesses feared to tread. And now, these prodigal sons and daughters of new immigrants were coming for him, harboring as they did, the false belief that he had, in turn, been exploiting them. He always tried to be fair, but still, not being able to buy in bulk, higher prices had to be passed on to the consumer. But he knew that some of them resented him for the shape of his eyes.

Mr. Kim knew from experience that the first generation of any immigrant group coming to America rarely succeeded in feeling at home. Eventually, the second generation, their children, would enter more fully into the new society. Perhaps they might not look the part, but at least they would be speaking the language better than their parents. The parents, like Kim and his wife, were permanent prisoners of the past, forced to remember and long for that which, in reality, did not exist anymore. They lived like Heinlein's *Strangers in a Strange Land.* At times, Southern California itself resembled a work of science fiction. South Central was much like another planet, he often mused, especially at night. But then again, the moon did not have over one hundred thousand gang members currently battling it out, block by block, for control of the local drug trade. This was the Brave New World he had brought his wife and daughter to. Sung, his beautiful daughter, so young and smart, had adapted almost too well, too easily forgetting some important cultural norms. She often spoke—hardly ever in Korean—as if Korea did not exist. He often wondered if all the sacrifice was worth it.

The mob was now one block away. Their voices rumbled then exploded into screams of terror and delight as a parked car suddenly burst into flames. When the owner of the vehicle came running out of his house wielding a baseball bat to protect his property, he was immediately surrounded and beaten with his own weapon. At that moment, under the watchful eye of a helicopter camera crew, just few blocks away, at the intersection of Normandie and Florence, the unfortunate trucker, Reginald Denny, was getting the same treatment with bricks to the head. And the police? LA's finest were nowhere in sight, neither protecting nor serving that particular day.

Mr. Kim called 911, but the lines were overloaded. He was tempted to lock the doors and make a run for it but decided that if he did, what little he had managed to build over the years would surely be destroyed. His small market sold fruits, vegetables, snacks, and drinkables of all sorts. Where were his employees? There were two of them—actually only one. The day before, he had been forced to fire big lazy Raul—for stealing—a practice that had been going on for some time. Kim had looked the other way as long as he could because he thought it would keep Raul's friends—who were mostly hardcore gang-bangers—from robbing the place. But now that the young man was gone—leaving with many threats—that left only Jesus. Chuche, as he was nicknamed, was too small and timid to be a *cholo*. Kim thought it odd but somehow endearing that Mexicans would have a nickname for their Savior. Chuche was quiet, a hard worker, uncomplaining even for less than the minimum wage. In the few conversations they had managed, the young man said he was saving his money, not for a car like all his peers, but for a computer and community college. After hours, over the past year, Kim endeavored to teach him tae kwon do. And the boy was an apt pupil, though he still lacked the sheer strength to deal with bigger, more experienced adversaries. Yet Kim sensed that Chuche was just a good kid from a decent family, one who had the misfortune of growing up in the *barrio*. It was better that the boy was not here to face this angry crowd.

Kim looked forlornly at his shop windows that had no metal shutters to protect them from thrown objects. The front door itself was glass. He had little insurance, so if they stole everything, that would be the end. He could not afford to borrow more money. What then could he do, move back to Seoul? His wife would be happy, of course, but his Americanized daughter would die a slow death there. Like Chinese water torture, drop by drop, day by day. Every moment away from home was like that. Kim did have a shotgun, and for a brief moment he thought of using it on himself. No, what little remained of his childhood faith—learned from the missionaries— forbade despair as being a worse sin than any temptations leading up to it. Going inside and pulling the heavy gun out from under the counter, he carried it back out front with him. He kept it always loaded, but even during seven previous robberies, had never fired it. A robber with a gun is infuriated at the sight of someone else with a gun. Kim sincerely wished he could use it but realized it would be better to put it away and face the mob alone and unarmed. But now, there was no time to put it back inside; they were too close. So he hurriedly shoved it into the trash can next to the pay phone chained outside the front door. He thought of calling the police again, begging them to save him, but he realized, with horror, that it was too late.

In the following days, the citizens of Los Angeles would learn about their police commissioner, Chief Daryl Gates, hobnobbing with the rich and shameless at a political fund-raiser up in Beverly Hills while the city burned. Because there was no help to be found in human beings, and though he felt it a useless gesture, Kim prayed to a deity who seemed just as distant as he did back in 1951.

The first rioters to arrive yelled something he couldn't understand. Then a thrown bottle smashed against the side of his head. He fell to his knees, fascinated somehow by the blood dripping between his splayed hands onto the sidewalk. Strangely, it was like he was standing in the window of a house nobody lives in and he was calmly surveying the scene outside. He knew he was surrounded, and they were reigning blows down upon him, but he felt little pain. Why? It didn't seem to matter. The past welled up inside him, suddenly overflowing into the present moment. The modern-day mob transformed into Chinese soldiers, of forty years ago, their voices like knives. How much time had passed, he didn't know, only that this was eternity. A single voice rose above the others. It was small at first but seemed to grow louder until it cracked through the droning. It was telling the throng to back off. Kim wondered if he had already died. Or was his halfhearted prayer being answered? Then, through the noise and pain, like the cadence of some demented poetry, Kim recognized his ex-employee Raul's voice, so he smiled ruefully. Looking up, he saw the young man's distorted features, the darting, wild eyes, and the veins in his neck pulsing with adrenaline.

"This *pinche* chink was my boss!" he shouted, arresting everyone's attention. "Yeah, and he fired me yesterday for stealing! He don't know what stealing is!" A roar of approval signaled the mad rush inside. So the looting began. Raul exulted, looking around the sidewalk for some blunt instrument. He spotted the butt of the shotgun sticking out of the trash can. "What do we have here?" he whooped, waving the weapon over his head. Kim envisioned the soldiers enter his ancestral family home back in the village, shouting when they discovered his mother, father, and sister hiding within.

At that moment, something interrupted his memory. A car screeched to a halt a few feet away. It was Sung, his daughter, screaming for the crowd to leave her father alone. "Poor, reckless daughter," thought Kim, "I cannot protect you. Why did you come back?" Many arms grabbed her, pawing her blouse, dragging her inside the market. Sung screamed, struggling desperately to free herself, calling for his help. It was odd how her voice sounded exactly like his sister's when the soldiers had taken her. He could do nothing then either. Held by strong arms, he was equally as helpless now.

Raul watched all this and didn't know what to do first. Aiming the shotgun at Kim's head, the feeling in his loins fought for control. Wouldn't it be nice to rape the daughter in front of the father, he thought? The old bastard couldn't speak English worth a damn, but then again, neither could he. In school, they insisted on teaching him in Spanish (which he already spoke at home anyway) instead of in English. Thus deprived of fluency in both languages, the resulting *pidgin* hybrid left him—one of many thousands—unfit for universities or higher-paying jobs. That left only gang life on the meanest of streets. Controlling turf meant inspiring fear, the only thing he was good at. After losing some respect in the hood for having been gainfully employed for a brief while, he was ready to make up for lost time and redeem his tarnished reputation.

Kim cried, "Please—I beg you, Raul—take what you want, but leave my daughter alone! Please . . ."

The crowd imitated his accent, while dragging him inside too. "Prease! Prease! Ret my daughter arone!"

Kim looked up to see tattooed arms holding the struggling Sung down, pinning her back on top of the checkout counter. Sweeping everything on to the floor, one hooded figure emptied the register while two others pulled off the girl's blue jeans, forcing her legs apart.

Raul dragged Kim closer, saying, "You get a front-row seat, old man."

Kim groaned. Nausea engulfed him. The unthinkable was happening again. Vivid memories of his beloved older sister, constricted his chest, cutting off his breath. They had held her down too. The Americans, overwhelmed, had retreated, leaving his family behind. The same nightmare was being replayed, but in America. The three were pushing each other aside, each vying to be the first. Their ringleader, Raul, yelled at them to hold her for him, and began pulling down his pants. Kim closed his eyes but could not close his ears to his daughter's desperate cries for help.

Waiting, everything seemed frozen in time. A fitful noise made amid the confusion shook him. A slight disturbance in the air made Kim open his eyes. He realized suddenly that once again, something new, someone unexpected, was pushing through the chanting crowd—through the door, to where he was being forced to kneel. Amid so many old memories, how could so many new things intrude? Now—whoever it was—was pulling Raul off his daughter. Kim looked up to see that it was Chuche. For a moment, he couldn't believe what he was witnessing. Despite being so much smaller, Chuche had managed to free Sung from all four of the gang members. Sung stood unsteadily, crying and trying to cover herself. Raul rushed at his former colleague, but with one lightning quick movement, Chuche tipped his balance so that the bigger man tumbled sideways, falling with a crash into a pyramid of canned goods. There followed that timeless moment when surprise leaves everyone paralyzed and silent. Huffing and puffing, and extremely embarrassed, Raul struggled to his feet, impeded by his baggy pants that hung halfway to his knees. The three husky teens who had been holding Sung looked at him, shocked. Chuche rushed to put a protective arm around her. The two of them began backing away toward the front door.

Suddenly, the three youths began to laugh at Raul, who was still having great difficulty pulling up his pants. Red-faced—he charged again, roaring at Chuche. Chuche let go of Sung, dropped to one knee under Raul's outstretched arms, and with the fluidity of much practice, grabbed the left arm, swinging it around so that his attacker's head slammed squarely into the front counter. Instead of helping, the other looters taunted their stunned leader, who, recovering quickly, lunged sideways at Chuche. But remembering one special move Kim had taught him, he stepped forward and tripped Raul's legs, this time sending him sprawling at the feet of Kim, his former employer. It happened so suddenly even the two guys pinioning the old man's arms let go in surprise.

Instantly, Kim Jung Lee grabbed the shotgun, which lay on the floor at his feet, and aimed it at Raul, who struggled to get up off the floor. Seeing this, his friends all backed away, turning to run out the back door. No use getting one's head blown off by some "crazy Chinaman." Kim shouted at them in Korean, and those few that heard him understood the tone, if not the exact meaning of the words. Kim was beginning to think that this war was almost over when Raul reached up and grabbed the barrel of the shotgun. Kim struggled to hold on while his adversary twisted it, toward his face, all the while groping for the trigger. Sung screamed. Chuche jumped at the two struggling bodies, desperately trying to yank the gun away from them both. Raul gained the advantage, forcing the deadly shaft up under Kim's jaw. Then with one frenzied effort, Chuche pulled the gun toward himself—just as Raul's fingers squeezed the trigger. Both barrels exploded into his chest, knocking him backward against the wall. Kim fell to the ground next to Raul, both gasping for breath. Raul stared at each of them in turn—Kim, his daughter Sung, and then finally over at Chuche, who lay in a pool of his own blood—before stumbling to his feet and running out the front door.

The Culprit Life

Monsignor Moreno woke in a bad temper like always. This time it was the Mexican family two doors down, celebrating a *quincenera* with loud music until all hours. Like all the times before, the police—when they finally did show up—slapped a few wrists but then went away, leaving the priest tossing, turning and grumbling till dawn. He wearily shaved, showered, went into his private chapel, mouthed his morning breviary and descended to the kitchen to digest the morning paper and a substantial breakfast. Doctors with all their pontificating diets be damned, he thought. A steady stream of assistants had learned from hard experience never to interrupt this waking process, or at least not before the second cup of *espresso*, especially imported from *Italia*.

Monsignor Moreno, a diocesan priest, incardinated in the largest diocese in the United States, in Los Angeles, California, was actually a *Romano*. He was related to—or so he told everyone—a long line of Roman ecclesiastics. His uncle had been a cardinal and was once thought to be *papabili*, or papal material. What an injustice that the man had wasted his life doing what amounted to grunt work as an undersecretary in the bowels of the Roman *Curia*, his once promising career buried deep within the Vatican. Young Anselmo Moreno had visited him often and, being particularly impressed by his revered relative's red socks, had chosen his vocation for life. But then, somehow, life had taken another turn. Just after his ordination, at some diplomatic function, the prefect for *Propaganda Fide* mentioned—over *antipasto*—how the Americans needed priests on their left coast. Cowboys chasing beleaguered Indians across movie screens came to mind. The whole table agreed that those brash *Americani* certainly did need saving, that was for sure. The young and zealous seminarian, ever eager to please someone of such obvious prestige, volunteered on the spot. His thinking was that, after a few years, they would beg for his return to the center of the world, and appoint him to some important administrative post as a bishop himself. This never happened.

Twenty-seven years passed in exile. Despite his many letters— or perhaps because of them—Father Anselmo Moreno received only brief replies, scrawled by various Vatican underlings. Anger over yet another injustice perpetrated against the family honor ignited the coals of rancor deep within the young man's breast. Resentment grew, day after day, into a towering inferno of stoic hostility toward his adopted diocese and his life's mission. To pour gasoline on this smoldering indignation, his first assignment was the Marriage Tribunal where he had to work shoulder to shoulder with the Irish missionaries who had also answered the pope's appeal to send pale-skinned Europeans to sunny Southern California. How he despised them. But after a while he found he enjoyed his work, turning down annulment applications. Habitual infidelity? Well, she should have known what she was getting into? Alcoholism? Well, Italians drink wine from infancy and we have no problem . . . Even legitimate impediments were not so easily overcome on his watch. It was no small consolation holding the line against the slipshod and sentimental decisions handed down by overly compassionate canon lawyers. "Life is hard, and we must all learn to live with it," he said to teary-eyed spouses on more than one occasion. Then, in the evenings, he would always return to his residence, turn up the stereo and hum along with Verdi, Vivaldi or Puccini. What did the Irish know about opera anyway? To them, opera meant singing drunken bar songs after playing eighteen holes of golf together on their day-off?

He returned yearly for a month to the deposit of faith. With the contacts he liberally watered during each summer's vacation, once again an episcopal nomination seemed like a sure thing. Yet with each opening, he was passed over. It was the Cardinal's fault. It was all the fault of those Irish. It was the written complaint from a coworker or a secretary. It was the whining from a few miserable failed marriages. Whatever the reason, when Rome chose its first Hispanic—his rival at the chancery, Arnulfo—as the new auxiliary bishop instead of himself, that was the last straw. Even the symbolic act of making him a *monsignor* did not pacify him. That's when he had asked for a parish. After years of sloughing through the stuff of human misery and upholding the sanctity of the marriage bond, he was finally given what he thought he wanted—his own parish. Ah, to be captain of his own ship, shepherd of his own flock! If the Church hierarchy refused to see the light then, by God, he would make his unsuspecting parishioners see it.

That particular morning, after breakfast, he went to the office and checked the previous day's mail. His young and embarrassingly earnest assistant, Father Nathanael, had received another letter written by an obviously female hand. The stationery was pink, a danger sign. Although tempted to open the envelope, he resisted, discretion being the better part of snoopiness. He made a mental note to speak with the young man later in the day, perhaps at lunch. Father Nathanael, still wet behind the ears, had arrived with big plans and such unbridled enthusiasm. It had taken several months to train him properly. Now, most days his assistant was docile enough, sitting with his head down, eating in silence, while listening to his pastor expound on one subject or another. The archdiocese was going to hell, as was the rest of the city. Both were being rapidly overrun by the hoard of new immigrants. It never seemed to dawn on him that he himself was once one of them. Father Nathanael would usually wolf down his food, even gulping the wine, before making some excuse or another to leave the table. He was always visiting the sick or some such thing.

But that morning, Father Nathanael was not at breakfast. Where in blazes was he? Monsignor Moreno was always a match ready to be ignited. And the secretary was late again too. Five minutes was five minutes in which he himself had to answer the phone and the doorbell, if some parishioner dared approach. The elderly Mrs. Logan simply wasn't an organized person and never would be. He had told her so many times, especially during surprise inspections of the files or the accounts. Perhaps it was time to start looking for someone new, younger perhaps, and a bit more presentable. While thinking this thought, at that precise moment, Mrs. Logan rushed in, the door inadvertently slamming behind her. She tiptoed down the hall to her little cubbyhole, hoping to bypass the Monsignor's office unseen. But the eyes and ears of the archdiocese could not be so easily fooled. He decided to give her his most sarcastic half-smile, designed to bring the poor woman to tears. He imagined her lame excuse: "My daughter's car broke down again, Monsignor . . . Joanie, my grandchild is sick again and . . ." Her voice would inevitably trail off into guilty silence. Monsignor would then say triumphantly, "Tardiness for work means you are robbing the poor and are cheating the Almighty Himself." But strangely, as he stood staring at her from the doorway, she took no notice of him at all. He pointedly looked at the clock on the wall—that was stopped. Now he was distracted—for his own watch too—oddly enough, did not seem to be working. He tapped it repeatedly, and ever more violently, but with no success. Leaving Mrs. Logan alone for the time being, he stomped down the hall to check the kitchen clock—it too seemed to be broken. Now, with his blood pressure rising, and after making a mental note about fixing clocks and docking Mrs. Logan's pay, he decided to go instead in search of the prodigal Father Nathanael who had missed his after-breakfast marching orders for the day. That was unthinkable. Something would have to done and immediately too, as he stormed out the side door that connected to the sacristy. No doubt, the culprit would be in there, praying again. What were they teaching seminarians these days?

Before entering the sacristy door, Moreno noted that several cars were parked in the Church parking lot. He wondered why, since his underling should have long since said the early Mass. The early Mass—6:00 a.m.—was good discipline for the unruly young man, and besides, only a few pious rosary-wielding old ladies attended. There, the newly ordained's idealism could do little damage.

Monsignor Moreno's *credo* was never allowing his assistants any slack. Many had come and gone. This one had been particularly difficult because it was Fr. Nathanael's home parish, where he had received "the call" under the previous administration. But throughout the years of seminary, and during every vacation, he himself put the guileless prospect through the proverbial paces, even making him paint the entire school, practically by all himself. There should be no rest for future shepherds of God's flock and the sooner this lesson was learned the better. The young seminarian, brimming sincerity and goodwill, had somehow succeeded in befriending the more disgruntled members of his flock. He even was learning Spanish in order to communicate with the Hispanic gardener, the janitor and their families. Monsignor prided himself on the fact that he—practically alone in the diocese—was holding the line, keeping the immigrant deluge from inundating his parish. "No way, Jose." No Spanish would be spoken during his tenure, no matter what the changing demographics were. He himself had had to learn English, so why couldn't everyone else. It was, after all, for their own good. His was a high and lonely destiny—to think only of the good of souls. Perhaps, in the rare moment of doubt, he wondered if he was being too hard on them all. Like when he asked Fr. Nathanael's aging mother to answer the phones whenever the secretary could not, mainly late nights and weekends. Imagine the nerve of the old lady who pleaded tiredness after working all day as a school librarian. Why, he himself was almost her age and was fit as Vivaldi's fiddle.

The last straw for Moreno was Nathanael's ordination for which the young man had invited a Spanish choir. Monsignor boldly sent them packing, telling them to cease and desist. It didn't help that Bishop Arnulfo, his old classmate and rival, would be performing the ceremony. How he made young Nathanael sweat, making the whole preparation for the ordination process, which should have been the joy and consolation of a lifetime in his home parish—as laborious and grim as a midweek funeral.

Shortly after the ordination, when Fr. Nathanael's mother was diagnosed with cancer, Monsignor deigned to visit her and prepare her properly to meet her Maker. He would never forget that scene or be able to forgive what happened. It was the only time he had ever visited his assistant's nearby family home. There was the antiseptic smell of death, with the teary-eyed family bravely gathered round. When he entered they all became silent, clearing a path for him to approach the deathbed. The older sister turned her back on him, her eyes puffy and red. The old woman herself, gaunt from the ravages of the final stage of the disease, held her son's hand while she held Monsignor's gaze. The silence—and her eyes—became uncomfortable after a minute and unbearable after two. To break the stalemate, Monsignor put on his best bedside manner, launching into his "consolation" mode, telling her about the purifications of purgatory and the punishments of hell. While doing so, he got the distinct feeling that this family knew more than he did, having lived through them both. The sick woman's intense eyes, on the other hand, spoke of the future joys of heaven. She seemed to look right through him as if trying to . . . to what? . . . to save him. When he was finally finished, all she said was, "I forgive you . . ." At first, he was surprised, and then offended. He was the one to forgive her—why should he ask forgiveness of this shabby, old woman and her half-baked priestling son. He left in a huff, muttering and cursing under his breath in Italian. Ever since, he had made Fr. Nathanael's life one long lesson in mortification.

That morning, when Monsignor Moreno finally entered the sacristy—the door seemed so heavy!—no one was there. But sounds coming from the sanctuary drew his attention. Evidently there was a Mass going on. But there should not be, at this hour? He started to get angry because he had not been informed beforehand. He went to the door and peeked out. To his immense surprise, he saw the altar area packed with his fellow priests. But there were very few people in the pews themselves. And Bishop Arnulfo was the main celebrant. Young Fr. Nathanael was sitting next to him. The readings were just about to be read.

St. Paul was first: *"If I speak with the tongues of angels but have not love I am but a clanging gong . . ."*

The responsorial psalm followed: *"The Lord is my shepherd I shall not want . . ."*

"Aspetta un attimo, wait a minute," said Monsignor Moreno to himself. "This is the funeral liturgy!" Sure enough, there were a couple stands of wilting flowers in front of a casket that looked like it was made out of cardboard. His first thought was that Nathanael's mother had finally had the good sense to die and that they all were celebrating her final obsequies. It was customary for all priests who could attend, to support their brother priest and his grieving family. But why hadn't they invited him? After all, he was the pastor and this was *his* church.

The bishop read the gospel: *"I am the good shepherd who lays down his life for his sheep . . ."* Monsignor wondered why his classmate chose this passage and not one more appropriate for the occasion, like the widow begging crumbs from the table of the chosen people.

Bishop Arnulfo took a deep breath and expelled it with words: "Friends, this is a painful and a difficult moment for all of us. Much could be said but so much more is better left unsaid. Our faith tells us God is love, that He is full of kindness and mercy. So let us remember the deceased in a moment of silence."

Monsignor thought, "Not even worth a decent sermon, was she?" He gleefully searched the faces in the pews. There were a few parishioners whom he recognized. Sure enough, there were the old ladies churning their rosaries. He even imagined that he could hear their silent prayers: *"Holy Mary, Mother of God, pray for him, a sinner, now . . ."*

"But wait!" he thought, "Isn't that one old lady in the wheel chair, over by the door—isn't that Father Nathanael's mother?" Next to the janitor and the gardener? But that was impossible. It must be his imagination. She could not be attending her own funeral unless she was a ghost? Moreno even wondered for a moment—perhaps her vindictiveness knew no bounds, not even those of death, and she had returned to haunt him from beyond the grave. The silence after the bishop's short homily seemed eternal. He looked at Bishop Arnulfo, now seated so smugly in his own chair, amid all his fellow priests with their heads down in concentrated prayer. Amazingly, he felt he could actually hear their interior pleas:

"Lord, have mercy . . ."

"Sweet Jesus, you died to save all people . . ."

Then looking at young and zealous Father Nathanael he heard: "Dear Father, thank you for these past few months together in which you have taught me to love the Cross."

Monsignor's mind reeled. Now he was really angry. "What are you fools all talking about?" he shouted. Stalking out into the middle of the sanctuary, red-faced, he gesticulated wildly. But no one looked up or took the slightest notice of him. He touched the bishop on the shoulder but the man didn't stir. "Ha! Ignoring me like always!" he screamed. He then rushed over to the coffin and tried to pry open the lid but it would not budge, despite his best efforts. He ran back and forth for what seemed like the longest time, wringing his hands and staring about him in disbelief. Pulling his hair he moaned, "What is happening to me?"

When the bishop and all the priests stood to continue the Mass, he ran back into the Sacristy, suddenly ashamed of what he had been doing. *"May his soul and all the souls of the faithful departed through the mercy of God rest in Peace . . . Amen."* Holy water was aspersed and the final prayer was said.

Monsignor Moreno thought, *"His soul?* I thought the deceased was a woman! Enough is enough!" he yelled, rushing again out the sacristy door headlong at Father Nathanael. But his assistant seemed to walk right through him. When his fellow priests hoisted the casket up onto their shoulders, struggling under the weight of it, he ran down the aisle ahead them to block their way, so the procession could not leave the church until all his questions were answered. The six pallbearer priests walked right through him, as if he wasn't even there. At the entrance to the church, the funeral director and the hearse's driver snickered at an inappropriate joke one of the Irish priests made about the weight of the body. "What nerve!" protested Moreno. "Stop! All of you! Where are you going? No one informed me about any funeral this morning . . ."

Seeing that his bellowing had no effect whatsoever, it finally dawned upon Monsignor Moreno that he actually did know the person in the coffin. All the pieces suddenly fell into a terrifyingly clear picture and he gasped. Seeing the few mourners' relief at being outside in to the bright California sunshine—he just knew. *He was the one. It was his own funeral—his own body lay inside that cheap casket.* He had always pictured his own funeral as somber and solemn where even the sun would refuse to shine, and where even the biggest church could not contain the countless mourners. The pallbearers commented back and forth over his dead body, confirming this sudden and jolting realization.

Fᴛ. Meehan from nearby Incarnation said, "Truth be told, I came just to make sure he's dead . . ."

"He's here all right, and he weighs a ton!" grunted Fr. James, the Pastor of Sacred Heart across town.

"He was pretty hard to bear in life too!" joked a third, Fr. John Keller, one of Monsignor's former assistants. He lasted only three months before begging a transfer.

"Yeah, the old bastard," intoned one of the Irish priests, "Better to be in heaven a half hour before the devil knows you're dead." Several knowing smirks followed this irreverent comment but were stifled by the bishop's exit.

A few cars followed the funeral train out of the parking lot with their lights on. The birds in the trees chirped cheerily and uninterruptedly. Almost worse than the thought of his own death was the awful truth that struck him, resounding louder in his brain than the ringing church bells—he was not even buried yet and he was already forgotten—what he struggled and slaved for his whole life was all for naught. Cold beads of sweat formed on his creased brow with the realization that he had spent his entire life doing neither what he liked nor what he was supposed to do. For all had been done without a spark of real charity. He was, in truth, what St Paul had described—a banging gong.

Monsignor ran back into the Church and threw himself down on his face before the tabernacle, breathing in gasps. He heard nothing and saw no one. He only felt a fierce, agonizing, burning sensation passing slowly throughout his body. The last thing he remembered was heading for his room in the rectory with that scalding, intense heat increasing. He wondered if he was already in hell.

It was dark when he finally opened his eyes. He started to panic, because, at first, he thought he was waking inside the coffin. Sweating profusely, his shirt soaked through. He wished he could weep for his past life and be sorry for everything but he felt no remorse. Then there was a sudden knock on the door. No, it was more like a prolonged rapping. Hardly daring to breathe, he remained silent, hoping it would stop. Was it the devil come to claim his soul? He thought he heard a key rattle in the lock. The door opened and in came a solitary dark figure haloed by a golden light.

"*O Dio misericordioso!*" cried Moreno desperately.

"Monsignor . . ." said a voice, "it's only me—Father Nathanael. Sorry to disturb your sleep, but when you didn't come down for breakfast this morning, we thought . . . that is, Mrs. Logan and I, thought that someone had better check on you."

Monsignor cowered under the covers, trembling, not believing what he was hearing. The young priest went to the window and pulled back the heavy drapes so that a burst of light illumined the scene. He was in his own room after all. In his own bed. And it was morning.

His assistant continued, "I thought perhaps you were sick, Monsignor. You looked a bit florid last night" Monsignor quickly felt his own forehead. It was indeed hot. What he had experienced was all just a nightmare caused by the fever. Yet how could that be? It was all so real. He took several deep breaths, already shaking off the lingering effects of his morbid dream.

"Monsignor, I took the liberty to bring you some of my mom's home-made blueberry muffins, fresh-baked . . .," said Fr. Nathanael with unfeigned goodwill.

Monsignor Moreno looked at his visitor, uncomfortably poised between bed and door. Then, looking at the muffins, he felt himself softening a little like melting butter.

Something was bothering him, however, something buried deep down was trying desperately to escape. It was a hazy memory of his childhood long ago, surfacing after all these years. In that moment, remembering seemed like a matter of life and death. Thus, he wavered for the briefest instant on the edge of the abyss. Then, with relish, he said, "I'm allergic to blueberries. Take them away! And close the door on your way out."

A Harrowing Grace

No one ever thought that one orange thrown from two hundred and seventy feet up could cause such havoc—certainly not the three college roommates living on the eighteenth floor of one of four towers at Boston University. BU was known far and wide as a party school. And although, during the week, some studying did occur, most freshmen did their best, especially on weekends, to uphold the school's most dubious distinction. These three realized, in the fleeting moments of sobriety that if they kept it up, the early onset of alcoholism would put them in danger of flunking out of school, a disgrace which would haunt them for the rest of their lives. Up in the rarified air of the eighteenth floor of the fourth tower, however, mass quantities of the golden amber continued to be downed daily, as they joked about what their parents would say.

One Saturday afternoon, in the glow of several uninterrupted hours of inebriation, they wondered what might happen if they threw various and sundry objects out the window. Did all falling objects really plummet at the same rate of speed as Newton said? The most zealous imbiber, Walter, from Connecticut, with a Polish last name containing no vowels, opened the dorm window and leaned out precariously, staring down at the ant-like forms traversing the sidewalk far below. He picked up a paper clip off the desk and dropped it out the window. Not being able to follow its descent with the naked eye, he decided to try a bigger object. He casually picked up a large naval orange that was sitting on the window sill, felt its weight in his hand and then, without warning—indeed, without thinking—launched the bright round projectile out the window. His two companions leaped to their unsteady feet, intent on following the fruit's trajectory downward, fully expecting an audible and impressive "splat" eighteen floors below.

Their blood-shot eyes followed it in rapt attention for a second. Then, to their everlasting consternation—at that precise moment, as said piece of fruit plummeted like a meteor inexorably downward, a nameless, balding man—without a hat—chose to exit their building below. He was surely entering their line of fire, directly beneath their room. Involuntarily, the three freshmen screamed an incoherent warning, which did not go completely unheard. The man, obviously noting something, tilted his head upward for a fraction of a second, but kept on walking, completely oblivious to his collision course with the streaking citrus. All three sucked in their collective breath, anticipating an impossible impact. The naval orange, having fallen eighteen floors, hit the unsuspecting pedestrian square on his shining pate, knocking him instantly to the ground. The suction sound produced upon impact was similar to a rubber boot being pulled out of the thickest mud. Two nearby passersby gazed alternately in confusion at the downed man and then in disbelief at the offending orange pulp that lay conspicuously next to the inert body. As one person, the two witnesses then looked up at the dormitory, espying the three guilty gawkers, paralyzed like rabbits caught in the highway's headlights in the fourth tower. Realizing that they had been discovered by the two, as one, the three backed quickly away from the open window.

They stared at each other, trying to breathe and absorb instant sobriety. There was no time for blame. Without saying a word, the unholy trinity fled, each to his own room, for fear that the authorities would soon come looking for them. Sure enough, ten minutes later, while paramedics attended to the fallen man below, the Boston Police invaded the entire dorm, initiating a thorough search. Closing off all exits and entrances to the beehive-like structure, they began by interviewing any students found in their rooms. All professed ignorance of the misdeed. But by the time the University Chancellor arrived, the cops had already homed in on the eighteenth floor.

Walter, his conscience smarting like a morning after, opened his bolted door at the sound of the authoritative knock. Before even being asked a question, he confessed to the crime with copious tears. Alcohol on his breath did not help his case, nor did the fact that he kept trying to hug the Chancellor. To his credit, albeit under extreme pressure, he managed not to inform on his two friends. The policeman had a hard time spelling his name.

The Chancellor's Cheshire cat frown seemed permanently fixed on his puffy, red face, as he prognosticated doom. Walter's two buddies looked on lamely as he was led away in handcuffs. The police took the young man—who promptly vomited in the back seat of the squad car—down to headquarters where he was given bitter black coffee along with a big helping of the third degree. Charges were filed and his parents were called in. The prosecutor was quoted as saying, "Hanging is too good for such a miscreant." Expulsion from school would only be the beginning. There existed a very real possibility, even if the unfortunate victim did manage to survive, of murder charges being filed or at the very least, manslaughter and aggravated assault. That meant a jury trial and real prison time. There would be no open windows in the slammer that was for sure. Even though

Walter had no prior criminal record, he would be punished—made an example of—to the fullest extent of the law. The next day, the Chancellor of the university held a press conference, expressing communal outrage: "Believe me, the crack down on excessive student drinking has begun! Drunkenness will not be tolerated at our institution." That morning's Boston Globe ran an editorial that stated: "Student alcoholism is only a symptom of a bigger problem—a sociopathic generation of undergraduates."

To make matters worse, the man whose head made contact with the flying orange was a well-known and a highly respected member of the physics department, one that had recently been considered for a Nobel Prize. Coincidentally, his particular field of specialized research was gravitational pull and the impact of falling objects on stationary ones. A host of internationally renowned colleagues also expressed shock and outrage that a fellow scientist, carrying on the research of Isaac Newton and his apple would succumb to an orange. Local radio talk show hosts and their irate constituency were incensed by the irony of the incident.

The ambulance had rushed the victim to Boston General. The best doctors awaited his arrival. An MRI-CAT scan revealed what everybody already knew to be the case—severe trauma to the cranium. Although these tests before emergency surgery were standard operating procedure, something in those particular images caused another involuntary intake of the collective breath. There was a large round blur in the left frontal lobe which none of the experts could explain. So a new set of x-rays was ordered, yet these too revealed the same strange anomaly. In the operating theater, after cutting off the top of the professor's skull, the team of surgeons discovered a large but operable brain tumor. Perhaps it was the operating room light or the sheer amount of blood, but more than one observer—sitting up in the observation deck—thought the color and texture of the tumor distinctly "orange-ish." After the four hour procedure to remove the growth, three biopsies were rushed to two different labs, amounting to one positive diagnosis of malignancy. Consulting physicians agreed that the whole mass had been completely and successfully removed. Two days later, out on bail before his hearing, Walter, now very sober indeed, went straight to the hospital. He snuck up the backstairs, to avoid stray reporters. Furtively entering the professor's room, he burst into tears, stammering an apology apparently without vowels.

It took a couple of minutes, but after realizing who the young man really was and what he was attempting to say, the professor managed a smile. He had not witnessed anything so pathetic since his own college days. Having been informed of his positive prognosis, the professor looked at Walter, whispering with some effort, "If you had not thrown that orange, and if it had not hit me, they never would have discovered the cancerous tumor. Although I have based my entire life and career on the scientific method and empirical proof you have made me believe in a higher power."

After twelve days of recovery in intensive care followed by acute care; Professor Headley, for that was his name, was carefully loaded in a Boston University van and sent home to begin an unplanned but not unwelcome sabbatical. He planned on writing a book on the theory of relativity.

Because of the professor's insistence, all charges were subsequently dropped and Walter returned to the university after only a two-week suspension. He went on the wagon permanently, applied himself to his studies and received an "A minus" in his physics class. Encouraged by these results, he decided on his future career in life. After graduation, he moved to Florida and landed a job as a mechanical engineer at a citrus processing plant in Lake Wales. Walter's two friends—whose guilt was never discovered—eventually graduated with honors as well. They visited him every winter, where they would sit around for hours and reminisce over tall glasses of orange juice.

That Woman and Her Boy

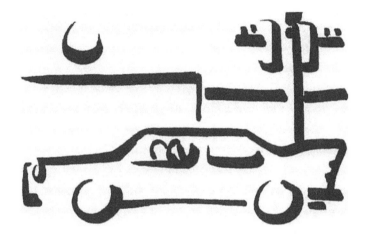

J unior looked around anxiously. The sun was setting and even he knew that this was no place to be after dark. Rivulets of sweat ran down his neck and were absorbed by his Lakers' jersey, which he had worn every day for a week. His momma sat behind the steering wheel staring straight ahead, her jaw quivering slightly. Junior had seen her like this a couple times before but never in the middle of rush hour. Horns blared when they didn't move.

"Mom, where are we?" he asked. Dolores evidently did not hear him, so Junior did what he was good at, repeating himself patiently until the meaning of his slurred words eventually became clear. Odd, his mother always understood him, even when his questions had no answers. Like when he was twenty and asked her, "Are you nobody too?"

"Two nobodies from nowhere," she answered ruefully. Dolores knew she didn't exactly come from out of nowhere, but rather, from a little black Catholic bastion outside New Orleans. Her daddy had moved the family—all nine in one old Buick—to California after the second Great War. California, sprouting oranges, spaghetti freeways and jobs was the land of promise. Back then, South Central Los Angeles wasn't the war zone it is today, but a decent—if not poor—place to raise a burgeoning family. And though Baptist churches sprouted like mushrooms on every street comer there was one Catholic Church nearby, St. Martin de Porres. Junior, growing up "challenged," as they say, was permitted the freedom of walking the three-blocks to the church so he could talk with Jesus.

"God understands you," his mom would repeat, trying to calm him down after kindergarten when the other kids made fun of him.

Worse than that was first grade—in the "special school." The kids there asked Junior why he talked funny, why he was so stupid and where his father was. The latter just up and disappeared one day when he was two. When Junior asked Dolores why he didn't have a Dad like all the other kids, she told Junior his daddy loved him very much but, unfortunately, died of a heart attack. Junior accepted the fact simply because his mom said so, without drama, even though when alone in his dark room at night, he would cry. Dolores always lit a small candle on the dresser so Junior could see the small statue of St. Martin.

Now, many years later—in the midst of terrible traffic with his momma acting funny—he prayed even more earnestly: "St. Martin, help!" But his mother had always said prayers were not enough. He knew he must also act. She said Martin, the Dominican brother, son of a mulatto mother and a Spaniard father who did not want him, always heard his prayers. The thought of Martin feeding mice and helping the sick calmed him down. Thinking hard, he grabbed the wheel of their vintage, robin's egg blue Cadillac, and turned it sharply to the right.

"Take your foot off the brake, Momma!" he yelled, while putting his left foot where hers had been and his right on the gas pedal. The big boat of a car leapt forward then lurched to a halt. This definitely was not as easy as maneuvering in the driveway back home. With fits and starts, and many yells from the fuming motorists

34

behind them, in this way the unrelenting flow of Los Angeles traffic was finally unblocked. Angry fists and obscene fingers gave way to blurs of motion passing them by. Once parked, with the right front wheel up on the curb, Junior reached over and turned off the ignition. Still, Dolores stared into space. She did not seem to know what was happening.

"Where are we, Momma?" Junior asked again, stroking her cheek.

The woman mumbled something he couldn't understand. Normally, Junior could understand everything his mother said.

Dolores suddenly looked toward the west. An angry orange orb sank behind the palms, elongating shadows which resembled clawing, purple fingers. Junior thought, at that moment, that his dear mother was old, something he never noticed before. How thin she had become. The harsh California sun had created a map of wrinkles on her face rivaling the freeway system. Dolores, suddenly realizing that Junior was calling to her, also knew she was not thinking clearly. Why was he talking to so damn loud? The smell of his rank sweat was like smelling salts. The old familiar fear appeared before her, like a taunting ghost: Who would care for her precious twenty-seven-year-old retarded baby when she was gone? Who would pray for Junior when she was dead? Recently, this thought had consumed her every waking moment and, of late, had even entered into her dreams. She knew that for a long time now, things were just not right with her. Avoiding the doctor was the only way to pretend she might out-live her only son. Named as she was after the *Mater Dolorosa*, she stared at him like the mother of sorrows. He was a late baby. She had him when she was already forty-five. But better late than never. She envisioned his tiny blue body with the umbilical cord wrapped tightly around his neck in the cold delivery room. Oxygen had been cut off for just long enough to make Junior "special." Slow but sure. Tough to understand but somehow always completely understandable—at least to her. A joy from day one. One son of a gun doctor told her to abort him but Dolores stuck to her guns. She was tempted to use one on that doctor too. Life was life, no matter what. After a couple turbulent years replete with arguments, her rat of a husband chose to jump ship. A retard kid was too much for Mr. Macho. No, the man had never had a heart attack; he just didn't have a heart. So she introduced the boy to Saint Martin so he would have a good male role model. Martin was black too, was rejected by his daddy, but accepted by the Father. Neither he nor Martin had an idea how to properly parallel park a '63 Caddy.

Growing up with two left feet, Junior was clumsy and left out of most things. He broke a lot of things too—glasses, dishes, and his mother's heart—mostly by accident but occasionally out of frustration. Forbidden to touch so many things, little Junior grew up desiring only to be touched. He was the object of many public displays of affection from his momma even at the age when most kids are embarrassed to be seen with their parents. Dolores didn't care because she cared so much. Love could never be hidden. The stove, and later, the Mike-Row-Wave were off-limits, but under her watchful eye, there was no limit to his creative cookery. Bananas cooked in mustard sauce followed by drunken chicken, marinated in Kentucky Bourbon.

Seeing them always together, some mean spirited folks said Dolores didn't want him to grow up, but wanted to keep him by her side forever. Like most gossip, it stung because there was at least a grain of truth to it. The truth was, he was completely dependent on her, destined by his Creator to be a child forever, a little kid rambling round in a body several sizes too big.

One of the big crises of his teenage years came when Junior asked to ride the bus—by himself—downtown. That was definitely a "no-no." He would get lost sure as shooting. And there was a lot of shooting going on out there. The world was full of bad folks who would not think twice about taking advantage of a slow kid all by his lonesome. The neighborhood was full of gang members who regularly robbed him of milk money, candy money and most recently, his glasses. She meant to get him another pair but her Social Security check wouldn't come for another week. He'd just have to sit two feet from the TV until then.

Junior opened the car door, squinted, and looked around hesitantly, for somebody or something familiar. No, this was definitely not their neighborhood. In fact, he had the sinking feeling that they were very far away from home. Most of the signs here were in Spanish. He recognized the words "taco" and "burrito." Obediently, his stomach growled. It was past dinnertime. Unrolling the window, he asked two teenaged mothers pushing baby carts on the sidewalk where he lived but got no response in either English or Spanish. They just looked at his wired hair that looked like he's gotten his finger stuck in an electric socket. That was one of the first "no nos." There were no police in sight and no other African Americans that he could see. He tried to get his mom to look at him. Tears flowed down the ravines in her drawn cheeks. She was trying to say something but couldn't. Something was definitely wrong all right. Now, he knew he had to do something all by himself. He remembered his mom always telling him that he had to be the man of the house even when the house was nowhere to be seen. He didn't really know how to drive and it seemed his mom was in no condition to, so they would just have to stay put. It looked like a bad neighborhood but there was no choice.

"You stay here, Momma," he said, "I'm going for help . . ." In response, she stared down at her hands. Just in case, he reached across and took the ignition keys. It wouldn't do to have his mother driving around LA in the dark without him. If they were lost, he wanted them to be lost together. That had always been one of their chief consolations in life. Junior spotted a Korean market. And there was a telephone outside. Getting out of the car, he checked his jeans' pockets and came up with fifty cents, enough to make a call. But when he slipped the two quarters in, it slowly dawned on him that if he and his mom were here, nobody would be home to answer his call. No, this was like that one Sunday when he got lost taking the Metro bus. He had just hopped on the first one passing Main Street. That one took him downtown, where he got out to walk and wonder for a while, never having been so free before. When he finally realized it was getting late, he boarded another bus thinking it would magically whisk him back home. Hours passed and he just kept transferring buses. Well after midnight, a kind stranger had found his home phone number written on a card stuck in his wallet and even allowed him to press the phone buttons. Dolores almost died of worry when he hadn't showed up. She called the local police station, but it seems you have to be missing at least three days or you aren't considered officially lost in this country. When his call finally came and she got him home safe, she didn't know whether to laugh or cry, so she did both.

Now, Junior stared hesitantly at the phone. He was about to do another forbidden thing. He dialed 911. "Emergency! We're lost," he said, "Mom and me, we went to K-Mart, but then something happened and she can't drive. We don't know where we are, and it's dark outside. And I'm hungry . . ." A woman's professional voice kept repeating, "Please repeat, I cannot understand you, Sir." Junior obeyed but after a few minutes, he hung up in frustration. That lady didn't know him well enough to love him, so how could she be patient enough to decipher his way of speaking. Junior entered Kim's Market and bought a bag of potato chips and a Coke. The thin Korean man looked suspiciously at him at first, out of fear, but after money was revealed, the man said something Junior didn't understand, smiling and bowing. He evidently didn't know much English. They would have to share dinner in the car just like on their one big trip to Las Vegas three years before. Junior, old enough to play the slots, won eighty dollars in quarters, a half year's supply of giant gumballs. In their present situation, that was a comforting memory. Walking back to the car, he stopped short, seeing their Caddy surrounded by several hooded figures. Their shaved heads, tattoos and baggy clothes identified them as gang-bangers. Spotting big Junior coming toward them, they stiffened, tightening their circle. Junior prayed silently to St. Martin, because Momma had said that the black saint knew Spanish too. He towered over them, but did not recognize this fact reflected in their faces. The leader of the gang said, "Hey *Morenito! Que haces aqui?* Whatchu doin' down here in our hood?" Try as he might, the only Spanish words he could recall from his Sesame Street days were numbers. So he just smiled at them and said, *"Uno . . . Dos . . . Tres. . . ."* Their eyes widened, and they looked at each other, unsure if they were being threatened. Meanwhile, inside the car, Dolores looked like she was asleep, her head bent forward, her face hidden by fallen gray hair. The gang members wondered if on the count of "three" the big black guy was going to pull a gun?

"Morenito, no tenemos miedo de ti . . . We told you ya—this is our turf, man!" said one *cholo*. Junior scowled at the sight of his switchblade. Momma never let him touch a knife. Remembering the time he cut himself bad enough to be rushed to the hospital for stitches, Junior stuttered, "B-B- BLOOD!"

This one word had a sudden and strange effect on the gang. Their eyes narrowed and they backed away very slowly. Their leader said, "Homies, he's a member of the Bloods . . ." With that, the other *cholos*, now with real fear in their eyes, started walking away more quickly. Junior stood perfectly still because he didn't know what was happening or what to do. How come they weren't pushing him around like all the others had done so often in the past? That's when the car horn blared, long and loud, not letting up. He peered inside the car to see Dolores's forehead pressing against the steering wheel. Mr. Kim popped his head outside the Market. The *cholos* yelled at him in Spanglish, "Hey, Chinky, this boy's a Blood, be careful man!" With that, the man disappeared back inside the market Junior had no idea they believed him to be a member of the infamous and ultra-violent, black "Bloods" gang. All he knew was the dark hoods were gone. He tapped on Dolores's window again, but she didn't move. Panicking, he started pounding on her window with his fists. This roused her somewhat. She looked at her son and made a halting effort to unlock the door.

"Are you OK, Momma?" He asked several times, but receiving no reply, repeated himself. "I'm in charge. I'm the man of the house now. Gotta do something . . ." He just wanted to cry.

"Momma, drink this Coke, eat these chips." He locked all four doors and hunkered down in the passenger-side front seat, trying to think. But thinking too hard just made him hungrier. No, this wouldn't do, he sensed that they both were too visible, too exposed. What if the street-gang decided to come back—with guns? First, he had to get both of them into the darker back seat where passersby couldn't see them. This took some doing, as his mom didn't seem to want to let go of the steering wheel. It was like she was hanging on for dear life. Finally, prying her fingers loose, and with much coaxing, Dolores climbed in between the front seats, mussing her hair and skirt before landing in the back. The only thing to do, thought Junior, was to sit tight until help arrived or until morning, whichever came first. His momma always said things looked different in the morning. The hours dragged on. He held her, rocking back and forth, softly singing the songs she used to sing to him. Eventually Dolores fell asleep. But he knew he couldn't afford to. He had to protect his mother. The noise of sirens from fire trucks, police cruisers and even a helicopter punctuated the night, oblivious to the invisible young man and his mother in the dark back seat. The gangbangers made another appearance around three in the morning but the tinted windows prevented their seeing inside. Junior prayed like never before, and then breathed a sigh of relief when they finally went on their way.

At last, morning dawned. Dolores, was awake. But she still seemed confused, not saying anything. It would be up to him to get them home, after all. At six o'clock, a Metro bus rumbled by and stopped at the comer. Feeling around the bottom of her purse for spare change, Junior got an idea.

"Come on, Momma!" He pulled her out of the back seat, locked the car, put the keys in her purse, and then guided her by the elbow to the corner where they waited. The next bus showed up a half-hour later. The bus driver couldn't understand Junior's explanations or questions but just pointed impatiently straight ahead. After feeding some quarters into the metal box, he grabbed two transfer tickets, and then stumbled backward, holding his mother to his side, as the bus lurched forward. After seating Dolores in the handicapped seat—the one he himself normally would have occupied, he stood in front of her, hanging on to the railing. She seemed to need it more than him now anyway. With no idea what number the bus was or where they were heading, Junior hoped he could remember where they lived. He searched his mind for the bus schedules he had studied after getting lost that first time. Without his mother's knowledge, he had indeed ventured out on his own several times on the bus to practice getting lost. He became something of an expert. So now, they rolled out onto a freeway. Soon the high rises of downtown LA loomed large on the horizon. Junior knew how to get lost there, if they could only get that far. With many twists and turns, at long last, they were deposited on Broadway in the middle of downtown. Junior and Dolores got out, almost getting run over crossing the street, and then walked until they reached Olympic. Junior recognized that sign. From there, they boarded another bus that happened to be passing by, riding until Junior realized they were heading west toward Santa Monica, the wrong direction! They got out at the next stop, crossed the street again, and then retraced their path, catching the next bus going the opposite way. Then, just east of downtown, they got out again and went to the nearest stop, this time headed south toward Compton. Another bus arrived and carried them ever deeper down into the hood. Scanning the sky as they rolled along, Junior wondered what to do next. Then he saw something familiar. His squinting eyes saw what looked like a big, brown finger pointing heavenward. It was the bell-tower of their Church. St. Martin had guided them home! Their pastor, Father Peter, exiting the rectory at that very moment, turned to see his two favorite parishioners getting off the bus. Coming over to greet them, he soon realized that something was amiss. Junior embraced the priest, their adventure gushing out of his mouth like a broken water main. The priest sat Dolores down on the church steps, with concern in his eyes. Then after Junior finished, he drove them both to Martin Luther King hospital, saying, "Don't worry, son, your Momma is going to be all right . . ."

After practically a whole day of waiting for various tests, Father Peter drove them home, asking, "But how about you, Junior? Are you going to be all right?"

Junior smiled, saying, "Yes, Father. We're home now." Then turning to his mother seated beside him, he added, "Momma, do you want some breakfast?" She always told him it was the most important meal of the day.

Dolores looked around and seemed to come back from wherever she was, her memory jogged by the sight of the roses in the front yard. With halting steps, she moved slowly up the walk, with the priest and Junior holding her arms. Once up on the porch, Fr. Peter opened the door for her, and sat her down on the living room couch. Junior headed straight for the kitchen where he made a mess cooking scrambled eggs. It took almost an hour to feed them to Dolores. When Father Peter finally left, he knew in his heart that everything was different now. A new heaven and a new earth had somehow been created overnight. Junior's Momma wouldn't be taking care of him anymore, but just the opposite—her son would have to take care of his mother. The next week, when the Doctor said it was a stroke plus something else called Alzheimer's, Junior didn't even blink.

One Mitred Afternoon

T he three priests sat around the dining room table, shaking their heads. After a couple minutes of glum silence, Father Morton, as pastor, spoke first, "I don't understand it. How could she have found out?"

"Don't ask me," said Monsignor Jim Sherman, pastor *emeritus*. "I'm fit as a fiddle."

"A regular Stradivarius . . ." chuckled young Fr. Brendan, recently ordained and the only one wearing clerics. "The only thing I can think of was that it happened during the nine o'clock Mass on

Sunday . . . My sinuses were stuffed up and . . . Mrs. Green was in her usual seat, front row on the St Joseph side . . ."

"And you sneezed!" snorted Morton triumphantly. Having survived the tumultuous years after the Second Vatican Council, his theology veered to the left just like his golf swing.

"*Mea culpa* . . ." Brendan, ever desirous of returning to the Church's time-honored traditions, struck his breast with a clenched fist.

"Now boys—chimed in Monsignor Sherman—it could happen to anyone. We just have to buck up and accept it. Lent is approaching—think of it as well-deserved penance for our many sins."

"Speak for yourself," argued Morton, who, although the appointed pastor did not ascribe to the Church's teaching on original sin. "I don't see why we all should have to suffer for what one guy did . . ."

Emeritus Sherman cocked a knowing eye at young Brendan, with whom he held the theological common ground, saying, "Genesis, chapter three."

"Why do you have to spiritualize everything?" countered the middle-aged Monsignor.

"Because, dear Father, everything is spiritual," prodded the older man.

Fearing another battle over breakfast, the newly ordained Brendan interjected, "Let's not argue. The fact is, now *Thelma Green thinks* that one of us is sick—and just as sure as day leads to night—will bring it over personally—just in time for our lunch today." Gloom settled over the room like a funeral pall. Brendan tried to cheer them up. "C'mon guys, it won't be so bad—it's just chicken soup. We've all been through this before. After a few days it'll be gone and life will go on."

Morton choked, as if reading the latest papal encyclical, "Just chicken soup! Are you so sure? Did you ever see her make it? How do you know the main ingredient's not some scavenging animal she caught crawling under the porch? It could be opossum or even rat soup for all we know. Certainly tastes like it!"

Although his stomach agreed, to be charitable, Brendan defended Mrs. Green, "That soup is homemade—just chockfull of quality ingredients fresh from the garden, just like your mother used to make."

Morton chose to be offended. "Leave my poor mother—God rest her soul—out of this. She never tried to poison me!"

Always the voice of reason, Jim Sherman picked up the *Times* and said, "Nor is Mrs. Green trying to do us any harm either, but rather, the *summum bonum, the greatest good*. So let's accept it with a smile and be gracious about it, shall we?" He exited the room with a flourish, the sports section tucked neatly under his arm.

Fr. Brendan and Father Morton stared dully at each other, realizing that more separated them than differences of theology. The inevitable would arrive by high noon, when they would be forced to sit across from one another at table. Both got up, crossed themselves in silence and went about their morning duties. Fr. Brendan took his dirty dishes to the sink and washed them, while Morton just left his at his place.

At quarter to twelve, the doorbell rang. Lupe, the secretary, answered, and ushered Mrs. Thelma Green down the dark rectory hall back into the ample kitchen. The woman held a huge, steaming pot in her oven-mitted hands. Luisa, the Mexican cook, looked on, somewhat taken aback, imagining that the pot had grown in size since the last time she encountered it. The shiny metal seemed to expand and contract with its own unique exhalations. Fr. Brendan, who happened to come down the backstairs at that exact moment, realized that he was the one who would have to formally thank their benefactor. Though he truly loved this lady, for that is what she was— fine, gentile, and generous to a fault—he realized that he would have to lie through his teeth in order to be kind. Grinning like the village idiot, first he thanked Mrs. Green profusely, and then protested that his Sunday sneeze was just a chance, allergic reaction, not deserving of her culinary arts.

"You poor darlings need some mothering. Eat my special chicken soup and it'll take care of what ails you," Mrs. Green smiled knowingly, returning down the dark hall. "I'll pick up the pot

Wednesday," she added, as the door clicked behind her. Through the office window, Fr. Brendan watched her get into her stately white Lincoln parked at the curb. Then the bell tolled lunch.

In the dining room, three large, steaming bowls awaited.

"Only three days," Morton murmured, in his mind questioning the doctrine of the Resurrection after three days in the tomb.

Large spoons lay ready on the right of each bowl. They said the blessing, really meaning it, and began the ritual performed so many times in the past. The question of not eating the soup never arose, because they were priests, after all, and there were still starving people in Africa. Pity—each thought to himself—the stuff couldn't be expedited to their needy confreres on that noble continent. But then again, thought Morton, heavily steeped in liberation theology, didn't the poor have enough problems already?

The first scalding spoonfuls, blown upon for proper cooling, went down surprisingly well. The grainy and greasy taste could be assuaged by mouthfuls of bread. The oldest, Monsignor Sherman, persevered, offering it up for the poor souls in purgatory, whom he pictured sitting round a dimly lit kitchen table eating the very same soup until their eventual release into paradise. Slurping involuntarily, they continued on doggedly until all was consumed as a midday oblation. Then, they looked at each other grimly but not without satisfaction. These were the times that brought their disparate personalities together. Knowing that a second helping was not possible, each man left the table pensive, digesting the experience. All were thinking the same thing: two more days. To make things worse, in the last deanery meeting reliable rumors ran that the Cardinal was making surprise visits to the parishes again. All the pastors thought of preparing sumptuous meals for his Eminence, but the problem was, no one knew the day or the hour the red hat would choose to drop by.

The second day, Tuesday, was harder to swallow than Monday, since the soup had had a chance to cook down, thus consolidating its juices. Why it was this way no one knew, but the second bowl was always for the stoic. The aroma of the viscous substance filled the entire rectory. Lupe closed the office door. Luisa hid in the kitchen hoping not to be fired. All were tempted to throw perfectly good food away, but resisting the urge, none did.

On Wednesday, just after celebrating a funeral, just before lunchtime, the *Emeritus* Sherman burst through the back door into the kitchen, his cane raised above his head like an Old Testament prophet "Out front . . . coming up the walk!" he shouted.

"Mrs. Green—so soon?" asked Morton, wide-eyed.

"But we're not finished eating it yet," protested Fr. Brendan.

"No, not Mrs. Green—the Cardinal! Mulrooney has descended upon us!"

A groan rose out of their collective depths.

All three were instantly struck by urgent interior misgivings. Monsignor Jim Sherman hated any surprises; changes of any kind to his daily schedule made him irritable. Morton worried about whether disgruntled parishioners were writing letters to the diocese about his last sermon saying hell did not exist; perhaps the Cardinal was coming to send him there. Fr. Brendan, realizing that the parish books were not quite up to date, hoped that the Cardinal would not ask to see the ledgers. A raised eyebrow meant a pointed letter from the Cardinal's personal secretary, a humorless Scotch Irishman named Father Hamish Berger, or the Hamburgler, as he was known throughout the diocese.

The three rushed to the front door, not allowing Lupe to answer the doorbell. Taking a deep breath, the older two pushed the younger one forward. Fr. Brendan screwed on his best car salesman smile and opened the door. As the imposing Prince of the Church entered, his two companions did their best dancing bear impressions, padding round the man like he was a May pole.

"Just dropped in to see how my favorite parish is doing," piped the Cardinal, "I would have come last week but I'm just getting over the flu. You know that St. Michael's was my first assignment many years ago . . ." The tall, handsome man launched into a story they were all familiar with. This gave them time to regroup. But His Eminence was too fast for them. Looking at his watch, the man smiled expansively while patting his formidable stomach, "The first stage of priesthood is *'Big Head'*"—he smiled—"the second stage is

'*Big Stomach,*' and the third is '*Big Funeral.*' I know I've passed the first but don't want to skip the second to arrive prematurely at the third! So what is Luisa cooking up for lunch today?" Leading them back into the refectory, the Cardinal sat down at the head of the table while the nervous little Mexican woman set another place. Leading the prayer in his deep, rich baritone, Mulrooney gave thanks, for what his companions of the moment couldn't imagine.

Their diminutive cook entered, perspiring under the burden of a soup tureen the size of a birdbath. And it was the third day too. The three priests blanched at what would surely be the Cardinal's reaction. His subtle palette was renowned throughout the diocese, and feared too, since no cook ever fully managed to rise to the occasion. He seemed to delight in making comments about the various parish offerings: "Oh, no thanks, one course of *that* was more than enough, thank you . . . I love simple and humble fare like *this* . . . *That* was indeed a unique taste sensation . . ." One could judge the state of the official visit by the number of antacids His Eminence requested afterward.

Their doom arrived. John Cardinal Mulrooney loudly slurped his first spoonful. Although it was not polite, the three could not help staring, open-mouthed. A second attempt was partially lost on the man's chin. But like the old campaigner he was, the successor to the apostles kept his eyes down, totally concentrated on the task at hand. The three priests, with their own spoons laden and poised at lips' edge, awaited judgement, all the while admiring their spiritual leader's tenacity. Here was a true shepherd laying down his life for his sheep. Perhaps this was why Rome and the Holy Spirit had elevated him to the red hat. For much to their amazement, their red-robed guest was putting down spoonful after spoonful, practically without pause. Luisa trembled, almost paralyzed by the thought soon she would be shipped back across the border to Tijuana in an unmarked van. Then, just before his Eminence scraped the bottom of his bowl, the doorbell sounded and footsteps were heard advancing down the corridor. Mrs. Thelma Green herself poked her head in, smiling seraphically. The three clerics arose from their portions, greeting her as if she were the Second Coming.

"The Cardinal just stopped by for an impromptu visit," offered Fr. Jim, *pastor emeritus.*

"His Eminence was just enjoying a bowl of your wonderful soup," added their pastor, Father Morton, half starting to believe in the need for confession.

Young Fr. Brendan said the first thing that came to his mind, "Why don't you sit down and join us, Mrs. Green . . ."

She politely refused, saying, "Oh no, I've got work to do in my kitchen." But then, thinking better of it, she sat down at the table anyway with an eye to watching the four of them finish.

It was Cardinal Mulrooney who picked up the baton. "Chicken soup is indeed good for the soul! Reminds me of my own dear mother's recipe, God bless her." Three Thomases stared at him, doubting what they were seeing.

"Good to the last drop," gulped *Emeritus* Sherman, reminding himself that the devil was a liar.

Monsignor Morton ventured, "Your Eminence, would you like to try some of Luisa's enchiladas now?"

Wiping his mouth with a contented sigh, the Cardinal responded, "No, I think not. But how about another bowl of that soup?" Mrs. Green sucked in her breath with delight Luisa, giddy with relief, held the very last bowlful at arm's length while apologizing in broken English, "Sorry, Padres, no more soup for you!"

"It seems gluttony is making a comeback, boys!" joked Mulrooney.

"No problema . . .," replied three generations united as one.

When the Cardinal finished, they all awaited expectantly, not sure if the world was going to end.

That's when *it* happened. John Cardinal Mulrooney, the great man himself—*sneezed.* Not once, or twice but three times, consecutively, with each explosion reporting like a neighborhood drive-by shooting. In their living rooms, nearby neighbors ducked behind couches and stuffed chairs. Kids out on the school playground hit the asphalt. Caltech, in far off Pasadena, registered a not inconsequential blip on their Richter scale. All were much taken aback by the shattering power of these starnutations—all, that is, except Mrs. Thelma Green.

That kindly lady frowned with concern. She turned, and squeezing his Eminence's arm maternally, said, "Don't worry, honey, I know what's best for you." With the empty pot under her arm, she led the man down the corridor, out the door, down the sidewalk to her Lincoln, where she was overheard promising him a batch of her finest that very evening.

A Pleasant Day to Die

Maria Josefina pronounced herself alive on arrival. She had crossed the border from Mexico, like countless others before her, looking for a better life in the United States. It was not the land of *leche and miel*, but anything was better than the dirt-poor *pueblito* and the shadowy life she had left behind. For some years she took the Rapid Transit bus downtown to labor in sweat-shops owned by immigrant Chinese. But as hard as those days were, there was something enduring and honest about them. In time, she was joined in South Central Los Angeles by several younger siblings who all crossed the same border from Tijuana, eventually getting married and starting families of their own.

Maria Josefina, remaining single and remembering the adobe church of her *pueblito,* became active in her mostly Spanish-speaking parish, St. Michael's, or *San Miguel,* volunteering to be an unpaid catechist. As was the Mexican custom, selling sweets to the kids on Saturdays between religion classes, she began to see brighter days ahead. Little by little, she ingratiated herself with the DRE (director of religious education), a busy Spanish nun named Sister Angela, offering to do more and more, all out of the goodness of her heart. When the nun was transferred to Mexico—and with no other, more qualified candidate to be had in such a poor parish—Maria Josefina was offered a modest salary as the new Sister Angela. This was the opportunity she had been patiently waiting for. Knowing that Fr. Tony, the elderly Italian missionary, being an overworked pastor, would never question her—so grateful was he for all the help she was giving—she got down to the serious business of grand larceny.

First, she volunteered to help count the Sunday collections, an onerous weekly task for pastor and staff alike which required straightening out and stacking one-dollar bills in piles of one hundred—for hours on end. This she did without complaining since it was possible to pocket the bigger bills without arousing the least suspicion. When the weekly "take" showed a slow but ever-increasing decline, it was thought that the economic downturn affecting the country as a whole was now trickling down to the poorest *barrios.* "They just can't give as much as they used to," said the unsuspecting priest. After all, Maria Josefina suggested, they had to eat and pay the exorbitant rents of South Central slumlords. That gave her another idea—someday soon she would be able to experience the American Dream and buy a house, renting the illegal garage apartment behind the main house to newly arrived immigrants, exploiting them for a good profit.

Maria Josefina collected the annual thirty-dollar fee from the parents of nine hundred and fifty-one catechism students when registering them that September. The grand total amounted to almost $21,000. The fact that she only handed over about a third didn't even raise a blip on the unsuspecting pastor's radar. This success prompted bolder ventures. She began asking parents to write their payment checks directly out to her—in her name—saying it was standard operating procedure in *Gringolandia* and that she would duly hand the money over to the parish. Since the old fashioned pastor had no finance committee and no oversights, it was like taking candy from a baby nearing senility.

By far, her greatest exploit was in chairing the parish *fiesta* committee. Half of all proceeds, mysteriously, never made it into the final tally. Maria Josefina, feeling quite content at having made such headway in her newly chosen homeland took advantage of a government amnesty program in the mid-1980s and became a bona fide United States citizen. After proudly making the pledge of allegiance, and snapping a few photos, she went down to the Bank of America and took out a loan on a house in the neighborhood. It needed some work but she knew she could easily parlay it into plenty of future cash in the form of loans and second mortgages. Somehow able to also collect welfare and food stamps for a fictionalized family she invented complete with *documentos*, things went so well over the next several years that she bought not only one but two houses, held extravagant parties there and started flashing wads of cash around—even around the parish. She would take the catechists she liked best out for champagne brunches and even took on a boyfriend, half her age—dear Felipe. Now on the cusp of her fiftieth birthday, she smirked at the easily scandalized because she could easily have been his mother. The fact that he was dealing drugs to kids in her Confirmation class did not seem to bother her in the least. Once, when he was arrested in a police sting operation, she was questioned because they were living together but after a few hours she was released. And all the while she kept stealing from the poor. She liked to say, "Jesus Himself said that *the poor you will always have with you.*" There was a reason they were poor, after all. Yet the aged pastor noticed less and less, if that were possible, so more and more funds disappeared. The more successful she became, the more she became the object of envious gossip. But it felt good to be a recognizable personality just like in one of the *telenovela* soap operas on Spanish-speaking television.

At the high point of her career, the very pinnacle of success, there was an unexpected change of administration in the parish, not a new pastor, the old Italian was still Mr. Reliable—but a new assistant, a young Gringo priest, fresh from the missions overseas. Also, a young seminarian, still wet behind the years would be with them for the summer. These three, she surmised, would present no undue difficulties. After all, she had not been caught yet and it was still *her parish* no matter what the archdiocese might believe.

One Sunday morning, when she and Felipe were counting the 11:00 a.m. Mass collection basket, the young seminarian volunteered to help. *"Esta bien, padrecito,"* she laughed at the "little father." Dollar bills were such a nuisance to uncrumple anyway; they could use the help. At a certain point, she and her boy-toy Felipe disappeared into the restroom together—taking the collection bag with them. They returned after a few minutes with an empty bag. The three of them finished counting the remains after which Maria Josefina generously offered to take both Felipe and the young seminarian out to lunch. The seminarian noticed that the bill was paid with a thick wad of one-dollar bills. Afterward, the three went shopping and Maria Josefina bought the two men new watches, paying again only with single-dollar bills. The seminarian, although definitely young, was not born yesterday. Very much bothered, he informed the *Gringo* assistant parish priest of what he had witnessed.

"Where there's smoke there's fire," said the Gringo assistant priest.

He informed the pastor who refused to believe anything bad of anybody but after insisting allowed his assistant—without making Maria Josefina or her companion suspicious—to collect the necessary evidence. Fr. Gringo immediately took all monies out of her hands. This was certainly a slap in the face for Maria Josefina. After all she had done for the people of that poor parish, the newcomer priest did not seem to trust her. Well, she had been around longer than he had. She had crossed the border without a *Coyote* guide! This new, grossly unfair policy would put a definite crimp in her monthly mortgage payments but she would soon find other ways to keep the cash cow flowing with green milk. She tried selling religious articles in the vestibule of the church but Padre Gringo said, *"The Church is a house of prayer, not a marketplace."* She tried sneaking into the office at odd hours to siphon the petty cash, but it was risky and the results were somewhat disappointing.

That's when she got a good idea, remembering what her mother used to do to their family's enemies back in old Mexico. She went down to the local *bruja* or *Santeria* witch, ordering up a big plate of poison for the problematic prelate. It would not be a pleasant way for him to die. She smilingly delivered a steaming plate of delicious looking, steaming enchiladas to the door of the rectory, saying she hoped they wouldn't prove too spicy for *el padrecito*. "Hahaha." The unsuspecting clod ate the whole "enchilada" as it were, that very night for dinner. But to her disappointment, over the following days—there seemed to be no adverse effects on him at all. No stomach cramps, no skin lesions or headaches, all of which portended an inexplicable death. What she had personally witnessed years before was not working as well north of the border. Hardly anything seemed to happen to him at all. To be sure, the assistant pastor complained of a stomachache but in the succeeding days did not wither away like he was supposed to. In fact, after three days, the damned Gringo seemed fit as a mariachi's fiddle.

Obviously, stronger measures were called for, a more direct approach perhaps. Felipe contacted his *"homeboys,"* from his old gang, any one of whom would disembowel their own brother for a dime bag of crack cocaine. Felipe instructed them to eliminate the interfering cleric. And they did indeed try on several occasions, but the man seemed to always be in the right place at the wrong time. Just when they were about to assault him—late at night in the parking lot—members of the youth group or choir would suddenly appear, surrounding him like a legion of protecting angels. Oddly, the Gringo seemed to be wise to their plan. One day he even changed all the keys and locks throughout the parish and set alarms in the rectory too, so there was little chance to get to him that way. Maria Josefina thought and thought about the best way to kill him. After all, he was ruining her dream. Her bank accounts were dwindling and her family members were always voraciously demanding more.

Then one day, Fr. Gringo called her into his office. On the desk was a one-inch thick manila folder. The heartless man then presented all the evidence he had painstakingly collected over the months since his arrival. At first, she did not bother to deny anything since she felt she had done nothing wrong. Then when denial didn't seem to work in the face of documented evidence, she tried her womanly arsenal. An attempt at being seductive only made him laugh. Then she tried reasoning with him. The previous pastor was really at fault for not instituting any system of accountability. She tearfully begged him not to prosecute. Her lover was in prison, she didn't want to end up the same way. The young priest did profess to have compassion on her, by merely taking her keys away and telling her never to return to the parish. If she continued in this way, he warned, she would surely either go to jail or come to a bad end.

Very sorry about having been caught, Maria Josefina exited the rectory, turned off her tears and began counting her lucky stars. An alternative plan was already forming in her coifed head. She decided, then and there, to take the Master Catechist classes offered by the Archdiocese *gratis* at nights. With her CCD certificate in hand she would simply do the whole thing over again at another parish. After all, there were two hundred and sixty-eight of them in the greater metropolitan area, each one ripe for the picking.

Several months later, she found herself comfortably ensconced in a veritable plum of a parish where the clueless Irish pastor, a certain Father Reginald, gratefully gave her free reign. Since he knew little or no Spanish, she knew he had to depend on her. It was exactly what she had been looking for. Like the first old Italian, this guy was so busy he had no time to worry about her. A year later, according to schedule, she was appointed the new director of Religious Education, and in addition, put in charge of the annual fundraising "fiesta." *Alleluia!* Finally, things were getting back to normal. And no one was the wiser. Felipe had even been released from prison early, not because of good behavior but because of overcrowding. The LA Central Jail would release Jack the Ripper and Attila the Hun early if they needed the bed space. Maria Josefina's main squeeze was out on the streets again, squeezing cash once again from hapless, drug-addicted teens.

Then one day, a thick envelope arrived addressed to Fr. Reginald, marked "Personal" and "Confidential." Passing through the office, she was tempted to steam it open and see what was inside—perhaps a few checks—yet she did not do so. It was probably from one of the dolt's younger siblings who were always calling him and sending him useless things from the Old Sod. The next day, Fr. Reginald called her into his office and read a letter from the very same Gringo priest who had persecuted her in her last parish. The Gringo had discovered her whereabouts and was—*in conscience*—warning Fr. Reginald of his peril, who undertook an investigation of his own books, which duly uncovered her pattern of thievery.

In his charming Irish brogue, Fr. Reginald fired Maria Josefina. Her copious tears did not dissuade him either. She handed over the keys and cursed them all—all these self-righteous priests—all the way out the door. Then an encouraging thought occurred to her— she must finally take her revenge on them, especially the Gringo. A simple plan was plastered all over the daily headlines. She would simply go to the Archdiocese and accuse her enemies of sexual abuse. Yes, that would be perfect. There was no way they could prove otherwise. For a holy priest like the Gringo or the Irishman, it would be a fate worse than death. They would remove them immediately from ministry—forever. Even if they were eventually exonerated later on, they would be ruined for life. Why hadn't she thought of this earlier? She envisioned herself, the very image of tearful sincerity, testifying in a court of law: "*saw the man in dark corners with children . . .*" Practically drooling over the money her nemesis's imminent demise would generate—without looking left or right—she stepped out on to the busy Main Street. A Rapid Transit bus carrying new immigrants back to South Central from the Chinese sweatshops downtown hit her broadside. Her body flew almost a hundred feet before landing in the opposite lane of oncoming traffic. Three cars were unable to avoid running her over. As a formality, the paramedics took her body to California Hospital where she was pronounced dead on arrival.

A Blaze of Butterflies

Eager black faces pressed against the glass, leaving nose prints. Thirty-three students strained to see the small ivory triptych that had been carved in Medieval France eight hundred years before. The center panel showed Christ on the cross with Mary, John the Beloved and the Magdalene.

We were making our way slowly down the long central corridor of the Art Institute of Chicago toward the famous Chagall blue windows at the end. Then it would be on to the main attraction, to the right and up the stairs—a retrospective of the work of the great American painter, John Singer Sergeant.

Breathing deeply, I only half-believed that we had actually pulled it off. All the weeks of planning and preparation were now bearing fruit. Miss Henzel, a second-generation Polish blonde, and the kid's fourth grade teacher controlled the perimeter while I spoke loud enough for all to hear "This is a devotional piece made for private patrons. That means, for rich people who could afford it."

At the sound of my voice the kids looked at me and then back at the work of art in question. Noting no notable responses, I asked a question: "Does anyone know what it is made of?"

Jamal, the shortest boy in the class answered without hesitation, "Ivory."

"And where does ivory come from?" I said a bit too loudly.

"From Africa," a couple voices responded.

"And from what animal is it taken?"

"From elephants," several answered simultaneously.

"That's right. Is it legal to make such things today?"

"Noooooooooo," the kids intoned.

"And why not?"

"Because it's illegal," smirked Jamal.

Knowing full well that the nervous guards were watching us like hawks, expecting the worst and listening to every word, I began to show off a little: "Come now, Jamal, you know perfectly well why it is now illegal to transport ivory out of most African countries . . ."

He looked at the closest guard, one burly grey uniform, who, after sizing up the young Miss Henzel, looked directly at him, as if to say, "You're not that smart, kid."

Jamal answered, "Because elephants are a protected species." He shot a meaningful glance at the guard.

I smiled magnanimously, and not without some pride at the elephant guard who returned my smile. At least this was a change from the normal, dull routine of standing in the same place each day, overseeing the usual clientele who all looked like they just fell out of their limousines. These kids were definitely not elderly, wealthy, white socialites escaping the end-of-winter doldrums of the near north side of Chicago.

"And why is it illegal, anybody know? Don't shout . . ." Several hands waved in front of my face expectantly. I called on Trisha, the shyest and biggest girl, the only one who had not raised her hand. Jamal frowned, feeling betrayed but content because *he knew that I knew* he liked Trisha. She looked at her feet "I don't know."

"Sure you do, Trisha," I coaxed, "What do they have to do to get the ivory tusks away from a live elephant?"

"Kill it," she mumbled.

"Correct," I began, "In the nineteenth century, they were killing all the elephants just for their ivory. So now, in order to preserve the species from extinction, international law forbids the export and sale of ivory . . ."

"One more thing," I paused for dramatic effect, "Where does an elephant keep all his clothes?" There were a few quizzical looks. "In his trunk, of course." Everybody groaned at this lame attempt at humor, even the guard.

We moved on to a suit of armor. The boys pretended to fight with imaginary swords and shields.

"We could use these in our neighborhood," said one of the brightest students, a kid named Anthony. All nodded. The near west side of Chicago was far more dangerous for these kids than Africa was for elephants or the Crusades for knights. There were killings every day, in the projects, on the streets, especially amongst gun-toting, rival gangs.

Precious Blood Parish and Elementary School were located just off the Western Avenue exit of Interstate 290. Although just a few miles from the museum, as the crow flies, it was a world away. Most of the neighborhood youth had never even seen the Lakefront. The idea of making a class trip to the fabled Art Institute, at first seemed an impossible dream, akin to flying to the moon. The principal, Sister Santina, belonging to an Italian missionary order, doubted it could work. Gesticulating wildly with her hands, she enjoyed playing the devil's advocate. "But when would you go? It would have to be in the spring, not too early but not too late . . . Because there is the state testing and inspection . . . Oh, and you would need permission slips from the parents . . . and what about the cost—the tickets and lunches. And the chaperones and . . . *Mama Mia!* The buses! They are so expensive." Despite the litany of difficulties, Sister Santina gave Miss Henzel and myself permission to try.

First, we picked a date—Tuesday of the last week of April. Not a Monday because the museum would be closed. I really wanted the kids to see something special so it had to be before the traveling Sargent exhibit left town. Once given the go ahead by Sr. Santina, I asked Fr. Bill Warman, the pastor, to write a letter on our behalf, asking the Art Institute for complimentary passes for our poor but deserving children. Handing me a copy, he shook his head, saying, "I hope you know what you're getting into."

I had no idea, but that had never stopped me before. As a former student of art history and now a seminarian—the new religion teacher—I walked by faith not by sight. All I knew was that God loved these kids. They were growing up in an ugly, brutal world of drugs and violence and I desperately wanted to show them something beautiful. My mother, having worked for years at the Art Institute, had brought me and my siblings there many times and those memories lingered. I was hoping for the same kind of lasting impression for our fourth graders. Most of them were black and only a quarter—children of Hispanic immigrants—were Catholic. But all were hungry for attention, for love and for knowledge. What they lacked in social graces, they more than made up for in their desire. Their biggest problem, however, were not the mean streets, but their beleaguered families, many of which were comprised of overburdened mothers, with oftentimes absentee fathers. This class trip could be just what the doctor ordered—if we could pull it off.

The following week, a polite letter arrived from the Museum saying that all complimentary passes had already been distributed to the public-school system. It was signed by a certain, Mrs. Elizabeth Wentworth, Trustee. Miss Henzel, daughter of immigrants, was not to be put off so easily. She wrote the following response:

Dear Mrs. Wentworth,

Thank you for your prompt and gracious reply. We ask you, however, to reconsider our worthy request. We know that we are a parochial school, and our kids all come from poor families, but they are extremely well behaved, and will be well prepared for the occasion. I assure you that they will cause no trouble whatsoever.

If you still find it impossible to grant our humble request, our only other option will be to tour the Chicago Tribune offices downtown where there are plans to interview our students. The series of articles will be entitled "Chicago's Cultural Heritage and the Neglect of Inner-City Youth." Some of our children—stung by the rejection at the hands of our fair city's cultural institutions—will, no doubt, feel obliged to relate their disappointment.

Sincerely

"Miss Henzel, I do declare—that smacks of blackmail," I said, after listening to her read it aloud.

She laughed. "My father stood by Lech Walesa during the Solidarity days in the old country. You think his daughter will back down so easily? Now, let's get to work. You know about God and art. Besides letter writing, I know other useful things. How do you think I survive living in this neighborhood?" She had a small efficiency apartment three very dangerous blocks away. Her conscience getting the better of her, she asked, "Is it a sin to exaggerate?"

"You mean to lie?"

"Well, yeah, but then again you're not a full-fledged priest yet, so you can't give me absolution."

"Do you really have plans to visit the Tribune?"

"No, but it's a good idea, isn't it? Speaking of which, they don't pay us the big money to sit around chatting . . ." Just then, the bell for the next class rattled our teeth.

Glancing out the window, I saw a bright, shiny red Porsche 911 with three white teens from the suburbs pull up across the street. A hooded man emerged from the shadows, and leaned down to exchange a small white packet for monetary reimbursement. One teen in the back seat glanced my way then quickly turned away.

An envelope with the requested tickets arrived a week later. The love note from Ms. Wentworth was notably absent.

Obtaining the use of a bus was our next big obstacle—because, our not being a public school plugged into public funding would cost us plenty. It was imperative that we obtain a free bus to haul us down to Michigan Avenue, wait several hours for us there and bring us back on time for the kids to be picked up after school hours. Since there was no budget for class trips, it had to be *gratis*. Begging for light, my first thought was Hubie Green. The Honorable Mister Hubert Stanton Green III. "Brother Hubie," as he was affectionately known by his constituents, had a local storefront office on the other side of the projects where he held court three afternoons a week. He was all smiles but no fool. I walked over that very afternoon, fingering my rosary, and wearing my Roman collar, not to impress the Councilman but for protection. The sharks were even known to feed upon ministers in broad daylight. Bleak, broken windows in the Projects stared darkly down at me. A couple gang members looked my way but waited for bigger fish. I thanked my guardian angel when I finally arrived at my destination, doubly grateful to find Mr. Green's office open for business. Two super-sized male attendants, with the misfortune to have been born without necks, narrowed their eyes upon me, asking what I wanted. Although tempted to blurt out the whole story, I decided to play it cool, refraining from explaining my business, but asking to see "the Man" personally. I was informed brusquely that "the Councilman" was indisposed and would not be attending any of the faithful that day.

"That's just fine," I smiled, "I'll wait." And wait I did—almost three hours. I could hear laughing in the back room. The security guards eyed me suspiciously every few minutes, but after a while, seemed to forget I was there. Then, just before the stroke of five o'clock, there was a rustle of movement coming from down the hall. A tall, elegantly dressed black man emerged, followed by an obviously formidable older woman. They stopped short, surprised to see an apparent priest standing before them. The bouncers tensed.

"Brother Hubie!"—I intoned, smiling widely while moving forward to shake his hand. "Good to see you again." (I had never met the man before, although I had seen him pass by once in a parade and many times on TV.) Now that the element of surprise was used up, I had to keep his attention. "Your many supporters in our church were overjoyed to hear of your recent reelection to which we contributed in no small way ourselves. Not only with financial support but with people power, pounding the pavements, getting the vote out, calling on the grassroots . . ." I truly hoped that exaggeration was not lying. Having learned much from a black Baptist preacher in the neighborhood, I naturally slipped into my Sunday best. The object of my sermon recognized the style if not the content.

"Yes brother, tell the truth . . ." he said, chuckling, and looking at his companions. His beefy cohorts, at first suspicious of my becoming so talkative all of a sudden, began to relax a little. The rather large, but extremely dignified, older woman dressed in bright red, listened attentively.

Although it was obvious that I had impeded the couple's egress from the door, I pressed on undeterred, "Brother Hubie, when our children found themselves in dire difficulty and asked me to whom could we turn, at first—I admit it, O' me of little faith,—I said to myself, "Who can help us now? There's no one to champion our righteous cause. Then, I thought, ain't nothin' impossible for God Almighty, isn't that so?"

Judging by my assembly's unequivocal vocal affirmation, it did indeed appear to be the case. Brother Hubie, although enjoying the novelty of the situation, all the while kept inching his way toward the door. If he left before I had a chance to present my request, all was lost. I correctly surmised that he wasn't quite sure if this crazy white man would pull out a knife or something. There was no more time to lose.

With my voice rising in evangelical fervor, I said, "Seeing the insurmountable obstacle. I was doubtin' just like you are now, brother! Like the apostle Thomas . . . until . . . I saw the light. The Lord Himself inspired me to come over here and stand before you now, seeking your advice . . . Seek out the wise man saith the Good Book! I believe, yes, like you believe, Brother Green, that God would never let our poor fourth graders down!" I stopped for dramatic effect, sweat beginning to run down my temples, then forged ahead, not oblivious to the fact that he was showing signs of beginning to lose his patience. "But who—I asked myself—WHO would get us the help we need? No, not money—did I ask for money? The root of all evil—Heavens NO! All the poor children need is . . . one bus. That's all our poor kids are asking for. A ride to the lakeshore. To get out of this cesspool of a neighborhood for a few short hours of fresh air. To breathe free. To wonder at God's creation and to see the beautiful artworks created by the hand of Man at our own Art Institute of Chicago . . . It's true that a Trustee at said museum refused us at first . . . but we shamed them, all right, writing letters . . . Ask, and you shall receive . . ." I was just starting to believe myself when Brother Hubie laid a hand on my shoulder, stopping me in midsentence. "Son, what is it you are asking Brother Hubie to do for you?" Like the pope in faraway Rome, he always referred to himself in the third person.

"Not for me, Brother Hubie, for the poor kids in our neighborhood. Thirty-three fourth graders need a bus on April 26 for a class trip to go to the museum, but the bus company turned us down."

"Now why would they turn you down? Your money is as good as anybody else's? Is it because the kids are black?" He said, indignantly.

"Well, there's the rub, Brother Hubie—we don't have the money."

The big lady dressed in red sighed. Now, I was certain she was Hubie's Mama. So I whispered, "You know how it is, Brother Hubie, the only thing these kids have are Mamas who love 'em. We can't afford no bus." Finally, the moment of truth arrived. Hubie hesitated, looked at his watch, ready to deny my request—but then he made the fatal mistake of glancing over at his Mama who was eyeballing him fiercely. Hubie's mouth puckered, and Mama gave me a sympathetic nod, as if to say, "Hubie is his Mama's son, no doubt about that!"

"Son, I like your style." He laughed. "You're not afraid to make a fool out of yourself in front of strangers to help poor folks! That's why Brother Hubie is gonna help you. The Lawd helps those who helps themselves. The bus will be there, you just make sure you and those kids are."

When Mama said "Amen!" the service was concluded. I hugged Mama first, then her son, but drew the line at the bodyguards. About the only thing I hadn't done was roll my eyes back into my head and flop around on the floor. But my mission was accomplished. And now, all we had to do was convince the children's parents.

The varied reactions we received from the permission letter we sent home with the kids were instructive. Some parents signed right on the dotted line. Others scribbled comments above or below the signature: *"Good luck! More power to you! Keep him the next day too! Now, I know you Catholics are crazy! . . . I send my son to learn not to waste his time in some museum! Do what you want, I don't care! Just get her home on time!"* And so on and so forth. Many parents did not answer at all. When Miss Henzel and I called their phone numbers, kept on file for just such a necessity, several had been disconnected. Others were not home and might never be. One little girl said her dog, a large Rottweiler named Gunther, had eaten the permission slip right after snacking on the mailman.

As sad as some of these nonresponses were, seeing the failure of family life, we were more determined than ever to succeed in our venture.

Then the immediate preparation began in earnest. I brought in art books that had reproductions of the most important paintings represented in the Art Institute's collections. It was imperative that the kids be able to recognize the work of each artist by sight. There would be real satisfaction in that for them. We used postcard reproductions of famous masterworks like flash cards. We talked about the history of art from antiquity up to the present day—prehistoric, Egyptian, Minoan, Greek, Etruscan, Roman, early Christian, Byzantine, Gothic, Renaissance, Baroque, and the moderns. The kids got to the point where they could recognize almost all the principal painters. They could tell the difference between a Manet and a Monet, between Georges Braque and a Picasso, and between Thomas Hart Benton and Grant Wood. They could even distinguish Chinese porcelains from those of the Japanese. They knew why Van Gogh cut off his ear.

As the big day drew near, the kids got more and more excited. They were tired of seeing small dark prints and wanted to test their knowledge on the originals. Finally—thanks to Brother Hubie and his Mama—the bus awaited us in the schoolyard. Thirty-three neophyte art students counted off and we were on our way. The bus driver let us off right in front of one of the Art Institute's famous bronze lions and the kids blinked as if emerging from a cocoon. Traffic on Michigan Avenue swooshed by northward toward the Miracle Mile. It certainly seemed like a miracle to me. The trees flanking the many-columned edifice burst with pink spring buds. In two orderly lines, we climbed the stairs, free passes in hand. Once inside, I gave them all a final pep talk.

"OK, class, you know what we talked about. How these folks aren't used to seeing kids from our neighborhood in here. They're expecting the worst, so let's give them our best. The guards will be waiting for you to touch the paintings so they can yell at you—don't give them the satisfaction. I want you to remember this day your whole life . . . Now, let's go look at some art!"

We filed in, two by two, proceeding through the glass doors into the inner sanctum. After the Medieval pieces, we proceeded directly to the Sergeant rooms. The guard's fingers twitched on their walkie-talkies. We climbed the stairs and entered straightaway. Several large portraits faced us. The kids looked first at one and then another, in an awed, almost reverent silence. No one said a word or got too close. I smiled because I had told them, "Let the painting talk to you . . . Don't rush up to them, first see them from a distance . . ." And that's exactly what they were doing. One bespectacled, rouged, blue-haired, old lady, from some wealthy suburban enclave froze—aghast—as the kids surrounded her, trying to get a closer look at a portrait of a nineteenth century socialite. Instinctively grasping her purse to her ample bosom, she seemed ready to call for help but calmed down when the kids started discussing the work before them.

Jamal said, "I like it. I mean, this one seems to be more of a painting than that portrait over there. That one could be a photograph. But this one, the paint is nice and thick."

Miss Henzel agreed, "It does seem more painterly and the face has more expression."

Much to her amazement, the rich lady could not help but become involved in the discussion. She and Jamal both leaned forward to inspect a particular detail of the hand. The guard jumped, shouting, "Young man, don't touch!"

The old lady frowned at the guard, reproving him in no uncertain terms, "Why are you picking on us, my dear sir—we didn't touch anything?"

The guard was taken aback and said, "Well . . . er . . . Mrs. . . . It looked like he was about to touch the painting."

The lady, now peeved, defended Jamal, "We were merely looking at the painting more closely, weren't we, young man?" Jamal smiled up at her, thinking that this white lady had to be somebody's Mama.

"I was just trying to figure out how he made the ring look so shiny with just one brush stroke," Jamal said simply.

"Me too." Nodded the lady. She then did something that made us all laugh. She reached out her hand, pointing her finger at the canvas, purposefully bringing it within a hair's breath of the painted surface. The guard's eyes grew wide, and he involuntarily sucked in a great breath. The suspense was killing me too.

"Ma'am, do you want me to call security?"

"My good man," she said elegantly, "you are security!" All the kids laughed. The guard turned red, and made his escape into the adjoining gallery, but not before the old lady's added cheerily, "Now go on about your business, young man, we have paintings to discuss."

She then turned to Jamal and asked, "What do you think of that small one over there?" The two sidled over to the corner, to an intimate portrait of a young black girl. The information card read, "Moroccan girl with hat." The whole class gathered round the two of them. Jamal looked at it for a moment, then said, "That's one of Sargent's watercolors. I like them better than his oil paintings . . ."

"And why is that, may I ask?" she said, sincerely interested in his opinion.

"Because the girl's cute!" laughed Jamal.

"You're right. But is there any other reason?"

Jamal hesitated, looking at me. I nodded encouragingly. He said slowly, "Well, he painted those portraits—if you'll forgive me for saying so, ma'am—for rich people. I guess he had to do it for the money. But these watercolors, he did them just because he liked to. He was outside and having fun. They feel free . . ."

The old lady seemed lost in thought for a moment before saying, "Young man, you know, you're right again. And I completely agree with you, but up until this moment, I never knew why."

Accompanied by the nice old lady, who obviously knew a great deal about the collection, we methodically made our way through the rest of the exhibit unmolested, enjoying everything, but spending more time with our favorites. The guards even joined in a couple times. With time flying, our sack lunches beckoned, and we breezed through the different period galleries, joyfully recognizing the great artworks we had studied. Each encounter was like meeting old friends unexpectedly. Having gone full circle, nearing the front doors, Miss Henzel organized everybody into two exit lines. But before filing outside, I approached our new friend and companion, who stood there enraptured at the sight of these thirty-three, living, breathing masterpieces.

"Thanks for coming along with us this morning," I said.

"No, Father, I am the one who should be thanking you—it's been a real eye opener for me. Not the paintings, but these beautiful children."

"I'm not a Father yet . . ."

"It seems like you're well on your way," she said, touching my arm.

"You know, ma'am, I do apologize, you've been so nice to us and we don't even know your name . . ." Calling the class to attention, they all stared at her expectantly.

The lady smiled and said, "My name is Mrs. Elizabeth Wentworth. I'm a Trustee of the Museum, volunteering part-time as Tour Guide in the galleries."

Miss Henzel and I gasped. What is often referred to as an awkward silence ensued. Then Jamal suddenly stepped forward and gave the lady a quick hug. She just stood there, surprised but touched.

Our art class waved goodbye to our new friend then exited through the front doors, down the wide steps and out onto the expanse of green beside the museum. They flitted to and fro like a blaze of butterflies amongst the blossoming trees.

The bus driver was punctual, picking us up and bringing us back to school right on the button. The next week, Miss Henzel received a letter in the mail. It was from Mrs. Wentworth. She informed us that, not only were we always welcome at the museum, but that her Foundation would be funding art appreciation classes at the Institute—beginning that very summer—for underprivileged, inner-city youth.

Anecdotes of Air
in Dungeons

Father John Baptist O'Brien sighed in between penitents. As much as he truly believed in the life-transforming effects of the Lord's mercy, hour upon hour in a cramped, airless confessional could be wearing. Saint John Marie Vianney—the patron saint of priests—appeared in his mind as the next person entered and knelt on the other side of the screen. It was probably another old lady with rheumatoid arthritis, and an all too vivid memory of the past. She would no doubt complain about her husband as well as her grown-up children who long ago had abandoned the faith of their ancestors.

Saint John Marie Vianney, had been sent to that backwater, Ars, to about 250 ignorant, ungrateful peasants. Through prayer and penance—he was known to boil potatoes at the beginning of the month and eat them until they were green—he managed to convert the whole town as well as about half of France. Fr. John Baptist always felt a little guilty thinking about his favorite saint since he ate much more than rotting potatoes and spent too little time on his knees. Padre Pio was a similar case—now officially sainted—who was also known for his long labors in the confessional. Word was that the Lord had gifted both saints with the scrutiny of hearts, that is, a clairvoyant knowledge of a penitent's hidden sins. God forbid a sinner tried to hide anything. The two saints would voice out the omitted sins, usually loud enough to wake the other penitents waiting in the long lines outside the confessional box. Both saints had been persecuted and even attacked physically by the devil and his minions for freeing so many captives from their sins. Fr. John Baptist smiled ruefully at this thought. His long line was usually made up of the same people with the same sins Saturday after Saturday. Confession was a liberation for the sinner but a weight at times for the Confessor. He had, however, been blessed with an extremely poor memory. In the outside world that was a detriment, but inside the confessional, it was a blessing. Usually, two minutes after giving absolution he could no longer remember anything the penitent had said.

Some would enter and say, "Well, you remember, Padre . . . last week . . ."

And he would be forced to respond, "No, sorry, I don't remember . . ." After all, if the Lord forgave and forgot, why shouldn't he? There was a story of the famous Doctor of the Church, Saint Teresa of Avila who, while praying in her cell was visited by the Lord in all His glory. She, feeling her sinful humanity reportedly said, "Lord, please forgive that sin I committed last week . . ."

Jesus asked her, "And what sin is that, my daughter?"

"Well, you know, Lord, the one I confessed to the priest . . ."

This was when the Lord interrupted her, "If you confessed it to the priest, then I no longer remember it." That thought more than any other, gave him the courage to face yet another sorrowful soul. It was a joy to set the captives free, even if a terrible bore at times. Many of his confreres hated hearing confessions. He suspected that a few rarely darkened the door of a confessional and so saw little need for others to do so. He had heard real complaints from people about how other priests told them that their sins were not sins at all. Many clerics who had survived the post-Vatican II exodus no longer clung to traditional beliefs about Original sin. If nothing was sinful, there was no need for a Savior or to waste a sunny, Saturday afternoon in a dark confessional when one could be golfing.

The next penitent began with the usual words, "Bless me, father, for I have sinned . . . I am a married man and have not been to confession in ten years . . ." Normally, these were the big fish one lived for. Big sins, big conversion, big graces. All the angels in heaven would be rejoicing in heaven over this one penitent sinner. But Fr. John Baptist opened his eyes. Something was different with this fellow. There weren't the usual embarrassed initial pauses. The man went on almost as if he were reading from a script. "Well," thought the priest to himself, "some people did write down a laundry list so as to overcome natural nervousness. By the end, however, they are feeling happy and free enough to state things spontaneously." This one said, "Father, my biggest sin is that . . . I molested my niece." The priest sat up straight, not only at the gravity of the sin but thinking that the man's voice sounded somehow unnatural—as if he was issuing a challenge. "When I entered this country, my brother and his family let me stay with them. Well, I was feeling so lonely one night, I went into her room and . . ."

"What exactly are you telling me? You abused the girl sexually?" asked the priest, now very much alarmed. With this information, he knew he would have to protect the victim as well as the confessional's sacred seal of silence. Getting the man to talk openly about his crime outside the confessional in order to be able to report it to the authorities would be tricky and difficult—but somehow he had to obey both Canon and Civil laws and protect the poor child from further abuse. And the only way to do that was to get the penitent to freely give himself up to the police so as not to violate the sacred seal of the sacrament.

The man went on with the disgusting details. The story seemed credible and the words he used bordered on contrition and amendment of life, if not true sorrow.

To be sure, Fr. John Baptist asked him some clarifying questions, then said, as forcefully as he could, "To receive the Church's absolution, you must remove yourself from your brother's house immediately . . . and have a firm purpose of never sinning in this way again. Furthermore, you must try to make some restitution, even if the damage is irreparable, by going to the authorities."

"What do you mean?"

"You must tell your brother about what you have done and then surrender to the police."

"Sorry, Padre, I can't do that, Miguel would kill me. *La policia* would arrest me, put me in prison or deport me. It was an accident. I didn't mean to do it. It just happened. Only a few times . . . What about God's forgiveness, anyway."

"Wait a minute! You just said that it happened only once!" His danger antennas went up. There was something very wrong here. The man had slipped up, proof that he was lying.

Calming himself with an act of will, Fr. John Baptist said, "It would be better if we spoke about this matter outside the confessional—in my office . . . I have only fifteen more minutes left on duty—please wait for me, so we can talk. Then and only then could you possibly receive absolution."

The man mumbled something in the affirmative. He exited and another penitent entered. Fr. John the Baptist impatiently waited until the old lady left, so he could deal with the man's case. A sinking feeling in his stomach told him something was going horribly wrong. Child molesters were also murderers, since they first killed the body by abusing it, but far worse, they often times killed the innocent soul. He hung up his purple stole and came out of the confessional, peering around the dimly lit church for the penitent. He looked in front of the statue of Our Lady of Guadalupe and the Sacred Heart but he was not there. The place was empty except for the Presence in the tabernacle. He knelt down to pray for guidance.

He asked God what he should do, repeating the whole scenario over again in his mind. Was there something that he should have done differently? Starting to panic, he thought perhaps the man would be waiting for him in the parish office. But he was not there. The man had seen the danger for himself and simply vanished. He would probably forget about the whole idea of confession. What about the poor abused girl? Seminary training had not prepared him for this. He closed his eyes again and prayed harder. The law said he had to report the offender, but if he did he would violate the sacred seal of secrecy demanded by confession, and lose his faculties to practice as a priest. But how could the man be reported when he did not see his face? He didn't even know his name, much less where he lived? No brilliant ideas came to him, only a dull ache at the back of his head. Who was the man?

Fr. John Baptist could not sleep that night. The thought that the man might be molesting the poor girl again made him toss and turn. But there was no way to locate the culprit. What else could be done?

The next morning he showered, dressed, prayed his office in the rectory chapel and went out front to get the *Times*. Even though it was notoriously anti-Catholic he liked the sports page. On the front page there was a headline at the bottom that stopped his heart: "PRIEST FAILS TO REPORT MOLESTER'S CONFESSION."

As he read on, it was as if he were being sucked into a nightmarish, parallel world. Everything seemed to slow down as the awful truth dawned on him—that the man had not been a penitent at all but a plant. A *Times* reporter had concocted the whole phony confession to see if the average local Catholic priest was complying with the law to report all sexual abuse immediately to the authorities. Of course, both the priest's scruples inside the confessional itself and his desire to resolve the difficulties outside it were glossed over and seemed lame. The reporter had worn a wire and had recorded the whole thing, but conveniently had edited the dialogue, slanting the story to show Fr. John Baptist in the worst possible light—as yet another cleric only too willing to avoid his civic duty in favor of antiquated formalities of the Catholic Church, so as to protect the so-called inviolable confessional seal. The priest was indeed sworn to secrecy while the reporter was not. The Vicar for Clergy for the archdiocese called before nine that morning, the local bishop phoned by ten and the archdiocese's attorney just before noon. All said the same thing, basically—you're on your own. Get a lawyer. But he had no money to hire one.

The police knocked on the rectory door around two in the afternoon. They wanted to ask him about other possible cases. Their reasoning being, if you concealed the man's guilt in this one case, how many more might there be?

Throwing his body down on the chapel floor he pleaded with God. But after his panic receded, slowly it dawned upon him that the whole scenario was an opportunity for martyrdom. The new persecution against the Church had arrived at his door and he was being asked to pay the price. He was all alone and could reveal nothing. No one took his side except for his family members who lived far away. During the endless interviews downtown at the precinct, he realized it was useless to continue trying to defend himself verbally. At first, the detectives said more questioning would be necessary but no arrest was forthcoming. The case was still under investigation. A series of Time's articles based on the incident followed. No one ever questioned the journalist's motives or ethics. There was even talk about a possible Pulitzer Prize. Meanwhile, Fr. John Baptist was left to deal with trying to find an attorney and calming scandalized parishioners. Word came from on high that he was being immediately removed from ministry—until things were resolved. But how could things ever be resolved? No, he realized he was being sacrificed. But "why?" he asked himself, over and over again? When the answer finally came in prayer, issuing from a dense darkness within, it had an unexpected calming effect upon him: *Because you have been freeing the captives . . .*

This was the small chink of light in the whole dark scenario. This was the reason the devil had seen fit to bother trying to destroy him. The evil one had despised both John Marie Vianney and Padre

Pio because they set the captives free in droves. So the old scoundrel would engineer just about anything to stop the process.

He had to move out of the rectory and was forced to sleep on the couch of a professor friend. Not able to afford a decent lawyer, and with his meager savings exhausted, when the case finally came to trial several months later, the jury ended up believing the reporter. The judge, wanting to make an example of him, sentenced him to seven years of jail time, not in one of those comfortable, federal, white collar correctional institutions but in a hard-core state prison upstate. Upon arrival, he was immediately placed in solitary confinement since most of his fellow inmates believed that any jailbird priest was a sex offender against children, the most heinous of crimes, and thus was fair game to be raped, beaten and worse. He was locked up twenty-three hours a day and let out for only one hour's recreation and exercise in a forty-by-ten-foot chain-link cage. Rain or shine, it was always the same.

At first, he was incredulous, then saddened, horrified, then alternately angry, depressed and desperate. But eventually, a certain peace settled in. He prayed more than he had ever done before. He celebrated Mass, secretly in the middle of the night, by pocketing some bread and raisins saved from the rice pudding to be fermented into wine. The chalice was a paper cup and the paten, a paper plate. Sometimes it would take three or four hours to finish a simple daily mass. Despite his poor memory in the confessional he was able to remember all the prayers. When a zealous evangelical guard realized what was going on, they took away his Bible and breviary. Nevertheless, throughout the long nights he prayed with silent, inexpressible groaning. The threats that reached him from other prisoners frightened him, because they mistakenly believed him to be an abuser, not one who had been abused by the system. He knew with certainty that someday they would find a way to get to him. Although isolated for his own protection, there were always ways. An interior voice told him that, like the apostle Paul, he was being poured out as a libation for the guilty and the innocent alike, and that all would be accomplished soon. He felt as if, like his namesake, he was preparing the way.

Fr. John Baptist could see out the small square window only by standing on the sink next to the lidless stainless steel toilet. He stared at the sky, thinking of heaven and trying to forget the earth. He ate what was placed before him, and spoke only when spoken to. Mostly he listened, even to the whispered confessions of fellow inmates. How happy they were to be set free. How happy he was to be exercising his priestly ministry, knowing that no prison walls could stop something coming from above. Since he had ten fingers, they could not stop him from praying the Rosary. Despite his sufferings, he began to experience a constant joy welling up within.

Since the federal prison was located in the northern part of the state, he received few visitors, a couple family members travelling from back east and a few of his brother priests. After the first two years, the parole board—seeing his smiling face—issued a verdict saying he was not sufficiently repentant to be released. But how wrong they were, he thought. He regretted every offense he had ever committed against God and neighbor. He fasted and prayed daily, not only for his own sins but also for those of the Church and the whole world. He begged God's mercy day and night.

Occasionally, a letter would reach him. And he would pen a short response. He was amazed at how similar his own poor scribbling sounded like the epistles of Paul from his Roman prison. He knew that his words would be edited by the censors and most probably would never reach the person to whom they were being sent. But that didn't seem to matter much since he sent them out like doves seeking a place to land after the flood. He felt that his life, as ineffectual as it had been, was finally taking on a depth of meaning. He found that the less he slept the clearer his dreams became. Night was as clear as day. He awoke from a particularly clear dream in which the Lord gave him a red crown of thorns, absolutely sure that that day would be his last—the day of his final surrender. They would come for him to set him free. In the dream, he had seen it all unfold the way he knew would take place. So he forgave his murderers in advance.

He was normally allowed his weekly shower alone. But that particular morning, the door leading to the general quarters where the rest of the prison population was housed, was inexplicably left open. The guard who normally stood around the corner was nowhere to be seen. Fr. John Baptist showered, dressed quickly, and then waited for them to arrive. Three prisoners he had never seen before entered and, holding him down, beat him bloody before cutting his throat with a homemade blade made of sharpened plastic. The in-house prison investigation was never closed, but simply shelved. The same reporter who wrote the original stories about him buried a short blurb about his death on page seven of the second section, between the entertainment news and sports. The priest was buried without fanfare at his family's expense in a plot next to his parents. Very few attended the funeral. At night the stars shone down upon his grave. During the day, a few wild flowers sprang up. A steady stream of people began visiting his gravesite, getting down on their knees and sticking their petitions written on small pieces of paper in the cracks around the simple black granite marker.

Sounds of Eden

Behind the strip-mall at the bottom of the hill was a barber-shop. The familiar swirling red and blue pole beckoned like a siren. Even though the portrait of the artist as a young man depicted a disheveled, unshaven, misunderstood genius, he felt in need of a good, short haircut. He hated feeling his brown locks flopping into his eyes or over his ears and collar. The only reason he hesitated was because of the barber himself. Walking past the large window and door a couple times, it was clear that no one was inside but the barber alone. That could be good or bad. If the man was good at his trade, there should be people waiting—loyal customers willing to waste time to receive the artful touch of his clippers. Nevertheless, there he was sitting in one of his own barbers' chairs. They were vintage 1950s—silver, covered by black leatherette that had been sat on so many times each was split in the seat, revealing white stuffing. The barber himself was neither short nor tall, and had a reasonably good haircut himself. The young artist wondered if he cut his own hair or did he have his own favorite barber. If so, where was *his* barber, and how could he possibly be located. No, there was nothing for it, but to chance it, and risk a bad haircut. Taking a deep breath, he opened the glass door and stepped through. The barber did not immediately look up from the headlines. The Viet Nam war still dragged on. And the only guys still getting short haircuts were coming home—unheralded—in black body bags. Seamus thought that perhaps there was still time to beat a retreat to his 1963 pistachio green Rambler parked out front, a few spaces down.

Opening the door, a little bell tinkled. The barber looked up; his glasses perched on a sharp nose. He smiled, slid out of the swivel chair, and putting the paper on the narrow counter below the big mirror, grabbed the protective haircloth, shaking it like a toreador before a bull. "Morning, I'm Ron," he said affably.

"Hi, my name's Seamus. I was walking by and . . . Felt like I could use a trim . . ." Although a freshman in college, he still always felt like he had to give reasons for everything he did.

"Sit right down, friend . . ."

"You don't have another appointment or something," Seamus asked, half hoping that if it were so, then he would skip the ordeal for another week.

"Nope, you're it and you're very welcome. Now what can I do for you today?"

"I need a haircut . . ."

"Which one? Uh, sorry, incorrigible barbershop humor. You're not obliged to laugh."

Seamus did laugh, nervously, "I guess I want it short but not too short, long enough to be *combable*, a little longer on top than on the sides . . ."

"Gotcha," said Ron, shears in hand. The man himself was salt & pepper, perhaps prematurely gray.

"A little slow today," the young man asked, trying to find out why he was the only client.

"Oh, things have been slow since the Beatles," the barber said, like a farmer talking about the drought. "Six months after the British invasion, every kid and his brother convinced his parents that the 1950's flat-top would no longer due. At first, it was the teenagers—who let their hair down, so to speak—then the little kids, followed by the parents themselves, and now the grandparents. Everybody wants to grow it out . . ." Despite this grim news, his voice sounded bright and hopeful.

Seamus found himself wanting to console a barber whom he had never met before.

Ron clipped and chatted at the same time, "You know what that means, instead of a trim every couple weeks, it's once every two or three months."

"You got kids?" Seamus asked, without knowing why.

Ron paused for a brief moment, "Yes, as a matter of fact I do," he answered, "A son maybe a little older than you. Jimmy. Good kid, if I do say so myself. Smart. Takes after his mother. Not interested in the shop. But not interested in going to college either." Ron stopped and said, confidentially, "To tell you the truth, he'll be nineteen next month and I'm afraid he'll get drafted and have to go over to Southeast Asia. Now, don't get me wrong, I support our boys over there, but what a mess . . . I was in Korea myself . . ."

Seamus said, "I registered for the draft but since I'm in college, I don't have to go." His words hung in the air, floating down like wisps of hair slowly to the linoleum floor.

Ron clipped away, thoughtfully, for a while. Seamus felt the man's light touch measuring his cranium, getting the feel for its circumference. The clipping sound reminded him of a childhood memory, summers long ago, hearing someone cutting the grass down the street by hand, snip by snip. It soon became clear to him that Ron was an artist as well, not with paint but with hair.

Seamus said, "I picked a low number in the lottery for the draft. If the war keeps going on, though, my number might be called after graduation . . . Why didn't Jimmy go to college?"

"Well, he always liked cars, always wanted to be a mechanic. Works at the speed shop down on Walnut." Ron finished a minute later with a flourish, dusted him off, and delicately flicked stray hairs out of closed eyes and open ears.

Well that's how the first haircut went. Right then and there, Seamus decided, rather—he knew—that Ron was his man, and would be his barber for life. From then on, he would trust his head to no one else. He would never have to tell any other barber what he wanted, how his hair should be cut. Ron already knew what was needed.

Once a month, the two cemented their budding friendship.

Later that year, Jimmy got his draft notice in the mail. He asked his dad to give him a haircut fit for the marines. They'd be sending him back east to Paris Island for basic training.

Ron filled Seamus in on his son's journey, all the way to his arrival in Nam. Ron even read him a few of Jimmy's letters. As the months passed, it became obvious that there were several close shaves over there, but not of the barbershop variety. Yet with each haircut, Ron became more hopeful. "Only nine more months! . . . Only six months to go before Jimmy comes home . . ." Then suddenly the weekly letters stopped. Seamus could tell that Ron was worried that day, since he trimmed one side-burn a little longer than the other. Then, finally, the month before Jimmy was due to come home, a letter arrived in which he informed his folks that he had reenlisted for another tour of duty, saying something about a promise he'd made to a fallen buddy.

Although the disappointment and worry on the barber's face was visible in the following months, the clippers still sounded sharp, maneuvering around his ears with expert abandon.

"He's a veteran now, he knows how to survive . . ." Seamus said encouragingly.

"You're probably right," said Ron simply, pulling the hair covered cloth from my body like a magician from under a table full of expensive crystal.

"I hope this haircut does the trick, because I'm having my first show of paintings. And I don't want to look shaggy. Maybe people will buy a few. Then, I won't have to be the starving artist anymore and can even think of coming in here a little more often." He always felt a little guilty letting four weeks become six or eight. Seamus knew that the long hair trend was slowly giving way to even longer styles in the 1970s, which only meant more hard times for Ron.

The next month, Seamus avoided talking about his art show and instead asked Ron what kind of car he drove. The barber pointed to a gleaming blue 1957 Chevy Malibu convertible parked off by itself in the far corner of the parking lot.

"Wow!" Seamus said, truly impressed, "It looks like it's in perfect shape. You must garage it."

"And I change its diapers like she was a baby. The wife wants me to sell it, but it isn't worth much nowadays, with the gas crisis and all. It's a V8, so it guzzles. I let it glide down the hill in neutral every morning to conserve fuel."

"Oh yeah, I live up the hill too on Hastings."

"Hello, neighbor, we're two blocks over on Rexford."

Seamus smiled; it was good to know that Ron was not only his barber but also his neighbor. California had lots of people, but with the fast pace of life, it was hard getting to know any of them.

Just as he was finishing up the cut, Ron finally asked, "Hey, buddy—how did your art show go?"

"Didn't sell a darned thing."

"Why not? I'm sure you're a great artist."

"For an artist to sell a lot of paintings he pretty much has to be dead."

"The way of the world," said Ron, shaking his head, commiserating for a moment before adding, "Times are tough all over for a lot of folks."

Seamus grinned, "You know, I think the problem was the haircut you gave me." "Really?" Ron said, disturbed. He stopped clipping, and swung the chair around to look his friend in the eye. "I gave you a bad haircut?"

"No! I didn't mean that! But perhaps, you gave me too good of a one. You see, I looked too clean cut for their idea of an artist. You know how it is, Ron, people think that in order to be a good artist you have to look eccentric—long hair, unshaven, clothes with holes, hang-dog anguished look, etc. . . ."

Ron grunted sympathetically. And then, as Seamus was about to leave, he added apologetically, "Sorry, I just had to raise my prices. You can pay me later . . ."

"Maestro!" said the artist handing over some bills, "My head is your canvas."

A few months later, Seamus informed Ron that he would be having another exhibit of his paintings, and that somehow, someway he had to figure out how to sell some of them.

Ron said, "I got just what the doctor ordered—but will you trust me?"

Seamus nodded, saying, "My head and perhaps next year's tuition are in your hands." Not allowing his client to look in the mirror until the work was completed, at last the end result was unveiled.

Seamus stared at his reflection in the mirror, open-mouthed, "Well, it does look more eccentric. It's not punk—what is it?"

The barber took a small mirror, angling it with the big one to show the back of his head. "It's my genius artist cut. Guaranteed to sell paintings." Ron crowed.

Seamus gasped, "You've carved my initials in the back of my head! My mother will be horrified but I suspect the folks coming to the wine & cheese opening of my show will be suitably impressed."

"That's right, they will say. "This guy must be good. Look at his haircut! How eccentric. He's the next big thing!" The two laughed and said goodbye.

At the opening, dressed in a gaudy, multicolored Hawaiian shirt and paint-splattered khakis, Seamus did indeed sell several paintings for good prices.

Overjoyed, the next month, he gave Ron a big tip, saying, "That haircut was a doozy. But just a regular cut until my graduation, OK!"

An uneventful year passed, marked by their monthly visits. That summer, trying to figure out exactly what to do after graduation, Seamus popped in to Ron's Barber Shop for a quick trim.

The first thing he noticed was that Ron was not sitting in his chair reading the papers. He was standing before the mirror looking at his own reflection in the big mirror behind the chairs. The young man knew immediately that something was wrong. Entering, Ron didn't even turn to face him but seemed to be speaking to someone far away. His normally steady hands were trembling. When he turned to pick up the scissors, they fell onto the floor, which had not been swept up after the last customer. But Seamus greeted him, as if everything was normal, sitting down in the swivel chair. Ron's voice was subdued, like a fog drifting in. The young man wondered what was happening to his friend. Then he saw the reason. To his right, in the middle chair seat, on top of the newspaper, sat a telegram from the government.

"Last Saturday," he said softly. "And here I was cutting hair, like nothing was happening . . . clear on the other side of the world . . ."

Seamus didn't know what to do or say, so after a few long seconds said, "Just take a little off the top, Ron." He said these words in the most normal, even tone he could manage.

Instinctively, Ron began to work. He rotated the chair to face away from the mirror, wrapped his client in the black body cloth and then suddenly began to weep. Then after a minute, recovering himself, he began cutting hair. Able to read the telegram from his vantage point, Seamus, too, felt numb. The gentle clipping sounds reached his ears, but they seemed unreal, mingling as they did with Ron's voice, informing him of Jimmy's death. *"Clip, clip* . . . out on patrol . . . *clip* . . . a land mine . . . like a hero . . . *clip, clip* . . ."* Weren't these the sounds of Eden—thought Seamus—just after the fall—when God the Father went searching the garden for his lost son.

They didn't exchange another word. Seamus tried to say something but couldn't so he paid Ron by putting the money in the little antique register himself. Ron turned toward the mirror again and didn't say goodbye.

The next time he came down there was a closed sign, with an explanation: "Gone Fishing. Back in two weeks." Seamus thought a lot about Ron during that time. Their next meeting was almost normal, with Ron telling him all about his vacation in Northern Wisconsin, and about how great the fishing was in the lake. "It's so peaceful," he said, "but the mosquitos are as big as helicopters!" Then suddenly, Ron announced his own news: "I bought a farm back there."

"You're going to move?" Seamus asked, surprised.

"Naw, my brother's gonna farm it, but I'll own the land. He'll pay me rent . . . The plan is to retire there someday. I think that's where I'm supposed to be." Seamus nodded, risking the loss of his left ear. Ron held his head still. The two artists understood each other. Both were trying to carve out a place in the world, one head and one painting at a time.

A few months later, the secretary of State, Dean Rusk, announced the end of the draft. Antiwar protests continued, all over the country. Seamus noticed that Ron was no longer reading the daily paper. When there were no customers, he just sat there, eyes half-closed, his arms folded on his chest. By this time, a few more clients had discovered his talents, so he was a little busier and that was a good thing economically and emotionally. Long-time customers, however, still had to wait their turn just like everybody else.

The '70s dragged on. Nixon, Kissinger, the fall of Saigon, Ford, Jimmy Carter, disco music . . . But with the release of the big Hollywood blockbuster about a couple Navy flying aces, every kid wanted a short haircut. So business began picking up again, much to the chagrin of their ex-hippie parents. Imagine some kid, still wet behind the ears, asking Ron if he knew how to give a flat-top?

A few years went by with Seamus having exhibits all over the States and Canada. Returning home, and pulling up to the shop one afternoon, the first thing he noticed was that the '57 Chevy convertible was not parked in the corner of the lot. Looking up, he was shocked to see the barber pole gone. The barbershop had been turned into the "Hair Today, Gone Tomorrow" Unisex Styling Salon. Horrified, he walked the whole strip, but Ron's Barber Shop was not to be found in the recently renovated minimall. No doubt, the owners had raised the rents.

Seamus was crestfallen, and entering the Salon, asked a young woman with green hair where Ron's went. She didn't know. Neither did her neighbors since they were all new businesses. Seeing a phone booth, he checked the local yellow pages but with no luck. Where would his friend have gone? Perhaps to his farm and that lake in Wisconsin?

Seamus drove back up the hill and informed his mother. She suggested looking in the big mall. He shook his shaggy head disconsolately. "No, that's not Ron's style," he said. There was nothing to be done but to find another barber. He felt like a traitor. The next day, in the Unisex Salon, he realized that the green-haired girl wouldn't know a regular haircut if it came up and bit her on her pimply nose.

Seamus kept painting and traveling. But it always pained him to have to go to strange barbers for haircuts. He always had to describe what he wanted, over and over again, but none of them ever got it right. Whenever he managed to come home, he would drive around the area, looking for Ron's. The man was seemingly nowhere to be found.

He passed Ron's house on Rexford many times. But there was never a blue '57 Chevy Malibu in the driveway, just an old Ford camper parked in front of a closed garage.

One day, however, Seamus drove over to the adjacent town and stopped on the little main street to buy a newspaper, trying to decide what to do with the rest of the day, when he thought he could hear the sounds of someone clipping—-in a garden—far off. Curious, he walked down a little alley lined with small shops, seeking the cutting sounds. Searching the shop windows, he finally saw it, on the left—a swirling red and white barber pole. Holding his breath, he approached the glass door and window, peering tentatively inside. There was Ron slouched down in the middle chair, snoozing, a newspaper opened across his chest. When Seamus opened the door, a tinkling bell startled the man awake. Ron opened his eyes to see his old friend standing before him. Getting up out of his chair slowly, the two stood there beaming at each other for a long moment. Then

Seamus took his place in the chair closest to the window while Ron arranged the cloth over his chest and lap.

"I need a haircut," said the artist.

"Which one?" Smiled Ron.

Life, Death, and Giants

T homas Williams was one of the last surviving heroes of World War II. He was a member of the fabled Tuskegee Airmen, the black flyers who harassed Hitler's Messerschmitts in the European Theater. Although he always wanted to learn to fly himself, he had not been chosen to become one of the pilots. Instead, he was given the responsibility of keeping the flyboys airborne. As one of the head mechanics, the nuts and bolts of aerodynamics fell to his team, so the pilots wouldn't fall out of the skies. Surely, it was a matter of pride, for Thomas and for all of them, as was so often evidenced in after years when they would gather for their yearly reunions. Reminiscing, telling real war stories, laughing and crying, they also remembered the extreme resistance of the armed services to having an elite force comprised exclusively of African Americans. Each member was a hero of a battle younger generations could not fully comprehend. The reunions were becoming more and more like a countdown—who would die next. Soon it would be Thomas's turn.

He and Annie married down in Galveston after the war, very much against her father's wishes. Thomas felt, that if the Nazis couldn't stop him, her old daddy sure wasn't going to be able to. Poor but in love, they moved to the greener fields of California, where he got a job working for the Johnsonville Pie Company. He called it his "pie in the sky" job. If he could keep the doughboys airborne, the machines mixing pie dough would present no difficulty. The years produced millions of cherry, apple and peach pies—yet no babies. They did manage, however, to buy a modest home on Sixty-Eighth Street near Main in South Central Los Angeles. In those days, the neighborhood was mixed with blacks moving in and white Germans, Italians and Poles moving out. He tended the garden while Annie did the cooking, cleaning and bills. He was, as he would say, "the outside man" and she was "the inside woman." And that's how they got on together for so many years, working, loving, hoping, going to church—all through the fifties, turbulent sixties and on into the eighties and nineties. They became pillars of St. Michael's Catholic Church. Not too many African Americans were Catholic, but since most hailed from Galveston-Louisiana stock they would practice the faith of their fathers and mothers until they died. Thomas was chief usher and collected the offerings after the sermon while Annie stayed after Mass to help count it. The various priests serving there over the years counted on them, and they—especially in their last years— counted on the priests, not to mention their many friends in the dwindling English speaking community. After the riots of the sixties and later on, in the nineties, the Latinos moved in and many of the younger black families moved out to better neighborhoods all over the Southland. It was mostly the oldsters who chose to stay.

When Annie was diagnosed with stomach cancer, Thomas did his best to help her, as did a few closer friends from the parish. But when he himself had a stroke, the priests had to start coming to bring them both Holy Communion. A fine pair they made too. There was Annie in her little cot in the back room while Thomas lay in a bed in what was formerly the dining room.

Father Mark, the newly ordained assistant pastor, visited every week. He was a World War II enthusiast and loved to hear Mr.

William's stories about his famous squadron. Together, if the old man felt up to it, they would pour over old photos and articles. This made Thomas forget his troubles for a time. He often wept over the fact that he could not help Annie more.

That's when Doreen Nelson became a part of their lives. She was one of those smiling but unscrupulous persons who prey on the poor, the weak and the lonely in poverty-stricken areas like South Central Los Angeles. She would identify elderly couples or singles that had no children to help or protect them and befriend them, offering to do miscellaneous services for them: taxes, real estate deals, banking etc. Then, before anyone realized it—his or her assets would be neatly signed over to her name. If other relatives attempted to file a lawsuit, the legal costs usually dissuaded them.

One day, while Thomas was in the bed sleeping, Doreen Nelson entered their little bungalow through the side door and proceeded to the back room to where Annie lay near death. Instructing the nurse to leave them for a moment, she took some legal papers out of her alligator skin briefcase and, with honeyed words, managed to get the ailing woman to sign on the dotted line. Thomas awoke in the dining room as the front door slammed behind her. Their dear friend, Doreen, smirked, as she revved her silver-blue, late-model Mercedes—Caddies were chump change—because her mission had been accomplished. She was now the legal beneficiary of 25 percent of the William's estate, whatever that might be worth. Since they had no close family member really looking out for them, even if she got caught, chances were good that she would collect after their immanent deaths. Even if their church friends got wind of the scam, it would be too late to do anything about it, short of spending their own money on lawyers.

Since the smell of blood attracts many other sharks to a feeding frenzy, other people started coming around "to help" the elderly couple, claiming to be "cousins" or "in laws" twice removed. Of course, each one said that their only interest was to protect Thomas and Annie from unscrupulous people like Doreen Nelson. One after another, however, attempted to get power of attorney in hopes of obtaining control of their checkbook. Mabel Owens, a true friend from the first pew, and Fr. Mark realized what was happening and did their best to ward them off. It was at that time that they also had discovered Doreen Nelson's plan.

When Annie finally succumbed to the disease, Thomas was inconsolable and didn't seem able or willing to take care of all the paperwork involved. Mabel Owens did her best to help organize things but she was not an accountant. Father Mark, visiting Thomas, noted the constant decline in the months after Annie's death, so he felt that it was up to him to intercede. Mr. Williams needed to void Doreen Nelson's phony will obtained from Agnes under duress. Fr. Mark managed to obtain a *pro-bono* lawyer named Steve Yamaguchi from Cohen Legal Services to help Thomas put his affairs in order and write a new last will and testament. Judging by their thread-bare lifestyle, the priest thought Thomas to be practically indigent. Between the "meals on wheels" and the general dilapidated state of the house, the man didn't seem to have two nickels to rub together. The lawyer came and interviewed Thomas to see if he was mentally competent to make a will. Depression and the stroke surely complicated things but Thomas proved that a Tuskegee Airman could think straight when he had to. And now forewarned, whenever the so-called "relatives" hovered too closely he would send them scurrying, like so many Nazis fleeing back over the Alps. Yet these nebulous relations still represented a danger—because each was hoping to finish what Doreen Nelson had started. They all wanted a slice of his "pie in the sky."

One day, the *pro bono* lawyer called Father Mark to say that he had to drop Mr. William's case because the old man had too many assets to qualify for free legal services. Attorney Yamaguchi would not explain—because it was privileged information—but he did hint at the fact that Annie had been very shrewd indeed about investing their savings. No wonder the sharks were circling, they sensed massive holdings. Yet the old couple had always lived so frugally, to all intents and purposes, a hair's breath above abject poverty. But in reality, practically every dime Thomas earned on the "outside," Annie had invested on the "inside" with her friends at the investment firm of McCormack Millington and Funt.

Since Thomas was visibly deteriorating so rapidly, Fr. Mark immediately sought out another lawyer, one recommended by the previous one. Unfortunately, although the new attorney managed to get Thomas alone to sign a new Will, trying to milk them for his hourly fees, he dragged his feet on nailing Doreen Nelson. To the very end, Thomas never told a living soul what was in the new Will. As for Mabel and Father Mark, they didn't want to know. To their way of thinking, Thomas was a Tuskegee Airman, and he was free to give his money to anybody he pleased, even to the neighbor's cat if he so desired. They just didn't want the circling sharks to devour him.

When William finally died—on a bright Southern California Christmas morning—the whole parish mourned. The air force sent a bugler to play "taps" at the cemetery. A seven-rifle salute sent Thomas off to the wild blue yonder as one of America's unsung heroes.

After the funeral, Father Mark remembered something his elderly friend had said to him near the end. Just before he died, while lying there in his dining room double bed, Thomas had looked up at the priest and said, "Father, after I'm gone it'll all be your problem." The priest had been wondering what those words might mean. He found out a couple weeks later when Thomas's lazy lawyer informed him that everything—all the Williams's considerable assets—were being left to the Church and to the poor. A couple of the so-called relatives hired their own sharks for the subsequent legal feeding frenzy. Unfortunately, Doreen Nelson actually got her 25 percent. But Thomas didn't care because he was no longer part of the grounds-crew anymore. He had finally learned to fly.

The Duller Scholars

Father Gerard saw the freshman approach. The young man was small for his age and seemed to be holding back tears. "Uh-oh," thought the assistant principal, "an upper classman is already picking on the newly arrived."

The boy walked up to him, and waited.

Father Gerard prepared himself for another academic year, dealing with just about everything but studies.

"Good morning, Joseph," he said, reading the student name-tag, "Shouldn't you be on your way over to the chapel for the opening Mass?" A New Year always began with heart-felt prayer.

"Yes, Father, but I couldn't get into my locker."

Minutes before, the priest had instructed the whole assembly to place their books in their respective lockers so as not to haul everything into an already packed chapel. Since no more information seemed forthcoming from the boy, Father Gerard waited, not without compassion. The priest noted a tear trickling down Joseph's cheek.

"What's the problem?" he asked in as controlled a voice as he could muster.

Now the boy was actually crying, and did not seem to care if any of his new classmates saw him. "When I finally found it—my locker—there was already a lock on it, Father." Fr. Gerard knew the lad's colleagues would think he was being reprimanded for some infraction of the rules. If he only knew, thought the priest. Far from hurting him, it was a misinterpretation that would only elevate his stature in the eyes of his peers.

"What number is your locker?"

"Three four five," Joseph said, wiping his running nose on his sleeve.

"Easy to remember," answered Father Gerard. The priest made a mental note to ask the janitor to break and enter later on. But it was getting late and he needed to vest before Mass. "Don't worry, son, we'll take care of it. Now be on your way."

"Thanks, Father." Joseph gave a hint of a grateful smile and ran toward the chapel.

With that, the first minor crisis of the new academic year was handled if not resolved. Fr. Gerard walked off toward the chapel on the other side of the athletic field. He was thinking about freshman football practice and who might make a good middle linebacker. This gridiron revelry was interrupted, however, by yet another new face, not weeping, but nevertheless visibly upset.

"Yes?" said the priest expectantly.

The blonde-haired freshman whose name-tag read "Philip" said, "Father, I got to school this morning and I think I put my lock on the wrong locker . . . Then, after the Orientation assembly, the bell rang to go to Mass, so I didn't have time to open it . . . The number of the locker is . . ."

Father Gerard held up his right hand which told a student to speak no more. Teachers lived for such moments. There were few consolations in his line of work and most were of the spiritual variety, so he resolved to enjoy this one to the full.

"Don't tell me, Phil . . ." he paused for dramatic effect, "You accidentally put your lock on locker number *three four five* . . . is that correct?"

Philip's jaw dropped in amazement "Yea . . . I mean yes, sir . . . I mean yes, Father . . . But sir, I mean, Father, how did you . . . How could you know that?"

Father Gerard smiled benignly, savoring the moment without giving in to laughter, "It's quite simple, really—I know everything around this place." The freshman Philip stood there, appropriately stunned, not only that the priest knew his locker number but also that he even knew his name. Of course, he had forgotten about his nametag. Not knowing how to respond to these manifestations of the supernatural, he ran off to the chapel so as not to be late. The priest smiled, gazing up at the blue sky. It just might be a good year after all, he thought.

Indeed it was—at least compared to the trials and turbulence of past years. From those two little conversations, Father Gerard's legend grew. Two other incidents helped enormously, making the entire school populace and even some of the staff gaze upon him with reverent awe.

Besides freshman football and his other duties as vice principal, Father Gerard taught history. By midterm, he knew who were the achievers and who were the slackers. The obligatory exam was fair but not easy, and he knew there would be some attempts at cheating—even in a parochial school. He thought he was prepared for such distasteful things but hoped for the best. On the big day, he passed out the sheet of paper covered with questions, all of which were multiple-choice. It would not be difficult at all for those who studied. Then he began explaining procedures. At that moment—just as the students began the test—a voice over the intercom urgently requested his presence as vice principal down in the office. Sensing something serious, he calmly but quickly walked out of the classroom, saying he would be back soon.

It turned out that the crisis wasn't so urgent after all—just another vomiting, test taking freshman. Returning to his classroom, he saw, to his chagrin, that he had inadvertently left the answer sheet on his desk. He wondered, with a poker face, if any one of this enterprising senior class had noted the fact and taken full advantage. It was indeed possible, especially for the two kids sitting in the front row. Two plus two equals four. These two had been trouble for four years. Not only did he not trust them, but since they were not the brightest bulbs in the socket, in all likelihood, they would be more tempted to cheat than the others. Besides, he knew they rarely studied. The question was, how to discover the truth, if they had actually done so or not? Discretion being the better part of a vice principal's life, he formulated a plan. When all the students were finished, he collected the test papers, and, thanking his charges, informed them that they would have the results the following day. Some few groaned, but he could have sworn that others held their collective breath. Several looked at him quizzically, as if to say, "Father, don't you know you left the answers on your desk?"

After football practice that afternoon, Father Gerard ate a piece of cold pizza, then got down to grading that day's test papers. There were only two expected surprises. The two usual suspects in the front row had perfect scores, a feat never before accomplished in their high school careers. They obviously saw the answer sheet on his desk and interpreted its presence as an answer from heaven.

The next day in class, Father Gerard praised the whole class to high heaven, but especially the two culprits.

"Isn't it satisfying to see how hard work pays off?" he intoned. "When you roll up your sleeves, and really get down to some serious studying, it pays off. How proud I am of this class—to have two perfect test scores. Well done . . . Bravo!" The rest of the class looked at him in disbelief. Was it possible for Father Gerard—the ever present, all-seeing, and all-knowing—he of the famous locker incident at the beginning of the year—not to know about the two cheaters? If he did know, he certainly gave no indication of such knowledge. In fact, he seemed blissfully ignorant, going on and on, lavishing praise on these two new intellectual prodigies, that he alone had the glory of mentoring. Father Gerard read their faces, and stopped himself, because, he knew if he laid it on too thick they would become suspicious. And there is no creature more suspicious than a modern American teenager.

He concluded with a flourish, "And since you all did so well, we will have the second part of the exam today." He could hardly contain himself.

Before class, of course, he had paid a visit to the school secretary, asking her the favor of calling him down again to the office at the exact same time as the previous day. Like clockwork, after handing out a different set of test sheets, the secretary's distinctive voice—hitting just the right note of dramatic urgency—called him down to the office. And just as he had done yesterday, he left forthwith, leaving the answer sheet for the exam on top of his desk—once again—for all the world to see. Returning after about twenty minutes, he collected all the papers with all eyes riveted upon him.

The following day, he purposefully wore his patented look of grave concern on his face, the one that never failed to inspire hushed whispering and mass panic in his students. It was the look that said there was something wrong and that he was terribly disappointed in someone. Not only that, but he was determined to get to the bottom of it. Father Gerard took a deep breath, holding it for a second before expelling it slowly. He said in a low tone, forcing them all to listen: "Class, after your triumph in part one of the midterm exam I am at a loss to explain part two. Most of you did your usual exemplary jobs—but a couple of you failed altogether—and this, after having done so well in the first part . . ."

He paused for dramatic effect. The two in the front row looked at him, and then stole quick, desperate glances at each other. Squirming like worms on the hook, they both turned crimson red, and began to sink down into their respective seats, like adolescent Mastodons being sucked down into the tar pits.

Father Gerard now gazed directly at them. Gazing over his spectacles, he addressed the two together, "You both got every answer wrong. How is that possible, you two who studied so hard, doing so well on the first part of the test? Well, the truth is, when I got home last night, I couldn't grade the exams right away . . . because I realized I brought the *wrong answer sheet* with me yesterday."

The faces of the two in question, despite not being the brightest bulbs in the socket, lit up with a sudden realization. Their teacher had tricked them into cheating by leaving the wrong answer sheet on his desk. A sense of wounded justice forced them to simultaneously cry out, "Father, that's cheating!"

"Precisely," the priest answered calmly.

"But you can't do that!" they cried.

"Wrong again, I can and I did," he quipped.

"We're going to call our parents," they threatened.

"Good, that will save me the trouble. Have them come to see me tomorrow afternoon at five." He smiled. This incident did away with any lingering doubters in the high school. From that point, Father Gerard's legend grew exponentially. Word spread like wild fire, from class to class, that one didn't mess with the Man. Like the saints of old he could read minds and predict the future.

So the year proceeded, with all bowing to his prescient talents. Only he and his secretary knew the real story, and she had been sworn to secrecy.

Near the end of the year, Father Gerard found himself confronted by one last challenge to his authority. The senior class was expected to pull some kind of prank, something grand enough to make them legends themselves in the annals of school history. "Remember what the class of '79 did? Remember 1986? And how about 2006? That was unbelievable!"

Father Gerard was admittedly worried about this possibility. If the seniors pulled off a doozy, his own position would be compromised in the eyes of the underclassmen the following year. Since he was set to become Principal, it was imperative to detect the prank early on and foil the attempt while still in the planning stages. His future reputation depended on it.

The priest sent out his most trusted spies, those students who courted his favor, not because he would give them special privileges but because that's just the way they were. But these eyes and ears disappointed him, finding out nothing useful. And time was running out too—the last week of class arrived before graduation and still he had no inkling what mischief the seniors were up to. Obviously, they were taking extra precautions to keep things under wraps.

With only three days left before graduation, and beginning to doubt himself, Father Gerard stayed an extra hour after school, pondering. Finally, he locked up his office, with the intention of going home. Passing the mimeograph machine near the exit, one of the discarded sheets of paper caught his eye. He stopped short—something told him to dig down and search. Reaching down into the trash bin, he pulled out a crumpled, hastily printed sheet of directives. But these were not from the principal's office or from his desk—they were obviously and amazingly from the senior class leaders themselves.

The instructions read: "MONDAY, every senior must bring an alarm clock to class with them, setting the alarm to go off at precisely 10:00 a.m. without fail! All the alarms will sound simultaneously, thus interrupting second period! The resulting chaos will blow the rest of the morning! A long lunch hour will then be ours! This process will be repeated each day! Different times to be announced. Signed, the Fourth-Year Freedom Fighters."

This was what he had been patiently waiting for. Some enterprising seniors had obviously, cleverly, and surreptitiously managed to print out a clearly written course of action designed to disrupt the smooth functioning of his well-oiled scholastic machine. How clever of them, he thought—they did not intend to disrupt the graduation ceremony itself but the entire last week of classes. It was already almost impossible to keep the young heathen on track for the last five days. If they managed to pull this prank off they would have a very long laugh indeed—all summer long. Father Gerard quickly formulated a plan. Confiding again only in his trusted secretary, he instructed the worthy woman to ring the fire alarm at exactly 9:55

a.m., not one second sooner or later. Strict secrecy, of course, was imposed under pain of immediate excommunication.

The next morning it poured down rain. All the better, Father Gerard thought. He maintained his composure throughout the morning's mini-assembly in the gym and then all the way through the first period. He could hardly wait. As second period wore on, he duly noted his senior class's growing excitement. Looks and notes were being passed but he pretended to see nothing. He knew what they were thinking, however. They would finally get him—finally trump the teacher who had exercised a beneficial dominion over them for four solid years.

When the fire alarm bells rang, the din seemed impossibly loud. The whole student body jumped in unison but the seniors all groaned in disbelief! Father Gerard raised his voice above the noise, like an Old Testament Prophet, ordering all to proceed immediately outside—in an orderly, calm fashion by the nearest stairwell. Seeing the hesitation their disappointment engendered, his voice boomed, "NOW PEOPLE! Outside! No talking! Move it!"

The students rushed outside into the school parking lot, out into the pouring rain—without raincoats—totally unprepared for the day's inclement weather. Within seconds, they were all soaked to the skin.

As they formed ranks, according to classes, some of the seniors noted that Father Gerard had his raincoat on with his black umbrella poised gracefully above his prematurely graying head. The bedraggled, soaking seniors spoke as one person, "Father! It's raining! When can we go back inside?"

"When the alarm clocks stop ringing," he beamed, staring up at the ominous dark clouds as if it was the most beautiful day in the world.

The Third Sycamore

Father Bartholomew—Bart for short—liked cemeteries. He didn't care much for funerals, however, having presided over so many, in the missions of Africa, and now at home in Canada. But he did appreciate the silence of the dead. Walking amongst the headstones of All Souls cemetery, they did not reprove him for smoking, as his confreres so often did. It happened that there were five acres of green manicured solitude next to the little parish where he served as assistant pastor. After *lauds,* the Mass and coffee, he would take a walk in All Souls Cemetery, puffing on the first cigarette of the day, gratefully pulling the nicotine into his already clouded lungs. Knowing what lay in store for him if he didn't quit soon—he would someday have to face the dark specter of cancer. Nevertheless he liked to smoke whilst wandering the paths between the graves. It reminded him where he was going to end up. The engraved names, all unfamiliar, were oddly comforting, since, at least for the time being, none of them were his. Hailing from Newfoundland, he also preferred walking in winter rather than summer. The crunch of fresh-fallen snow under his boots felt like home, after the red mud of Africa.

At first, he just shuffled about, unaware and unthinking, but soon, he began using the time to pray. Cigarettes cleared his mind. It was a pity one could not smoke in church, he thought guiltily. Remembering what he had been through—war, famine, refugees, and so many deaths—his regrets rose up to heaven along with the tobacco smoke, which was not exactly like incense rising before the throne of God. As the months passed by, and as he accustomed himself once more to being back in his own country, however, the horrors he had left behind slowly began to fade. As he walked along each morning, at first all he could still see were their black faces everywhere—on the ground, in the trees, filling the sky—but after a few months, even these haunting visions became faint. Gradually, there emerged another vision, of a much colder world—the one he had returned home to—one that did not remember or care so much about the genocide in faraway Burundi. He just couldn't seem to understand how the killing had happened, how so many hundreds of thousands of innocents could be slaughtered in such a way. They said it was a "tribal conflict." As if that explained everything. Perhaps it went all the way back to Cain and Abel. But now, he couldn't help wondering why, why he was spared, and why he had been reassigned to the rich, industrialized North. They said he was traumatized. Perhaps that was why he was having trouble connecting with his new parishioners. Certainly, there were plenty of good, well-meaning people in his new situation—it was just that they didn't know how the poor lived, grieved, rejoiced, and died.

During Mass, his first tendency was to pray almost exclusively for his old mission station—he missed the people so much. Duty, however, made him also include the souls of the people in his new parish. Sometimes, he imagined he could see both groups intermingled, the living amongst the dead. But then, as time passed, without realizing it, he even found himself including all the souls in "his" cemetery. Yes, he began to think of the cemetery as his own domain, and part of his flock to tend. He wondered so often who they were and what their lives had been like, that he naturally brought them to the altar in prayer. That's when he thought he began to see them. But these instances were not quite like his memories of African faces. They would flicker at times like candles for a second or two above their own gravestones before fading out. He couldn't help feeling that they were not just figments of his imagination or the result of his traumatized mind. He was, after all, coming to meet them where they lived, day after day, two packs at a time. Surely, that was it—he was answering death's knell. Mysteriously, they were growing closer. And like him, were not these souls yearning for peace. The dead weren't judgmental in the least, for they were well aware of human foibles and fragility. After a year or so, walking daily, he developed a favorite route, where certain graves seemed to speak louder to him than others. There was one particular grave, under the third syca-more at the north end, near the crumbling wall, that always caught his attention, because once he thought he saw a woman's image there. When he tried conversing with the apparition, she disappeared. The marker was so old, and the engraved name so worn by wind, rain and lichen that it was completely illegible. He wanted to know who she was, although he accepted the fact that he might never know. Each day, he prayed specifically for *her*. That seemed to be the only way to communicate. He began referring to her as his "friend." Somehow he became certain that *she* was a young woman who died of scarlet fever in the middle of the eighteenth century. But how could he pos-sibly know that? One summer day, seeing a man trimming around the stones with a pair of hand shears, Fr. Bart asked the caretaker if he knew the name of the person buried in the unknown grave. He wanted to see if his belief was merely an illusion.

The grizzled old man took him back to a little shack hidden behind a hedge, and removing a battered notebook with yellowed pages from a deep drawer, rifled through it for several minutes before finding the right column of faded names written in a spidery scrawl.

"Let me see, seventh from the path, last row," said the man. "Says here a certain Marion O'Neal, born 1824, died 1843."

This information was, strangely, a confirmation of what he already knew. Even without being told, he had known all along that she was a young maiden. The caretaker also told him that the two weathered stones beside hers marked the eternal resting places of her parents who had survived her by ten and twelve years respectively. Oddly, he even knew her name would be Marion. Now, he found it easier to pray for her, since they had been officially introduced. That week, without any other intentions, he offered Masses for her soul, and then for her parents. It could have been his imagination, but a week later, he could have sworn that the sycamore branches swayed slightly, when he stopped to greet her. He told himself it was silly, thinking such things, so he never revealed to a living soul the words that formed in his mind while he stood there. Marion was getting through to him. There was an almost palpable sense of her feminine presence, as she thanked him for his prayers for herself and her family. Then oddly, he knew she was pointing to the other gravestones of her neighbors—buried there for many decades—who were also in need of prayers. He approached these graves, gradually getting to know them as well. He begged God to purify their souls, and give them rest. These new friends solidified into living images like developing photographs in the dark room of his mind. He just knew what they looked like. There was one widower—a certain Terrence Jones—who had died of loneliness after the death of his wife from consumption. He had had to give up his bitterness and forgive God for taking her. After much prayer and several masses, Fr. Bart knew that the man had been finally released. One bitter cold afternoon, as the sun set behind the naked trees, the priest could have sworn he saw a light appear then disappear over the man's grave. He knew that now *all the souls knew* about him. And all began asking for prayer.

There was a soldier who had become an alcoholic after returning from the trenches of the First Great War. He had left his bed in the hospital, only to be haunted by grim memories until the drink consumed his life. Father Bart wondered if this is what was really happening to him. The trauma of seeing so much death in Africa had unhinged his mind to the point where he was seeing the dead everywhere. Or perhaps his past experience had prepared him for the present one. Questioning did not help, only accepting afforded any peace.

The priest carried on in this way for several more years, praying for the many souls in his "underground" congregation, as he thought of them. Meanwhile his "above ground" parishioners tolerated him, thinking him odd—so quiet and thoughtful—always smoking whilst wandering alone in the cemetery. His Pastor was the first to agree with them.

Year after year, gray winter yawned into spring, which burst into ripe summer before erupting into a brilliant, painted autumn. He walked throughout all the seasons—mostly in the mornings but increasingly also at night. The more he walked, the more souls he got to know. And the more he got to know them, the more he loved them. He felt the nameless revealing themselves, pressing in upon him, begging his poor prayers, which he gladly gave. He even sacrificed his Marlboros at times, as penance for some particularly poor soul. A few of his parishioners began to complain that his Masses were becoming too long and far too contemplative. The Pastor reproved him for always offering *the Mass for the Dead.*

Then one winter, Fr. Bart developed a chronic cough. Expecting more than a diagnosis of bronchitis, his doctor told him that the X-rays revealed a few suspicious spots on his lungs. Almost joyfully, the priest knew that the moment he had been waiting for had finally arrived. Although it was already too late, he would finally be forced to give up his own addiction. Knowing he didn't have the strength to stop on his own, he asked—*his friends*—to intercede for him. He went first to the third sycamore, to Marion and her folks. A big snow had fallen during the night. While pacing the pristine white blanket between the gray stones, he took one last drag, inhaling it deeply, savoring the burn, the lightheadedness, before expelling it slowly. Marion let him know that she and her parents would have been gone long ago, thanks to his prayers, but they had remained, waiting for him to accompany them. Throwing the rest of the pack away, he thanked her and heaven for every breath of his past life and for whatever time he had left on earth. Then he marched back to the parish and made a good general Confession.

At Mass each morning, as his breathing became more and more labored, he started to see many more people present, more than would normally be sitting in the pews at that early hour. There were the usual smattering of daily communicants but there were also other visitors. As his hour approached, the almost empty church filled to overflowing with both black and white faces—who were now praying for him. Their prayers flowed through him and upward, enveloping him like a warm embrace.

In his Last Will and Testament, Fr. Bart had requested burial—not in the section of the cemetery reserved for the clergy—but near the third sycamore.

The Genesis of June

The first thing I heard about Jack was that we shared the same birthday in June. Moreover, being from Chicago, like me, he was a lifelong Cubs fan. The first fact provoked interest, thinking he could not be a bad guy, while the second, naturally, elicited only sympathy. I also discovered that he owned a small bookstore in suburban Elmhurst, Illinois—and that he had polio.

His coming out to California was an occasion for more woeful news. As if polio and the Cubs were not enough, his bookstore had folded. The big chains, selling more titles for less gradually seduced his small but faithful clientele, enticing them away from the deteriorating downtown area to the glitzy suburban mall. Jack prided himself on personalized service, for indeed, this is what had kept "Jack's Book Nook" going for so many years. His innate generosity went as far as loaning his friends money and giving his customers credit, which, when push came to shove, many could not or did not choose to repay. He was dead broke, fifty-nine years old and not dead yet, with no prospects and nowhere to go in his wheelchair. All he had was his ever-ready smile in the face of catastrophe, his gift of gab and the most extensive and detailed knowledge of horses in the Midwest. Jack knew the track. But he rarely bet for fear of becoming addicted to gambling and losing his beloved bookshop. One afternoon, after his bankruptcy sale, he was severely tempted to blow the final few dollars on the ponies at Maywood Park. Who could blame him? There is another thing Jack and I had in common besides birthday, birthplace and baseball team—Jack had once been a seminarian studying for the priesthood like me. Books, I had read a few, but as for racetracks, I had never been near one.

In his darkest hour, on the bleakest day of a January winter in Chicago, Jack called upon his best friend. My Uncle Bill was his classmate way back at the Dominican-run Fenwick High School in Oak Park, Illinois. He and my Aunt Martha, despite having reared ten kids together in Pasadena, California—and deserving a break—without any drama—decided to take Jack in. Jack was penniless and half-paralyzed but Marty and Bill never considered him a charity case. He was simply a good friend who happened to be in need. So without any hemming and hawing that I know of, they flew him out on the next plane, loaded the man himself, along with his few worldly belongings into the back of their Accord station-wagon and brought him home. At that time, he could sit up by himself, hoist himself into his wheelchair, wash himself and do just about everything without help. The only thing he couldn't do by himself was get in and out of the car.

My Aunt and Uncle, God bless them, did their level best to make Jack's transition to Southern California and their ground-level ranch house as smooth as possible. He was included in their busy social life, enjoyed their lively conversation, their ample wine collection, not to mention the visits of my cousins and their families. He won everybody's heart with his charming, gracious presence and sense of humor. He seemed even to have a winning way with the animals in the house. The Sheltie dog named Magic and the Siamese cat, Casey, would shamelessly compete for his attention and lap. They had never known another human being willing to sit with them for such pro-longed periods and they definitely approved.

That following June, after my introductory year of postu-lancy, before I was to enter the much stricter period of religious life, Novitiate, the time of preparation before making my religious vows, Marty and Bill decided to go on "walkabout" down under in Australia. Marty had relatives and friends in Sydney who promised them side trips to Alice Springs, Ayers Rock and Coober Peaty to look for opals. The only problem was—who could stay and keep an eye on Jack, in case of emergencies? All ten cousins either lived at some distance or were already otherwise occupied, leaving me as the only available candidate. Actually, I jumped at the chance of spend-ing some time in their air-conditioned, spacious house, within close proximity of their well-stocked refrigerator. Besides, I was looking forward to getting to know Jack well. Meeting for the first time at my Aunt and Uncle's annual bash the previous Christmas, we parked ourselves next to the mammoth bowl of peeled shrimp and had a fine *how-dee-doo*. In between mouthfuls of fifteen dollar a pound crustaceans, we talked about the Cubs, the track, and finally, in the waning hours—when just about anybody with any sense had already gone home—about our experience in the seminary. I was extremely curious as to why he joined and even more so about why he left. As far as I could see, the man had "priest" written all over him.

"I got as far as second year philosophy when I got polio," he said matter-of-factly. "Then I spent a year in an iron lung down in Georgia. There, my rector paid me a visit, informing me that I would have to leave the seminary. I could see their point, I mean, I wasn't technically yet a member of the order, not having taken my vows—so they did what they had to do . . ." I was incensed that his order could not see fit to stick by a brother in need. He paused and then added with a smile, "I keep in touch with all my class-mates who were ordained. We correspond regularly and I send them a little help when I can . . . but most of all, I pray for them, for their perseverance in their vocations. I guess that's what the Man upstairs wanted from me." He quickly changed the subject, going into great detail about his one big trip to Mexico back in the early sixties. Evidently, he and a good friend had driven down and had more than a good time south-of-the-border. Certain details were hard to come by because I don't think he wanted to scandalize me.

The next morning, I drove Marty and Bill to the airport early. And upon my return, I found Jack all dressed, breakfasted, with his weekly copy of *The Racing News* on his lap.

"I think it's time for a road trip," he grinned.

"What? I mean *where?* You need me to go down the hill and get you something from the store?" I asked, hoping this was the case.

"No, what say you and I give ourselves an early birthday present—by spending the day at the track," he winked like I had always been part of the conspiracy.

"But Marty and Bill . . ." I began haltingly.

" . . . are not here." He finished my sentence with bravado.

"But Santa Anita is closed this time of year," I said hopefully, not really wanting to take responsibility for something happening to my charge mere moments after my aunt and uncle were out the door.

"Of course it is, but Del Mar is opening today. It's the Jockey's Cup. Starts at one o'clock, so we better get a move on, partner . . ." He started rolling his wheel chair toward the garage at the end of the hall.

"But Jack, isn't Del Mar in San Diego?" I protested.

"What are they teaching in the seminary these days? Come on, it will be fun. I may be bankrupt but I still have a few bucks to blow."

Before I knew it, I was hefting him sideways into the front passenger seat of the Accord. After belting him in, I folded the wheel chair and slid it into the trunk. Barreling south on the 5 freeway, I was more than a little nervous. What if we had an accident or worse, what if Jack had some kind of attack? And now that I was a seminarian, I wasn't supposed to be going to racetracks. The Vatican tended to frown on that. It was vicarious fun to read about them in Dick Francis's mystery novels but actually to go was another thing altogether.

"Relax," Jack beamed, reading my mind. "We're going to have the time of our lives. Did you know Del Mar used to be owned by Bing Crosby? Ba Ba Boo . . ." Two hours later, we exited the freeway, found the grand entrance to the racetrack and parked. I could hardly believe that I was wheeling him out to the exercise paddock. Surveying the horses, trainers and jockeys, he breathed deeply, laughing, "Ah, there's nothing like the smell of horse manure." He pulled the daily forms out of his breast pocket and began scrutinizing the small print, marking the days' races.

"Pincay in the third on Baby's Breath . . . Chris McCarron in the fourth on Table Manners, four to one, not bad . . . Look who Gary Stevens is riding! Yahoo! It's like the cavalry coming to our rescue. Nothing but winners today, laddie! But hurry, we've got to place our bets." He went on for some time talking to himself, marking his paper feverishly. Wheeling him to a landing overlooking the finish line, I couldn't help admiring the track and the sheer liquid grace of the pacing horses in their colors against the green backdrop of the infield. Off in the distance, an Amtrak train zoomed by, full of people wishing they were us. I smiled, catching just a little bit of my companion's contagious excitement. Almost against my will I was starting to enjoy myself. Decades of work in a wheelchair had not made Jack a dull boy but one year in the seminary had certainly curbed my enthusiasm. Guilt drained away slowly until Jack handed me his wad of bills.

"Hey! Where did you get all that?" I asked.

"As I said, I may be bankrupt not totally broke," he said, looking around him, as if the IRS might be watching. "Put everything on Five Finger Discount TO WIN in the first," he said emphatically. "Can you remember that? Now, hurry! Chop chop!"

"But Jack . . . You might lose everything."

He looked up at me, and said with a serious smile, "You're looking at a man who has nothing left to lose." How could I argue with that? What was I expecting, anyway? Nobody in their right mind would come all this way down to the track on a picture perfect day at the beginning of summer *and not put their money down?*

Certainly, one thing I had learned in the seminary was to do as I was told. Obediently, I went up to the betting window, waited behind five grizzled, chain-smoking veterans of the track and put all Jack's money down on the well-worn counter. The man behind the grill barely looked up. Collecting the receipt stub, while retracing my steps I wondered where he had gotten two hundred dollars. Probably Uncle Bill had given it to him for emergencies. The ponies definitely didn't qualify as that. I prayed as hard as I ever did in my life.

"Jack, that's a lot of money to put down on one race, isn't it?" I queried.

"That's all I've got. If we lose, we go home sooner. You got any money on you?" That sinking feeling made a strong comeback. "About twenty-five."

"Ah, don't worry, we won't need it . . . Push me on up to that platform over there where we can see better." A line of elegant horses paraded out for the first race. "Look at her, she's a beauty, isn't she? So alert, ready to run . . ."

A minute later, they were off, thundering to the far side. Jack whipped out his binoculars, and yelled, "Go, baby go!" I started to scream too, "Run! Five Finger Discount! Run!" If only the Novice Master could see me now, I thought.

The announcer's streaming ramble said she was third, rounding the bend, coming into the final stretch. Jack stopped yelling and closed his eyes. I got the impression he was willing the horse to win. Five Finger Discount came on strong, edging the frontrunner by a nose. After a few tense minutes, a photo confirmed the finish, and I trotted happily off to collect our winnings. A cool grand, pocketed immediately, made me feel giddy and wary, as I had been warned by Jack to beware of pickpockets.

"Space Odyssey to WIN . . . Let it ride!" he whooped.

"You mean you want me to bet all of it . . . again?"

He smiled, "God is giving us a birthday present."

I plodded off and reluctantly laid ten one-hundred-dollars bills down on a five to two nag. Leaving Jack on the handicapped platform full of handicappers, I walked down to the rail bordering the dirt track for a closer view. I didn't want to be there to see his face when we lost. He had had too many disappointments in life already. Space Odyssey looked just about the same to me as all the other horses. Our bet started off slow, trailing most of the way until about the midway point, when, slowly but surely, she began pulling forward, passing one horse after another. They hugged the far fence with our horse behind by only half a length. Their thunderous approach made the ground tremble.

We ended up winning by two. I screamed, hugged an old lady next to me, apologized, and then went to find Jack.

"Next race . . . Lafitte Pincay, getting old but still a force to be reckoned with . . . just like me," he chirped.

Incredibly, Baby's Breath won the third race by five whole lengths. The wad in my jacket pocket bulged noticeably.

I couldn't believe our good fortune, while Jack seemed to be expecting exactly this outcome. He'd been studying these horses and their rider's histories for months. He knew their past, their breeding histories, their owners and their jockeys, chapter and verse. We won the fourth with Chris McCarron but only placed second in the fifth with Gary Stevens riding Emerald Ghost. But since Jack hadn't put much down on that one, we didn't lose too much. The sixth we sat out altogether, going off to drink a couple beers in the bar. "We're saving everything for the seventh," Jack whispered between sips, furtively checking to see who might be eavesdropping. At the appointed time, I trotted off to place our bet, a whopper. We went back down to the track just in time to see Diamond Rio prance by. "Looking good, honey," Jack called to her, as if to an old flame. She seemed to look back, snorting encouragingly.

This time Jack closed his eyes the whole time and remained quiet even through the nail-biting finish. I got the distinct impression he was praying for the grace to accept whatever happened. We lost by a head. I was shocked, as if the Almighty had let us down. Jack, however, just smiled, looking all around at the other punters. It didn't seem to faze him that we had lost almost all our winnings.

"I've lost everything before," he said cheerily, "Losing everything is always a new beginning . . ." I didn't understand what he meant, although I thought about it for years afterward. Breathing a sigh of contentment, we skipped the final race. Once back at the car I counted out what was left, handing it all back to him.

"Eighty-six dollars," I said, not able to hide my disappointment.

"Hey, we're Cubs' fans. We should be used to it! Besides, kiddo, you're about to take a vow of poverty anyway," he said. "It's enough for two decent steaks and a cheap bottle of wine. The Lord hath given and the Lord hath taken away . . . The story of my life!" he laughed. Then, unrolling the window, he breathed deeply once again. We could hear the crowd cheering the last race as we drove away.

On the way home we gladly stopped at a The Chop House restaurant to spend the remains of our day. Jack insisted we leave the waitress a big tip. "We're all winners today, "he said.

The next day, Jack woke up happy, although he said he wasn't feeling too well. Too much excitement or too much wine, I thought. I offered to take him to the doctor but he said he would wait for his normal scheduled appointment when Marty and Bill returned from Australia.

Two weeks raced by. We didn't have any more adventures. And to my relief, Jack didn't insist on any more road trips. He was his usual cheerful self, even though, to me, he looked more than a little tired. We relived every moment of our Del Mar birthday present, practically every day, with the understanding that not a word be said to my Aunt and Uncle upon their return. When Marty and Bill finally did get home, they made me feel guilty by thanking me profusely for taking such good care of Jack. Jack winked, saying to me as I went out the door, "Now, we're in the final stretch!" I thought he was referring to the fact that, soon, I would be entering the final phase of my formation before vows and ordination.

A month or so later Uncle Bill called me with the news. The doctor said Jack had a malignant stomach tumor. A second opinion confirmed the first, adding only that the cancer was quite advanced. Three months later, I got word that, after his operation, he could no longer sit up or get out of bed by himself. What with Marty and Bill's bad backs this meant Jack would be forced to go live in a nursing home down the hill. Then I realized that *he had known all along*—that our day at the races was to be his *last hurrah*. Through all the long, weary months in that nursing home, Jack remembered the ponies running to win on a bright breezy June day. Whenever I visited him, I could see that all the nurses loved it when he joked with them. The Racing News was always next to the Bible at his bedside.

Beggar on the Bridge

The jay landed on his hand and cocked an eye at him.

"Good morning, Johnny-come-lately," said the man, shaking his head. One feather glinted like lapis lazuli. The bird stayed for an appreciative second then flew a few feet up to perch on the bridge's girder.

An early morning jogger ran by, thinking the unshaven, shabbily dressed man perched precariously on the railing completely insane.

The bird looked down at him, expectantly.

The man addressed the jay again: "Sorry, fresh out of peanuts. And don't worry, my friend—there will be no jumping today. Unlike you, I cannot fly. Besides, I have a busy day ahead. I have to look around, and walk a bit and sit for a spell . . ." He laughed ruefully then climbed down with some effort to the sidewalk. A commuter, waiting for the bus at the east end of the bridge wondered how it was possible to be drunk so early in the morning, when normal people were just starting for work. Bus 541 better arrive before the crazy bird talker approached asking for money.

The man shuffled to the end of the bridge. He saw the commuter board the bus. At one time he would have done the same. During the day it was easier to imagine his former life, less so at night. For that's when the ghosts visited him. He vaguely remembered one night when three specters taunted him as he lay in his favorite doorway. The next thing he knew, they had materialized and come at him with a baseball bat. Arriving at County USC's emergency room, the only thought that occurred to him was that the three men resented finding one lower on the food chain than themselves.

But Stephen—that was his name once—never asked for money or sought trouble. Over time, he had learned to simply let everyone and everything come to him—birds, sunshine and even stitches.

From the bridge he proceeded on over to his "spot" in Old Town and hunkered down with his back to the cold bricks, adjusting his pea-green army-issue coat for the duration. Many people passed by just beyond arms-reach. With eyes heavily lidded, he felt the air stir, so he knew they were real. Yet he spoke to no one unless they spoke to him. It felt odd speaking to birds but not to people. "People are for the birds," he joked to himself. His own words had to travel a great distance and echoed in his ears. Repeating them to himself, he knew they used to carry the weight of meaning. But lately, they tended to scare him because whenever he directed them toward anyone, the person would flit away. He was learning that there was much to be said for silence.

That morning, he recalled something that once seemed to be a fact, that he had been a successful accountant with a wife, and three handsome if not beautiful children whom he thought loved him. At least they would say so. And in these reveries, he would say so too, along with his apologies for drinking too much the night before. He did indeed love them—that was the one constant, an ache that penetrated his bones more surely than the numbing cold of a hard sidewalk. He knew only too well that social drinking had led him down the slippery slope to full-blown alcoholism. Years of lies, masking the illusion of normalcy, finally dissolved his life—first his marriage followed by his career. And the funny thing was, he had seen the train wreck coming but couldn't or didn't want to get out of the way. His wife and kids, however, had jumped to safety just before the crash. After a particularly long binge—always on the fringe of memory— he discovered that he had remained away four whole days. When he finally did come home it was to an empty house. There wasn't even a note, which was appropriate since there was nothing left to be said. After that, it was simply a question of when he would hit bottom.

Musing on these things, the sun came around to his doorway. A Mexican immigrant, perhaps a day laborer, walked over to him and stuffed one, folded US dollar bill in his front pocket.

"Dios te bendiga, amigo," said the young man in his own language.

Stephen tried to remember his high school Spanish but nothing came out. As in a mirror, he watched this man walk away unthanked. After a few minutes he could no longer remember his benefactor's face. He was having trouble remembering anything lately, even the faces of his family—wherever they might be—even his former colleagues at work. There was a voice in his head that told him that if he allowed even one more thought to escape he would disappear forever.

Sitting there, he did manage to recall waking up many a morning, covered in his own vomit. His body had refused to die. He always knew it was just a question of time and time was the enemy. Each day was as long as his arm but still out of reach. Early on, he knew several months were spent on the sidewalks of downtown Los Angeles, sometimes sleeping outside at night, occasionally in one of the shelters run by the holy rollers. For the price of sitting through a half-baked sermon, a half-decent meal could be had—if one were hungry at all. It was during that period that he found and fiercely defended the corner near his old office, just to see if any of his former friends would pass by—and perhaps—recognizing him, stop for a little conversation.

"Hey, Stevie, boy, how ya doin'? Whassup?"

Although it never happened outside his fantasies, he would always answer, "Great! Super! Couldn't be better! Things are looking up . . . especially if you're sitting on the sidewalk."

Back then, one hot day, Stephen got tired of sitting down and roused himself to get up and walk all the way back out to Pasadena, his old hometown. It took him a whole day, but eventually he arrived in Old Town where there were many like himself. But it was not nearly so crowded or violent as downtown LA. He managed to get his daily dose of uncertainty there for what must have been several long years—so long in fact that, before he knew it, they were turning the place into upscale condos and fashionable restaurants. Dark doorways disappeared, as did his brethren. Rousted by the local cops, he was forced to move more often than was his want, if he wanted anything at all. At that point he knew for sure that he was just one of the ghosts seeking other haunts. He would wander around all day and half the night until he found a place to doze unmolested. Then, he came upon the boulders under the Arroyo Seco bridge, that long span overlooking the Rose Bowl, favored by so many jumpers. At first, he imagined the sound of some poor soul's death wish being granted. But the first few times he witnessed it, he didn't have to wonder what they were thinking, for he already knew. None of them had time to change their minds between the bridge and the rocks.

The sun rose overhead and the church bells tolled telling him it was time to go up to St. Andrew's near the 210 freeway. Kneeling in the dark, his head rested on the back of the pew in front of him. Flickering candles illumined the statue of The Lady—that's what he always called her—enfolded in her blue mantle. It was the same blue as the wings of his jay. Although he dared not look up at her, he sensed that she was looking down at him. He tried to pray—the vague memory of a nun in parochial school helped him remember parts of the *Ave*. Yet surely, he felt, his prayers did not rise like incense before the celestial throne.

When the Mass started, his eyes closed and his breathing almost stopped. He didn't join the line to receive communion, but did enter the confessional after the final blessing. A young priest, dressed in a black cassock, listened to his disjointed attempt to explain his life but seemed put off by the smell.

The priest said, "If you keep going like this you will surely go to hell."

Stephen responded, "I'm already there, Father." Thinking he was being mocked, the priest gave him his penance, hurriedly pronounced the words of absolution then disappeared. Three hours later, when the same cleric saw Stephen sleeping in the last pew, he attempted to persuade him to go outside. When Stephen did not immediately respond, the young man returned to his office and called the police. The cops arrived, cuffed Stephen, sat him in the back of their squad car and promptly whisked him down the Pasadena Freeway to downtown LA, dumping him out onto his old familiar sidewalk. As soon as the cruiser disappeared, he did something he had never done before. Getting down on his knees he wept, long and loud, clutching his head in his hands. Then after a long time, recovering himself somewhat, but still shaking, he turned northeast and slowly began the long trek back up to the *Arroyo Seco* and his bridge. He walked all day and well into the night.

On the way, he saw some of the brethren with signs promoting compassion and cash: *"Hungry . . . Will work for food . . . Vet needs help . . ."* They stood on islands under traffic lights, guarding their turf. One even tried the novelty of the truth: *"I need a beer. God help me if you won't."* He passed them by without a word. They did not even appear to see him.

Finally arriving in downtown Pasadena, he had enough change in his pocket to buy some Thunderbird at an all-night liquor store. Making his way slowly over to the Arroyo Seco he climbed under a chain-link fence and down to the huge boulders beneath. The cheap wine burned his throat. Under its influence he made one last effort to pretend that everything was normal. He even counted his remaining coins, like bullets, imagining himself an important accountant again. But instead of passing out as usual, he began to hear a voice from above. Somebody was on the bridge repeatedly calling his name. Unsteady, he got to his feet, and peering up, could only see the metal underpinnings of the bridge with the stars above. There was the voice again. He began to climb, his only thought being to discover who it was. Could anyone really know he existed? He knew if he didn't find out, the morning might not come. Then suddenly, he found himself perched on the railing of the bridge above, not knowing exactly how he got there. Peering across the dark abyss of the valley, thousands of cars flew by on the nearby freeway. The Rose Bowl in the distance stood dark and empty like an abyss ready to swallow him. One step could decide everything. Yet somehow he knew that he would be able to fly, just like his blue jay. A glint of blue flashed before his eyes. Tottering on the brink, the memory of The Lady appeared before him, and trembling like a candle flame, he climbed back down on to the pavement.

Where Dreams Are Born

Fr. Ray hated to speak in front of crowds, even small ones made up of small people. So he entered the first-grade classroom, looking around nervously. Finger paintings hung to his right, with the alphabet to the left. Rows of girls and boys stared up at him expectantly.

"Hi kids!" he chirped, a little too loudly. Sister Veronica piped in, "What do we say, class?"

Twenty-two first graders intoned the personalized welcome for important visitors: "Good Morning, Father Raymond!"

"You can all just call me Father Ray, OK?"

A couple wiseacres in the back repeated his name. Fr. Ray straightened his clerical collar as if it were a tie; a big bead of perspiration dotted his forehead like a Hindu's *urna*. He truly liked kids, but he didn't know what to say to more than one at a time. He had a moment to think while the much more experienced nun was in the process of settling them all in a circle on the big green rug that occupied the back of the classroom. When all the children were seated, Fr. Ray, approached the open end of the circle, wondering what to say. It was so much easier to talk to adults, who, in his limited experience, he suspected were not listening to him anyway.

A poster taped to the door read "National Vocations Month." That gave him an idea. So he said, "Now, I want each one of you to close your eyes. That means everybody. And no peeking. We're all going to sit for a minute with our eyes closed and listen . . . for the voice of God." This was a novel approach. A couple of the little girls near the window giggled then settled down when they felt Sr. Veronica's footfall approaching.

Fr. Ray went on: "I want you to listen for the voice of God in the silence of your heart." Then he didn't say anything more. More beads of sweat formed on his temples. After the longest minute, he asked, "Do any of you girls hear God calling you to be a nun like Sister Mary Veronica? . . . Anybody?" The priest waited, eyebrows arched expectantly. It seemed that either God wasn't talking that day or the little ladies couldn't imagine being like their teacher, who besides being well into her sixties was also the principal of St. Bartholomew's school. Beads of perspiration multiplied and collected into rivulets which ran down his neck, so that the young priest appeared to be drowning. His next words even sounded gargled, as if bubbling up from a watery grave. Yet to his credit, Fr. Ray did not panic. Forcing a smile, he doggedly pursued his original line of questioning, this time with the boys: "Now, you young men, do any of you hear the voice of God speaking to you?" He waited expectantly, unconsciously hopping from one foot to another, thereby giving a good impression of a first-grader in need of the bathroom.

Almost desperately, he looked at Sister Veronica for help. She, something of a traditional feminist who believed in torturing neophyte male clerics, suddenly seemed totally absorbed in picking a piece of lint from her blue veil. She was not being cruel necessarily, but was allowing him just enough rope to hang himself. Perhaps, he wondered, this was because he had given short shrift to the Convent's spiritual needs of late, saying he was too busy to say their early bird

Wednesday Mass in honor of St. Joseph. Hell hath no fury like a nun scorned, he thought. The young priest looked down at the circle of children, each head obediently hunkered down over the knees. But wait, what was this? One little boy was actually raising his hand. His name was Nicholas, but everybody called him Nick. Fr. Ray had seen him before. He was tall for his age and had a mischievous smile missing a couple of teeth, but seemed very nice. He had three older sisters in the school at that moment in various upper grades and an uncle who was a missionary working in Africa.

"Yes, Nick, you have your hand raised. Did you hear the voice of God speaking to you?"

Nick opened his eyes and looked up. "Yeah," he said in his rather thick New Jersey accent Sr. Veronica objected like a good prosecutor before the ecclesiastical court: "Nick, what do you saaaayyy?" She prolonged the last word like she couldn't quite get the thing out of her mouth.

Nick stifled a laugh. "Oh Yeah," he corrected himself, "I mean, yes, Father Raymond, I mean, er . . . Fr. Ray." Now everybody laughed. The kid had close-cropped hair and seemed to be serious enough. Nevertheless, Fr. Ray had a sudden presentiment that he was about to be made a fool of.

"We'll, what did God say?" asked the priest, his black shirt now completely soaked and sticking to his back. He was feeling more than a little impatient, and wanted to get out of there.

"He told me he wanted me to become a priest," Nick said matter-of-factly, looking Fr. Ray directly in the eyes. The priest released his breath and smiled tentatively, nodding while pointedly looking at the nun, as if to say, "See!" Still, he wasn't at all sure what this particular little boy was up to.

"And what did you say to God?" asked Fr. Ray expansively.

"I said, 'Sorry, I want to be a truck driver.'" All the kids cracked up and Nick's cherubic face split instantly into a broad smile at the reaction he was getting. Fr. Ray thought it best to nip this disaster in the bud, by beating a hasty retreat. He thanked Nick, saying, "Well, truck drivers can serve the Lord too!" Then he thanked the class, nodded apologetically to Sr. Veronica as the door clicked closed behind him. "Damn!" he thought, "I have to change this shirt before visiting the next class."

Hearing about this story long-distance from his sister, Nick's mother, Nick's missionary priest-uncle whom he called "Father Uncle" commented, "Well, we do have to drive a lot of trucks down here in the missions . . ."

The following Christmas, another Nick episode occurred.

All the costumes were readied, and the stage was set for the first dress rehearsal of the annual Christmas play. The town of Bethlehem was a painted backdrop.

Sr. Veronica patiently coaxed the two children playing Mary and Joseph and the two comprising the front and back of their donkey, into their costumes and through their lines. The two inside their beast of burden could not stop fidgeting. Nick was given a minor part as the innkeeper. When Joseph approached and knocked on the door of his inn, he opened it with a smile.

Without hesitation, the kid playing Joseph rattled off his lines, "My wife is with child and we have traveled so far for the census. Do you have any room for us at your inn?" A pint-sized Laurence Olivier he was not.

Nick looked up at the big painted star hanging above them, then eyeing St Joseph and the little girl playing the Virgin Mother, said with unfeigned compassion, "Sure, I have plenty of room!" He had a fine stage voice.

Sister Veronica, listening from the side curtain, caught the error immediately and came running over, her shiny black shoes clomping across the wooden stage. "Oh no! Nicholas! You can't say that! That's all wrong . . . You have to say—we have no room at the inn."

Nick's brow creased then furrowed. First of all, he wasn't used to being told he was wrong. Second, in his opinion, he did have plenty of room. Putting his hands on his hips like his father, he said, "Sorry, sister, but I won't turn them away." Again, all the kids laughed. Sister Veronica looked at him, half-smiling, realizing that the little boy was quite serious and ready to defend the holy family. She admired his resolve and it pained her to have to explain to him why he needed to turn them away. "That's how the story really went," she said kindly. "We all wish they were welcomed in, Nick, but they weren't."

After an anxious moment, finally, Nick—who had turned bright red—begrudgingly accepted her explanation with a nod. Not liking it one bit, yet seeing no other way—as the inn-keeper—he said in a hushed tone, full of embarrassment, "Sorry, we don't have any rooms left."

Nick had accepted the necessity of historical accuracy but went home disappointed, his face glum. His mother asked him if he was feeling all right. A few minutes later, the mother of one of the kids in his class telephoned saying only that she should ask her son what happened during practice that day.

Hanging up the phone, she asked, "How was the Christmas play today?" she asked.

Nick groaned, "Oh, I'm the inn-keeper."

His mom tried her best to cheer him up, saying, "Well, it's not the biggest part, but an inn-keeper has an important role to play. Is that the problem—you wanted a bigger part?"

"No, it's just that all the kids laughed at me."

"They did?"

"And Sister Veronica said I did my part wrong . . ." he said, his lower lip now quivering. "When Joseph asked me if I had any room at my inn, I said I had plenty of room."

"Oh, I see," she tried not to laugh.

Reluctantly, Nick repeated Sister Veronica's explanation. He still seemed to be having trouble accepting the injustice—how Saint Joseph, the Savior and his Blessed Mother could be turned away and have to stay in a smelly, cold cave. Nick's mother suggested he go outside to play awhile before doing his homework. He headed for the toy trucks he parked in the corner of the deck.

He really did love trucks. Given half a chance—even in December—he would be outside digging in the mud or snow, making an astonishing variety of truck noises. There were miniature metal replicas of International Harvesters and Kenworths, but his favorite big rig was the Mack. While other kids his age played with the latest video games, Nick preferred an eighteen-wheeler any day.

The play went off without a hitch. But that Christmas Eve, when the whole family arrived at church all dressed up for midnight Mass, Monsignor Caffey, their pastor and young Father Ray's immediate superior, approached their pew.

"I heard what happened at the Christmas play practice a couple weeks ago," he whispered to Nick's parents. Nick looked up at the gray-haired man, wondering if he was in trouble. Then Monsignor winked at him, asking, "Hey, Nick, would you mind if I use your story for my homily tonight?"

"Sure, no problem," he answered. The anecdote got a big laugh but also remained in the hearts and minds of many parishioners for years afterward. They knew they had to find room for the holy family in their homes too.

Life went on in the parish and for Nick. God continued to talk to him. Especially after his First Communion. He received the Sacrament of Confirmation in eighth grade, thus confirming his parent's original suspicions. The Almighty was with their growing boy in a special way. Ninety-nine percent normal, 1 percent was very different indeed, like a door opening onto some far horizon. He finished high school, a scholar athlete, then went on to graduate from college four years later with honors in mechanical engineering. After that, he got a good, well-paying job with a well-known firm in New York City. He liked his job because, occasionally, it brought him to the construction sites where, with some cajoling, he could convince their drivers to allow him to fulfil his childhood dream of actually getting behind the wheel of the big Mack trucks.

All this time, Nick kept in contact with his uncle, the missionary priest, occasionally writing letters to him in Africa. For years, Nick had promised his "Father Uncle" that he would visit him in the missions. Finally, one fall day, with the trees dropping their colorful leaves, Nick informed his employer and his parents of his plans to take an extended vacation. At the beginning of December, armed with quinine and a backpack, he flew by way of London to Malawi, a small country in the southeastern part of the continent nicknamed "the warm heart of Africa." He planned on spending Christmas there, to see how the tribes would celebrate it. His introduction to the reality was an eye-opener. Besides billions of malaria-carrying mosquitoes, the country had three million human residents plus another one million refugees fleeing war-torn Mozambique in the South. It was primarily with these people that his priest-uncle worked. Since more of the starving refugees streamed across the border daily, the need grew ever greater.

From the start, once his uncle picked Nick up at Blantyre airport, they were constantly on the move in a four-wheel truck, over dusty or muddy roads, from one camp to another, loading and then distributing emergency relief supplies. Nick had never seen such misery or such joy in life. Despite their dire situation, he was constantly amazed to see the smiling faces of the children. It made him think how, despite having every material advantage, so many kids in his home country did not seem happy.

"They trust," explained Father-Uncle.

"But there are so many," Nick commented, "and there aren't enough supplies for everybody. Doesn't that discourage you?"

"The government doesn't have the will, and the international community doesn't have the resources to deal with a problem of this magnitude. So the Church is doing what she can. We can't turn them away . . ." These words jogged Nick's memory, and he was very quiet on their return to the mission station south of Lunzu. By the time they arrived, it was dark. Pulling up the long dirt track into the compound, they were met by a tall, handsome African standing on the verandah.

"What? You don't recognize your old classmate anymore?" said the man, grinning broadly.

"What a coincidence! I was just telling my nephew about how much trouble you used to cause when we studied together in Rome. Nick, let me introduce you to Father Andrew Mpanda Chimwemwe. His last name means 'joy,' because that's what his mom felt after giving birth to him. Father Andrew is a Malawian priest working on the other side of the border in Mozambique, where all the land mines are . . ."

The three laughed and chatted for a while under the eaves of the mission house before Fr. Andrew suddenly grew serious. "I need some help, old friend," he said.

"Is it the leg?"

Nick had noticed Father Andrew's limp but then suddenly realized it was a prosthetic limb.

Seeing this sudden realization dawn on the young man's face, the African priest smiled. "Oh, it's healing up pretty well. But I'll try to avoid another land mine if I can."

He lifted up his pant leg to reveal a plastic calf and foot, connected to a bandaged knee, set into a muddy brown boot "No, my problem is not the leg. Tomorrow we have a small convoy of relief supplies going south. And we have to cross the border into Mozambique before dark—which is when the rebels come out—but we don't have enough drivers. This new leg can't depress the clutch very well, so we need a driver."

Father-Uncle scratched his graying beard, thinking aloud, "The men of the mission are all helping at the main camp, where we just came from. Too late to get one of them back for an early start. I suppose I could drive one truck for you. God knows I've had enough experience lately driving around these parts, but not anything so big."

"That would be great, my friend, but we're still one short."

The three companions looked up at the darkening African sky in silence. A few clouds were forming on the western horizon, presaging the wet season. The stars above seemed to blaze a swath from north to south. One star shone brighter than all the rest. "There's the star of Bethlehem," said Father Andrew.

"You're right," added Father-Uncle. "I'd almost forgotten that tomorrow is Christmas Eve." Inexplicably, Nick found himself remembering Father Ray, Sister Veronica, and the Holy Family years before arriving at his inn at Bethlehem.

The two priests continued to talk, trying to solve their problem. People's lives hung in the balance. Throughout this exchange, Nick got up and paced the railing, sweating and wondering why he was feeling so excited. From what he had read, it didn't feel like the onset of malaria.

Suddenly, he interrupted their discussion, saying, "I can drive . . ."

"Wait just a minute, buddy," cautioned his Father-Uncle. "Your mother—my older sister—would kill me if she found out that I let my nephew—her only son—drive a truck into an area full of land mines and rebel soldiers . . ."

Father Andrew looked him in the face and said, "Nicholas, you are either very brave, very rash, or someone who trusts in the Almighty. Thank you, brother, but you are just visiting, and I cannot ask you to risk it."

The three fell silent for a moment, before Father-Uncle said, "Nevertheless, we are in a real bind—people are hungry, and we have to get the relief supplies delivered before the rains which could begin any day—and when they do—it will be impossible to get anything through for weeks."

Father Andrew added, "I'm afraid your kindness would not help in either case, my dear young friend, because the truck we need a driver for is a big-rig, the only Mack we were able to finagle out of the Relief Agency . . ."

Nick smiled, feeling a rush of joy within.

Well before dawn, with his guide Father Andrew in the passenger seat beside him, Nick revved the colossal engine and said to himself, "I won't turn them away . . ."

An Overcoat of Clay

Behind the wheel of his sleek black Lincoln, the road opened up before him like a book of memories: his youth, the entrance into religious life as an idealistic seminarian, the rapid rise to prominence—first as abbot—then as bishop. Now, as he cruised along ten miles above the speed limit, his mind raced even faster. He who had become known as the conscience of the Bishops conference was wrestling with his own. He was going home, a rare occurrence—to visit his ailing mother, in what would certainly prove an unpleasant encounter. This was no ordinary vacation, sitting round the kitchen table, eating apple pie and drinking coffee. No, at the behest of his younger brothers and sister, all of whom lived conveniently out of state, his task was to convince dear Mom to leave her home and move into a nursing facility run by the neighboring diocese. The car purred like a sleek black cat, soundlessly eating up the miles. Although he was entitled to a driver, he liked to drive himself, since it afforded a sense of control. Turning up Beethoven's Ninth, he tried not to think about what must be faced. She always used to tell him "to do the right thing," and he hoped she would listen to him.

As he aged, he found it difficult, if not almost impossible to keep certain thoughts out of his head. Why did he always associate his own mother with Mother Church? Perhaps that is why he was always pointing an accusing finger at them both, since the two of them were obviously one, tied together by rosaries and dusty Tradition. After the Council, he became the voice of the world condemning the Church for hypocrisy, and the world listened to him, especially the media. He was always good for a juicy sound bite. After being a revolutionary abbot in an old traditionalist monastery in the Carolinas, he felt an almost palpable craving to destroy the icons of previous ages, in order to erect the brave new church. Many responded to his leadership, becoming iconoclasts more fervent than himself. By the late-sixties, his cohorts were busy ripping out tabernacles, altar rails and *baldechinos* all over the country. The Bishops' Conference, confused by the changes, desperately needed a prophet and he conveniently fit the bill. Any word against Rome was warmly received by the majority, but not by his mother's minority of one. She once told him that his words were like a knife in the pope's back. But as long as the dissident theologians loved him for it, he could put up with an old lady who didn't know any better. In public, he had just the right measure of outraged dignity in his voice when hammering away at the supposed injustices within the Church toward—women, minorities, the dispossessed, and the marginalized. But at home, face-to-face with the woman who gave him birth, he might not be so sure of himself. He who had been instrumental in dismantling the formerly sound spiritual practices of seminaries all over the country held little or no moral authority at home. If indeed he were to literally wear the mantle of leadership, his mother would always manage to find lint on his shoulder. He consoled himself by reminding himself that no prophet was a prophet in his own home.

Exiting the freeway, involuntarily his heart beat faster. The little, white, wooden house evoked even more memories, even smells. The front porch was where the family would gather on summer evenings to pray the rosary, with each child leading a decade. The front door painted red, open now as always, had never been locked, despite the neighborhood's obvious deterioration. The same old religious statues stood at odd angles in the garden—St. Francis, a cross, a badly repainted Our Lady of Lourdes and an oversize Saint Benedict medal—as reminders of the simple faith of his forbears. His mother insisted such reminders also kept evil at bay. What an antiquated notion, he thought—to even think that the devil exists.

How often he told himself that his mother's simple faith had long ago been superseded by the need for clarity. At that moment, he was seeing everything only too clearly. The whole place seemed rundown, shabby, in need of a fresh coat of paint. If given his druthers, he would gut the whole place, paint it and sell it in a wink of an eye. But he knew his mother would never allow that. She actually prayed before the small blue kitchen Madonna over the sink. She read the Bible, morning and evening, invoking the saints. Therese, Martin, Francis, Anthony, Kateri—these were her closest friends. Bishop Ronald Fielding shuddered at the thought of such backward ecclesiology, then rang the bell.

His mother shuffled to the door, opened it smiling, and embraced him long and hard, without a word of reprimand for not visiting in the last six months. She took off his overcoat, made of the finest Italian wool, revealing a light blue sport shirt, not his bishop's colors and pectoral cross. Even though he tried to stop her, she quickly genuflected before him, and kissed his ring before seating him by the fire which burned gaily in the grate.

"Please wait a moment, Ronnie, there are fresh muffins and tea!"

He hated it when she hung his boyhood moniker on him, while incongruously, just seconds before, recognizing the signs of his apostolic authority.

The diminutive, white-haired, sprightly old woman carried the loaded tray out of the kitchen, placing it before him with reverence. This was the part he hated most: having to chitchat and catch up on all the family news. He rarely wasted words on lesser subjects than social justice and service to the poor. This feminine form of selfless generosity now serving him was an absolute humiliation. He knew many a liberated nun who would love to set her straight. His mother smiled sweetly at him, waiting for him to begin, so she could carry on. This he dutifully did, talking about things he knew she could little understand. His world had grown so large while hers had shrunk so terribly—like her own body. It did seem that she was getting thinner, or was it because his girth was expanding. Waving that thought away like a bothersome fly, he listened benevolently to his mother's voice talking about the prospects of a spring planting in her garden. Her voice was sweet like the tea, but now wavering with age. He knew that the decision could not be made too soon. Never one to put off to tomorrow what can be done today, he broached the subject.

"Mother, dear? Did you receive the brochures I sent you about St. Joseph's Manor?"

"Yes, Ronnie, as a matter of fact I did." Then she was silent.

"Well, what do you think?"

"About what, dear?" The infernal woman was toying with him.

"About moving into a nice private room there . . . where you'll be nicely taken care of . . ."

"Oh!" She laughed, "I thought you were asking me, what do I think about St. Joseph?" She chuckled at this, continuing without missing a beat "You know, Ronnie, that I love St. Joseph. He provided for the Holy Family, he continues to do so for the whole Church and I have no doubt he will do the same for me." He had the feeling she was making a point.

"So you'll go?"

"Try to understand, dear, I believe in God the Father Almighty, in Jesus Christ His Only Son and in the Holy Spirit . . ."

Now he was openly irritated, "I know the Creed, mother!"

"Do you, Ronnie?" He turned as red as one of her ripe summer tomatoes.

"You taught it to me yourself, I should know it."

"Yes, you should, but I think you've forgotten parts of it."

What was she getting at? He was there to convince her that she was too old to keep living independently on her own, to sell the family home and to reconcile herself to her declining golden years and eventually, death. Rather, it was she who seemed to be on the offensive by being offensive.

"Mother, what are you trying to say?"

"I am simply saying, Ronald, that I will go when the Lord tells me it's time to go. This is my home, and the Church is my home."

She only called him "Ronald" when she was angry, which, admittedly didn't happen often. All the tripe about the Church and heaven was lost on the fact that she was unwilling to go to the nursing home. If he could only get her to go, then he would feel less guilty about not visiting her. She would be well taken care of. He smiled broadly, taking in the moment, until he suddenly realized she was weeping.

"Mother, don't cry, it won't be so bad. A community of Puerto Rican nuns take care of the place now. And they have a chapel and daily Mass."

"You don't understand—that's not what I'm worried about . . ."

"Well, then what is it?"

"I'm worried about you."

Now what could the foolish old woman mean by that? That's when his cell phone rang. It was the call he had been expecting, so he said, "Sorry, Mother, I have to answer this . . ." thus signaling her retreat back into the kitchen.

"Hello," he answered, his voice, tense, suppressed. "Yes, I will bring the check myself . . . Yes, tomorrow . . . Yes, I know the place . . . Goodbye." He closed the phone and his mother duly returned. He did not look up, but just sat there, breathing rather heavily, suddenly red in the face, staring into the fire.

"You're in trouble, aren't you, Ronnie? You always come home when you're in trouble," she said, matter-of-factly. "Ever since you were a little boy I always knew when you had done something wrong."

He couldn't look at her, and almost against his will answered truthfully. "I suppose I am, mother," he said, "But you wouldn't understand." He thought she was going to say, "Don't worry, dear, it's nothing God can't handle," or some pithy maxim like that, but she didn't.

She whispered, looking straight into his eyes, "That was your friend, wasn't it, on the phone just now?" She emphasized the word significantly.

"What friend?" he asked, just a bit too loudly.

She got up, walked over to the bookshelf and took an envelope from the Bible. Holding it up, she asked, "He sent me a copy of the same letter he sent you. You didn't know?"

"What are you talking about now?" he said.

"Do I need to read it out loud? Just tell me it's not true."

She could always tell if he was lying so he didn't bother to try. He sat there silently stirring his now cold tea. The fireplace felt suddenly hotter, as if the very flames of hell were licking his legs.

"You must first go to confession," she began, "And then you will have to resign your office. Then, return to the monastery, to your first love, and spend the rest of your days in prayer, doing penance." Her words, grated on his mind like fingernails on a chalkboard, but after a few minutes, began to sink in. She was speaking to him like she used to, many years before—in a soft soothing voice—whenever he was particularly troubled about something. Like the time he stole money from her purse, or when he broke the basement window, or when he got involved with some foul-mouthed friends. She was reading his soul like only a mother can, as if he had never stopped stealing, breaking and cursing. The embarrassment and shame wrapped him round and then—strangely—comforted him, promising warm redemption if he did not refuse the embrace.

"That bastard told you all about our . . . uh . . . relationship, did he?" his voice rasped, on the verge of tears.

"Everything," she said sadly, not able to hide the disappointment in her voice.

"Mom, I'm sorry for getting you involved with him . . . He promised me he would keep it secret, but then he got greedy . . ."

"He's blackmailing you, isn't he?"

The look on his face told her it was true and that things were even worse than she knew. He desperately wanted to change the subject, so he stammered, "Mother, I'm sorry about not visiting lately . . . But as you know, I've been so very busy . . . Many times I remembered too late and it is too late to call."

"I can see that . . ." she said, "But you didn't forget me," she said softly, "You have forgotten God and His Church."

He finally looked up at her, taken aback and snapped, "I realize that you disapprove of my relationship with him, but it's over, so you can stop judging me." He stood up and walked toward the front door, but stopped dead in his tracks.

"Oh, I'm not the one who will be judging you, Ronnie. But I will be the one to call the newspapers if you insist on putting me out of my own house." He stood there for a long moment unsteady on his feet, allowing the enormity of her words to sink in.

"You're blackmailing me too?" he gasped.

"No, dear, let's just say I'm helping you do the right thing."

"And what is that?"

"Resign, of course, before there's a scandal."

"Now, you're threatening me, mother."

"Better to never to have been born than cause one of these little ones to lose their faith."

He burst out through the front door and lurched unsteadily down the garden path, past St. Francis, the Cross and the Virgin, fumbling in his pocket for his keys, unsure if he would make it to the car. Opening the car door, he sat for a long moment, breathing heavily, and staring back at his mother who was now standing on the front porch looking at him. Putting the keys in the ignition, he started the engine and threw it into reverse. Pulling back and away, without waving goodbye, he sank into the smooth Corinthian leather seat, feeling the sense of unreality grip like a vise. He put a

Mozart CD in the slot and heard the first soothing strains sound. He merged on to the highway, and the miles began to flow by, his anger glowing like the dashboard. Who was she to tell him what to do? He was, after all, not only her son but also her bishop. After all, in his own eyes, he had done nothing wrong. It was the Church that told him he was wrong. Why, he *was* the Church and could do as he damn well pleased. How could some ignorant old woman tell him to retire, do penance, in a life of solitude and silence—-to end his career in disgrace—-in the very monastery where it had all had begun.

The following day, dressed in street clothes, dark glasses and a baseball hat, he met a slim, younger man between the stacks of the public library, handing over an unmarked envelope containing a check—in the vicinity of six figures—drawn from a secret account. Hopefully, that would keep his "friend" quiet for a few more months. Exiting the library, he did his best to forget all about his unfortunate home visit and went back to his plush office in the chancery to write an article about "Women's prophetic voice in the Church today." That afternoon he told the whole tale to his psychologist, asking if there was any way to get his mother declared insane or at least, incompetent. The psychologist asked him more questions about his mother and then wrote a prescription to calm his nerves. A week later, the scandal made national news, with the local reporter refusing to name his source.

Flesh Surrendered

Father Gregory's reputation preceded him to his new assignment. A young, earnest convert—just five years ordained—besides the faith, he also had "the touch."

Every time he gave the Last Rites—the anointing to the sick, the recipient inevitably expired as if on command. No sooner were the words—"Go in peace, Christian soul"—pronounced than the person would give up the ghost. In the mind of the Church and indeed, in his own mind, his purpose was to bring prompt succor to those teetering on the brink of eternity, allowing safe passage to the far shores. But the faithful clung to the old belief that the appearance of the black-robed priest at the door meant that the grim reaper was also knocking. The Last Rites, known formerly as Extreme Unction, or literally, the "anointing at the extreme" were presently known as the Sacrament of the anointing. No longer only for the dying, it was for anyone—aged or infirmed—who needed the healing touch of the Divine Physician. Fr. Gregory's experience was that the Sacrament always had both physical and spiritual effects. Many times the recipient, perhaps, even in the throes of death, would recover, living on to fight the good fight another day. This minor miracle allowed the anointed time to get their lives in order, to repent sufficiently of their sins, to pray and do penance before judgment. Father Greg knew this to be a great mercy. The spiritual effects were not so visible but were certainly potent. Even if unconscious and unconfessed, the anointed's sins would be wiped out and grace would surrender flesh to the Spirit.

Being newly assigned to the parish in North Myrtle Beach, Fr. Gregory's arrival was big news. The bulk of his parishioners, besides being Yankees, were also retired. Snowbirds mostly from New York, New Jersey, Massachusetts, and Canada flocked to spend their last winters in South Carolina playing golf. A young priest would make a good companion. The problem was, however, Father Gregory didn't golf, nor did he have the slightest desire to learn. He might miss an emergency sick call someday while out on the golf course.

Without a prejudiced bone in his body against Northerners, Fr. Gregory welcomed them all. They, for their part, seemed to appreciate him very much, his brief but insightful sermons, his reserved, prudent manner, not to mention the fact that he never mentioned money in church. He was a firm believer that if the preacher shared the Good News then people would naturally respond by opening their hearts followed by their pocketbooks. But after a few weeks, any newcomers would inevitably hear and usually believe the rumors about his unusual talent. Then their glad-handing Sunday morning demeanors would change. Father Gregory had the touch of death. A brave few would invite him to be the fourth in their morning round of golf but since he would always politely decline, such offers soon disappeared. Moreover, the young cleric was a teetotaler and so would be no fun at all at the 19-hole afterward. And he never accepted invitations to early-bird dinners the septuagenarian set was so found of. But mostly, they felt uncomfortable in his presence. He had a way of looking at a person, with those piercing blue eyes of his. Some said it was like he was reading their soul. So the golfers and their golf-widowed wives soon stayed clear of their new pastor because they were not yet ready to be confronted by someone whose only concern was preparing them for eternity.

Word had traveled down from his first assignment as assistant pastor up in Charleston. Evidently, it all began when—within a week of ordination—he rushed to the Cooper Nursing home to anoint a spinster, Miss Ann McCaffrey, who was in the last stages of cancer. After the administration of the sacrament itself, including a peaceful confession and the reception of Viaticum, the young prelate was asked to anoint Miss Ann's spinster sister, Margaret, who occupied a room at the other end of the hall. This he dutifully did. Margaret, pronounced "Maaaagaret" in the South, actually asked "Faaaather" for the anointing and that would have been that, had not two other Catholic women in the facility gotten wind of the presence of a priest and requested the same treatment. The good Southern Baptists, both patients and staff, shook their heads at this errant Catholic practice. They could not say it was not biblical because it was mentioned in the letter of James, but ever since Luther, for them, that particular missive was suspect. Yet "Faaather" Gregory, hailing from stout Methodist roots was prepared from his mother's womb for their purely prejudiced objections. His conversion began in public school in the fifth grade when he witnessed a Catholic classmate make the sign of the cross. Smiling and calm, they soon learned that they could not win a discussion with him—arguments did not happen in gentile society—since his logic always flowed from the biblical font.

He was so nice and good looking, that boy, why did he have to ruin it all and become a papist? From the womb, they had all been taught that any unfortunate soul who mistakenly ascribed to the teachings of Rome was destined for hell. It surprised them no end that Father Gregory's only concern seemed to be getting them to heaven. The ladies in the craft room spoke about him often, since his kindness was hard to condemn. A few even conspired secretly to have him meet their southern-belle daughters in the hopes of both saving his soul and arranging a grand wedding, whichever came first. Yet—the fact is within an hour of his visit first Miss Ann died, which was not unexpected. After all, she was the reason the priest had been called. But then a half-hour after receiving the news of her dear sister's demise, Miss Margaret succumbed as well. Whether it was the shock of no longer having her sibling within shouting distance or whether it was because the young man had the "touch" will be forever debated within the confines of the Cooper Nursing Home. Indeed, it became news citywide when the third and fourth ladies to be anointed died, one that very afternoon and one the following evening. "He has the touch—didn't I tell you . . . There was just something about him . . ."

The bishop, well satisfied with Father Gregory's exemplary service as a humble assistant in the big city, felt it was now safe to send him as administrator of a fledgling parish catering to the tourists down in North Murtle beach. There was no school, so the financial burden would not be overwhelming. Besides, there were a couple retired priests living in condos that golfed during the week but were willing to help out with a Mass or two on Sundays. There was even a retired bishop nearby. The young priest, though, admittedly shy of temperament and of experience, would manage.

When the retired priests introduced their homilies with jokes about the links and the Masters tournament down in Augusta, Father Gregory quoted Saint Augustine and Saint Thomas Aquinas. When the retired bishop spoke of politics and changing society, the young pastor made his congregation squirm, speaking about the need for the conversion of heart.

When Mr. John O'Neal from Lowell, Massachusetts, had a heart attack on the back nine, his two golfing buddies called the ambulance and then Father Gregory. Right on schedule, meeting the trio in the emergency room, after the priest's anointing, John passed on. Seeing Father Gregory in action and witnessing the loving way he comforted John's wife Jeannie, an entirely new rumor began to circulate. Evidently, the new priest had the touch—with living people too. Although young, he knew intuitively how to help people in pain. With the lonely and the grieving, he knew how to sit with them without saying too much. "There's just something about that boy," they all said, "He couldn't hit a golf ball if his life depended on it, but he's all right."

So gradually, despite the fact that he did not golf, Father Gregory became much loved by his parishioners because they sensed he loved them much. He never accepted their invitations to any of their social functions, preferring to walk alone on the nearby beaches. They knew, however, that if they called him for an emergency, he would be there. When things got really serious they never called the retired priests or bishop, especially if the end was near. After years of practice on their days off, they all had the right touch on the putting green—but not where it really counted—at the hour of death. The snowbirds knew that one day, sooner or later, each one of them would have to make one final migration. And they all wanted Father Gregory to be there when it happened.

Sacrament of Summer

Look up the word "big" in the dictionary and you'll find Gerry's picture next to those of Mount Everest, Jimmy Durante's nose and Ayers Rock in the Australian outback. Humongous, enormous, huge and every' other adjective the thesaurus might offer would still lack some essential quality about him. That's because, besides sheer size, the man had some additional, less quantifiable something. He had a big heart—as big as a baseball stadium, filled with cheering fans in October. He had a big voice too. At Mass, every time he proclaimed the first reading by one of the prophets, you could really imagine God talking. He was, however, the proverbial gentle giant, capable of making a Buddhist monk look bloodthirsty.

Gerry was my first friend in the parish. It's funny how, with friendship, you can always point to a precise moment where it actually begins. For us, it was outside the Church, one Sunday morning in late April. After greeting parishioners filing out to fight their way out of the parking lot, I suddenly realized I was standing in someone's shadow. Turning around, I looked up to see the big guy's smiling, bearded face. His head totally eclipsed the sun. If it weren't for the baseball cap he was wearing, I would have mistaken him for a mountain. But since my eye level was somewhere just above his stomach, next I found myself looking up at my favorite baseball team's logo—the Chicago Cubs—imprinted on his chest. Following my gaze, Gerry said, "Yeah, I was in a National League mood this morning."

I understood him perfectly. Coming from Chicago, where prevailing thirty-mile-an-hour southwest winds regularly swept both the old Southside Comiskey Park and Northside Wrigley Field, one is either an American leaguer or a National leaguer from birth. Being a fan of either team may accurately describe one's mood. Moreover, as so often happens, one does not necessarily need to hail from "the city of big shoulders" to be fatefully drawn to one team or the other. Like Gerry, a complete out-of-towner might tie their boyish hopes to either the White Sox, or more tragically still, the Cubs. It was something akin to being a fan of Notre Dame, for those who never attended that worthy university could vicariously live and breathe Fighting Irish blue and gold. These fans were called the "subway alumni," as if some secret subterranean system connected like-minded enthusiasts throughout the land. But the difference, of course, is obvious. Notre Dame has a history of winning. But for Chicago's two baseball franchises, the misery of losing attracts the same kind of company. Both teams always would begin strong in spring training, their bats popping with promise. And then, as inevitably as the turning of the seasons, the official season would begin, signaling the bursting of hope's bubble. Sometimes both teams would toy with the fan's affections, winning games all the way through the All-Star break in early

July, sometimes even leading their respective divisions. But invariably, like the turning of Summer to Fall and then to dread Chicago Winter, the long slow slide from one loss to another would crush the dreams of kids, both old and young alike——like so many paper beer cups under the "L" tracks. Anyway, to say Gerry was "in a National League mood," meant he was a Cubs fan. That statement established an instant and lifelong bond between us. It didn't seem to matter that I was perhaps the first priest friend he ever had. Faith and hard experience had taught us not to place our hopes in anything of this earth. Gerry nodded, and I understood.

"Do you want to go see a game?" Gerry asked, interrupting my reverie.

"Who's playing?"

"Dodgers and Giants."

"Not the Cubs and Sox but another good rivalry. When?"

"Tomorrow night, before the strike on Thursday," he answered ominously. This sparse conversation typified all our future conversations, short and to the point. In 1992, both the American and National leagues that year were threatening a walkout. Billions of dollars were at stake and the already rich players wanted more. Gerry nodded again—we both understood that greed threatened the purity of the game. One guy, barely hitting .230 was demanding 10 million a season. That came down to almost $10,000 every at bat. These players' whining news conferences, meant to induce support and put pressure on management and owners, had the opposite effect on fans. It's awfully hard to feel sorry for a multimillionaire complaining about how tough life is when you yourself are struggling just to get by. "How many BMWs, Bentleys, and Mercedes can one individual drive at a time, anyway?" Gerry asked rhetorically.

The next day, at precisely 5:00 p.m., Gerry pulled up in front of the rectory in his big black Cadillac Eldorado. It seemed to take up the entire block in front of the church. It was so long the front bumper arrived ten minutes before the back one. And there was not a scratch on that baby. Gerry treated that car like his best girl. Momentarily lost in the leather front seat I managed to buckle the seat belt before takeoff. We cruised up Main Street—the 110 freeway was a parking lot—slowly navigating downtown LA like a yacht through Marina Del Rey. Conversation was sparse as usual but focused mainly on the upcoming event. Good but cheap seats were had in the upper deck on the first base line. The Los Angeles Dodgers and the San Francisco Giants were archrivals and two of the better National league teams that year. Noting Gerry's apparel, I was surprised to see him wearing a complete set of Giants black and orange below his sunglasses. I kept my mouth shut, however, chalking this fashion statement up to another one of his National league moods. But I did wonder how this attire might go over, entering their archrivals home stadium. The big riots, just a few months before came to mind. The big man himself seemed unperturbed, turning the Eldorado's starboard rudder to exit off Sunset.

"I used to be a pro myself, Father," he said confessionally. "A pitcher with the Kansas City Royals . . . until I wrecked my knee." Disappointment flooded his voice. "I could hit too," he added. No need to go on. It was my turn to nod. A pitcher who could hit. "Now I work with kids in the neighborhood, getting them unhooked from gangs and drugs and hooked on the game," he said. I had heard from some neighbors how much good Gerry was accomplishing in this difficult area. Crime was down and hopes were up on his particular block. But the infamous Rolling '40s gang didn't appreciate losing prospective members and influence, so they harassed the big guy whenever they could. Gerry called them a "bad element." It was a grim truth in our neighborhood that a semiautomatic could cut anybody down to size, even the biggest. In later days I worried about him. But Gerry was not one to be intimidated, carting his recruits off in his cruiser to a local park to practice three afternoons a week. He'd hit fungoes, run them through their paces, patiently teaching the fundamentals like catechism at Sunday school.

We pulled into the miles of empty parking lot surrounding Dodger Stadium, roughly two hours before game time. This, I was learning, was an essential part of the ritual. We had to arrive that early so we could catch batting practice. Gerry then proceeded to park his oil tanker as far as humanly possible from the entrance gates. No one would want to walk that far to the stadium so chances were

148

no one would park next to him, therefore there would be no chance of scratching that sleek black paint job.

Once anchor was dropped, Gerry walked slowly around the car, inspecting the hull, caressing it, as if to say, "It's OK baby, don't worry, Daddy'll be back soon." He then opened the trunk and took out the biggest radio I had ever seen, one requiring nuclear powered batteries. With no small difficulty I hoisted the cumbersome apparatus up onto my right shoulder while he rummaged around the cavernous space, searching amongst various pieces of baseball equipment—bats, balls, gloves and the like—until he found two matching batters' helmets. Closing the trunk delicately, he turned to me and said, "We're wearing these." Refusal was not an option.

I looked at the Giant's insignia, aghast. "But, Gerry, they're San Francisco helmets. The Dodger fans'll kill us if we go into their stadium wearing these."

Gerry just looked down at me and said, "That's why they are hard." But then he added, "Don't worry, Father, you're with me."

Obediently, but with many an interior misgiving, I put on the helmet. Expecting it to be much too big I was surprised when it fit perfectly. Looking down on so many, Gerry was obviously a good judge of head size. We trekked several kilometers to the stadium, presented our tickets, and then entered the gates. I know I wasn't imagining the raised eyebrows from staff and the other early-bird fans as we made our way to our seats. I felt terribly self-conscious, and not because I was in my black clerics. Somehow Gerry wedged himself into his seat. I was hoping the seat next to me would be vacant so I could lean left and breathe. We admired the green field and the eucalyptus trees beyond the four-hundred-foot mark. Even if these weren't our favorite Chicago teams, it was a longstanding rivalry promising a tight contest. Besides, Barry bonds and Darryl Strawberry would be playing and they usually came through. Although the latter was proving one comedian's prophetic words to be more than true: "Cocaine is God's way of saying you're making too much money." Poor Darryl had already been suspended a couple times for drug use, but now seemed on the straight and narrow. As for Mr. Bonds, back then nobody ever suspected he might be pumping steroids to boost his home-run total.

After a country singer crooned the national anthem, everybody clapped anyway. Then, at last, the game began. The place filled up, and everyone began filling up on Dodger dogs, beer and chocolate malties. How to describe it? A kind of religious awe enveloped the crowd. Thirty-five thousand human beings, all from diverse ethnic backgrounds, cheering as one, all there for one reason only—for love of the game. It didn't matter how overpriced the foot-longs were or how lukewarm the beer was, how overpriced the tickets were, or even how overblown the egos of the players themselves were. What mattered was it was summer—and what could be better than catching a cool night game at Dodger Stadium after a hot day in Southern California.

During the game we experienced only one moment of tension. And this didn't happen in the game but in the stands. There were five, hefty white businessmen seated directly down in front of us, all liberally lubricated and shouting obscenities at the umpires. Well, because of this offensive language, Gerry turned up the mega-blaster to earthquake volume. It was strategically placed under his seat so he could better hear Vin Scully intone the play by play. Admittedly, it was pretty loud. If I was thinking at all, which is debatable, I realized the cranked up radio was irritating the heck out of the five slobs in front of us. I noticed them working themselves up to a possibly nasty confrontation. When the guy directly in front of Gerry's radio got sufficiently fed up—he turned around to angrily tell whoever we were to "turn that damn thing the hell down." He had just started to pronounce this unmistakable phrase when he realized that he was facing perhaps the largest human being he had ever seen. And that the behemoth he now faced was not smiling, was wearing the opposing team's colors, was obviously the owner of the offending radio, was intently watching the game, and was ignoring him completely.

I'll never forget the scene. The guy, no small fry himself, started to open his big yap as if to say: "Hey! What the hell . . ." but seeing Gerry, he stopped in midsentence, and said, "Hey . . . er . . . What a great game!"

Succeeding in getting Gerry's full attention, the man and his companions waited with bated breath. When Gerry smiled and said, "Yeah, it sure is!" the danger passed. Knowing the big guy, however, I knew there was never a hint of a threat from his end. But for the five obnoxious white guys from the suburbs, now all sneaking worried peeks over each other's shoulders, Gerry was their worst nightmare. One by one, they became suddenly interested in something else— the bottom of their popcorn bag, a mustard stain on a shirt, the girl walking down the nearby steps. One by one, they all turned around and sat up straight in their seats like good little boys.

A minute later, I shouted to my companion, managing to make myself heard above the din, "Hey Gerry, maybe it's a little loud, could you turn it down a tad?"

The big man readily obliged, reaching a hand the size of a first-baseman's glove under the seat to adjust the volume control, all the while keeping his eyes focused on the action down on the field. Another crisis averted. I felt blessedly like a peacemaker, who just might inherit the kingdom. The rest of the game proceeded without further incident. Fernando Valenzuela fired smoke from the mound for three innings before losing control. Mr. Bonds and company came back, knotted things up by the seventh inning stretch and won with a sacrifice fly in the ninth. We two waited for the crowd to disperse before hiking back to the car under the parking lot floodlights, a warm glow flooding our hearts. We drove home in companionable silence, awash with gratitude, for having gone to a game together. When Gerry dropped me off at the rectory, little did we know that the headlines the next morning in the *LA Times* would read: "Baseball Players Declare Strike." They were demanding a percentage of the television broadcast rights as well as the removal of all limits to their already scandalous salaries. There would be no more baseball for the rest of the summer. Worse still, there would be no World Series that fall.

Seeing Gerry the next Sunday, he proclaimed the Word like Jeremiah himself. It was a warning for the chosen people to turn back to God. Outside afterward, on the front steps of the Church, we greeted each other without saying a word. The big man then walked off to the furthest corner of the parking lot to fire up the Eldorado. His neighborhood kids would be playing the Rolling '40s gang that very afternoon.

"Another cross-town rivalry," he said.

Palace of Charity

I t was already a month into the winter 1991 semester and Matthew realized that he still had not met everyone in his class. All were black faces, seminarians sent from their dioceses in Africa to study in Rome—except for two.

That morning, in between Moral Theology II and Canon Law, as a true innocent abroad, he approached the only other white face in his class, standing alone in the long hallway. The huge windows afforded a wondrous view of Michelangelo's dome over St. Peter's Basilica. The bearded, young man he surveyed was tall, wearing a black cassock, and was totally absorbed in his reading of that morning's edition of the Corriere della Sera. Standing there, Matthew waited until the turning of the page to speak, "Hello, I thought I would introduce myself . . ."

The bearded seminarian looked at him and then glanced at the group of Africans starting to gather around. He said in Italian, "I am Sharbel. I am from Iraq. Where are you from?"

Now Matthew understood the reason for the ever-increasing throng of onlookers. Since the beginning of the first Gulf War, three days previous, the news was full of pictures of exploding "smart" bombs and lots of pictures of Iraqi soldiers surrendering. Matthew, taking in the headline blaring from the front page in Sharbel's hands—"MORE BOMBS!"—was tempted to lie and say, "I am from Canada." As they trekked through Europe, Canadians were famous for plastering red maple leaves over everything they owned so as not to risk being mistaken as Americans. Gathering round, a group of African students, rife with centuries of tribal conflicts, held their collective breath, awaiting Matthew's response. Evidently, they had all been hankering for this moment when the personal war would break out between their two white classmates. After all—one was Iraqi and one was American—and they were sworn enemies, now at war. Matthew looked up at the nearby statue of St. Joseph, and prayed a quick prayer for a happy death.

Taking a deep breath he grimaced, and answered with a gulp, "I am from the United States." He had learned that if he ever answered "America" all the Latin Americans in his religious community would be up in arms, informing him for the umpteenth time that their ancient ancestors were the first Americans. Practically in the same breath, they would then go on to remind him of the tragic fate of the Native Americans. But Matthew always acknowledged the truth. For him, true patriotism was a question of acknowledging both the good and beautiful as well as the shabby and shameful about your country's history. One could legitimately be proud of the former while trying to remedy the latter.

Sharbel's eyes narrowed. He stared fiercely but did not speak. The whole hallway, now filled with Africans, of all tribes and nations—about a hundred strong—had the sense that a volcano was about to erupt. Sharbel began by pointing to the picture on the front page of his newspaper. "You see this—woman and children injured by a bomb! Dropped by a US bomber . . . You Americans . . . are warmongers . . . everywhere . . ." Overcome by anger, Sharbel choked on the stream of Arabic expletives issuing involuntarily from his mouth. African eyes grew wide with every explosive curse, awaiting the American's response. Contrary to their expectations, and to their great disappointment, however, Matthew just stood there, hands at his side, patiently looking into the eyes of the man raving at him. Some of the Congolese pounded out a war dance on their textbooks. A few Eritreans eyed their Ethiopian counter-parts menacingly. Hutus and their Tutsi blood enemies were yet to have their day. When Sharbel finally came up for breath, Matthew addressed him, calmly, "I am sorry about the war, just as you are. Perhaps, when things calm down, we can talk about it—someday." At that moment, he was saved by the bell signaling the beginning of the last class of the morning. All the Ugandans, Kenyans, Eritreans, Ethiopians, Congolese, Burundians, Zambians, Tanzanians, Malawians, Mozambicans, Angolans and Sudanese disappeared, a bit disappointed at the lack of blood.

Sharbel stared at Matthew for the longest moment, before abruptly turning and walking away. That's when he got his second vocal wind. He turned around and—right there in the middle of the hallway, in the shadow of the dome of Saint Peter's—began scream-ing at the American once again. Some of their classmates returned to see the slaughter. Harsh words, full of frustration accompanied Matthew all the way down the hall as he gratefully slid into his next class. Then, suddenly, there was silence. The vitriol stopped alto-gether. Matthew wondered if his hostile colleague would enter the class to kill him with a scimitar. Suffice to say, it was not easy con-centrating on Canon Law that day. He told himself he would never introduce himself to anyone ever again.

The next day, Matthew stayed inside the huge *aula* classroom during the breaks, hoping to avoid another tongue-lashing. He did not feel like arguing with anybody about war. He believed what the pope had been preaching, that it's always better to seek diplomatic solutions rather than violent ones. Unlike so many in his home country, yet like his parents, and grandparents before him, he was a Catholic first and an American second. He was not a so-called Kennedy Catholic, ready to abandon the ship of belief in order to win an election.

On the third day, he ventured out into the hall, since Sharbel was nowhere to be seen during the two previous days. Matthew gazed out the window at the great dome, feeling homesick. It reminded him a little of the Capitol building in Washington, DC. There remained still one more long year of studies before ordination at home. That's when he felt the murmur rather than heard it. An almost palpable electricity surged down the hall. His normally jovial African classmates began to gather round again. Sharbel was coming down the hall and he definitely wasn't smiling. There was no newspaper in his hands but from the look on his face he was ready to make headlines of his own. Matthew turned and saw the enemy approaching, almost in slow motion. He couldn't help wondering if this was the way it felt just before martyrdom. He almost groaned aloud but didn't want to give the gawking onlookers the satisfaction. His dream had always been to be a martyr of the Church. But the last thing he desired was to be martyred simply for being an American.

Sharbel walked straight up to him and without warning, raised his arms, and then, suddenly, opening them wide—engulfed Matthew in a fierce embrace. The Africans gasped. Putting his hands on the American's shoulders, the Iraqi said, so all could hear, "Matthew—you know your name means 'gift of God'—you are an unexpected gift from God to me. You have made me reflect on my calling. And I apologize for what I said to you the other day. I am truly sorry. I was wrapped up in many emotions, I could not think straight—please forgive me. You and I are both disciples . . . As you said, perhaps we can talk . . . please, come, and allow me to buy you an espresso in the school cafe . . ."

Matthew, stunned, not quite believing what was actually taking place, walked arm in arm, in the European fashion, with Sharbel down the long hallway. The dome of St Peter's shone through the expansive windows to their right. All their black classmates stood by, watching in disbelief, wondering how peace could break out so unexpectedly. All the way down that endless hallway, the Iraqi and the American talked. Upon entering the little cafe, which pandered coffee to the poor seminarian crowd, they both ordered and stood at the bar, talking some more. This they did every day until the end of the semester. At first, it was just small talk but soon they came around to discussing the war and the prospects for peace. But as the days went by, as each came to know and understand the other better, their conversation centered mostly on their own life's journey, their families, and their hopes for the future.

Sharbel had been named after the famed Maronite hermit-priest-saint, Sharbel Makluf, the miracle worker. Matthew was named after the tax collector who left his moneychanger's table to follow the Master. The two learned many more things about each other. They were the same age, heard the call at about the same time, and recognized it coming from the same voice.

Sharbel explained his conflicting emotions: "Although I hate Saddam—he has persecuted us Maronite Christians almost to extinction—but I still love my country. That is why I reacted the way I did," Sharbel said.

Matthew nodded.

The man's eyes welled tears as he went on, "Many of my family have been kidnapped and killed over the years by the secret police. Most of us who remain have been forced to escape to other countries . . ."

"Where is your family now?" Matthew asked gently.

"In the United States," Sharbel said, looking at his American companion, as if struck by some invisible blow, one that did not hurt so much as humble. After a long moment, he said. "That's where my father and mother are now . . . and my two sisters and brother. In San Jose, California."

Matthew joked, singing the old hit song: "Do you know the way to San Jose?"

Sharbel answered seriously, "No, I have not been able to visit them yet . . . Your government makes it very hard to obtain a visa."

Matthew stopped singing and said, "Now, that's not my fault!"

"Of course, you're right, my friend," smiled Sharbel.

"But you know what?" said the American, "My family lives in California too—so we're neighbors."

During the course of that academic year, every time they met in the hallways, the two embraced as brothers, taking turns to treat the other to coffee. That summer vacation they visited one another's families then spent a most enjoyable week driving down Route One along the California coast. It reminded them of the Italian coast.

Sparrows Noticed
by the Father

Three months after his ordination, Fr. Brendan was sent by his order to the city of Manila. He was assigned to the crowded Murphy district, to Transfiguration parish, not far from Camp Aguinaldo. It was an inner-city parish, teeming with the usual problems inherent in the Republic of the Philippines: poverty, politics and plenty of people. His first impression was positive, however, for the latter were extremely welcoming and willing to work building the Kingdom in their barrio. There was much to be done, but the first order of business was for them to teach him Tagalog which had words longer than a basketball player's arm. For example, the word for "faith" is *pananampalataya*. You needed faith just to get to the end of the word, thought Fr. Brendan. He also thought that if Saint Paul was right, and love is first of all patient, then his parishioners were very loving indeed. The first time he celebrated Mass—sweating both buckets and bullets—he took twenty minutes longer in the native tongue than in English. At the end, after the blessing, in which the priest says, "The Mass is ended, go in peace" the faithful had never uttered a more a heartfelt "*Salamat sa Diyos* (Thanks be to God)" in all their lives.

Their word for "peace" is *kapayapaan*. The famous Filipino smile made him feel very much at peace, despite the fact that he was replacing a much beloved priest, Father Armando Reyes, who had been transferred to UP, the University of the Philippines, as chaplain. The weather, of the steam bath variety, was the only thing hard to get used to. It made him comment: "I feel like I'm constantly either getting into or out of hot water." His parishioners liked the young Irish-American because he didn't take himself too seriously. Also, about half the parish had relatives in his hometown of Chicago in the States.

As he got used to the place, slowly coming to understand the culture and the local reality, he began to notice many things. For example, he discovered that most of the people spoke other dialects, mostly Bicolano and Ilocano, not the one he had—with such pains—just learned. Exploring the neighborhood streets on foot put him into contact with the masses, especially the many street kids living under the viaducts and the Aetas, the small black aboriginal natives displaced by the eruption of Mount Pinatubo two years previous. The former numbered around sixty thousand citywide while no one had exact numbers for the latter. It broke his heart to see their misery and begging. He felt helpless, not knowing how to tackle such an enormous problem, especially since the local and federal governments seemingly could not or would not do anything. From the time of the Acts of the Apostles, the Church had always taken special care of the poor.

At first, walking the streets of his parish, everyone saluted him like they would any other American—"Hey, Joe"—a name stemming from the long time US military presence in the archipelago. The explosion of Mount Pinatubo combined with a growing nationalist opposition, not to mention an exorbitant—even by military spending standards—clean up, forced the US Navy to vacate the nearby

Subic Bay. But Father Brendan was actually happy that his compatri-ots were gone, because it gave the Filipino people their first real taste of freedom since the 1986 peaceful revolution which ousted then President Ferdinand Marcos. The miraculous stalemate, between tanks and People Power took place on the EDSA (Epifaneo de los Santos) highway just blocks from his parish. He saw that some stray Americans still came and went in pursuit of business interests while a few more ran nongovernmental organizations in the interests of philanthropy. It was to one of these that his brother John referred him, recommending a visit to a colleague—a certain Judith Lyons—who ran an NGO (nongovernmental organization) based in Honolulu that also administered projects in the Philippines. "Perhaps she can help with your street kid problem . . ." his big brother advised.

Fr. Brendan liked the idea, since he had been praying for guid-ance. And this seemed like a providential response. So he called up the number his brother gave him, talked to a very professional sound-ing secretary, and made an appointment for the following Monday, his day off. He was in luck, Ms. Lyons happened to be in town. If she couldn't give any financial assistance perhaps he could benefit from her experience working with the street-children population. Being just a beginner, and new to the country, Brendan knew enough to know he knew nothing—Socrates's definition of wisdom.

Since he had not yet visited the gleaming glass-towered business section of Manila called Makati, it took a while to find the City Bank building with its adjacent parking lot. The Richard and Rosamond Harris Foundation occupied approximately half of the tenth floor. Upon entering the plush, carpeted offices, Fr. Brendan felt like he had just entered another world, with an abrupt transformation from black and white to glowing Technicolor—like Dorothy setting out on the yellow-brick road to the Emerald City of Oz. Secretaries and other employees smiled and scurried in their busy post-*merienda*, prelunch routine—whatever that was. The receptionist directed him to the right, to the desk of an obviously more important secretary, judging by the plaque on her desk. This "personal assistant" asked him politely to take a seat and wait. After about five minutes, a tall, blonde, well-attired woman about his own age came out to greet him.

"Glad you could come," said MS. Judith Lyons, Director of the foundation, her eyes meeting his for the briefest instant before flashing around the impeccable, bustling scene before her. The glass wall of windows offered a spectacular view of the world below.

"How is your brother? When he called to say you now live here in Manila, I was hoping to get together. Please come into my office . . ."

Fr. Brendan allowed himself to be led into what looked more like a living room than an office, complete with couch, comfortable chairs, and a low table appropriately adorned with rare orchids and fresh coffee.

"Impressive," he said, a little awkwardly. His own comparatively shabby surroundings came before his inner eyes. All at once he felt ashamed at his worn collar and scuffed sandals. But MS. Lyons seemed not to notice, launching smoothly into an explanation of the foundation's "mission." A twelve page, four color brochure showed the lady herself surrounded by grinning street children, all well clothed and better fed. There were pictures of her with both the past President, Corazon Aquino, and the current President, Fidel Ramos, as well as with Jaime Cardinal Sin, the spiritual leader of the nation.

"What a great work you're doing, MS. Lyons," he said, now really impressed, taking a steaming cup of the fresh brewed Lipa blend, while sinking down further than he wanted into the couch.

"Call me Judy, please. Knowing your brother, I feel like I already know you. Perhaps, as you can see, we like to maintain a family atmosphere here, for the staff as well as our dear children."

"Please, Miss . . . I mean, Judy—tell me about your work with the street kids because in my parish, I'm quite at a loss what to do . . ."

"Well, our foundation was founded by Richard and Rosamond Harris. She was a native of the Philippines who immigrated to Hawaii and had the good fortune to marry the very wealthy Mr. Richard Harris, not the famous actor, but nevertheless from one of the most important families in Oahu. Pineapples, sugarcane and land—miles and miles of prime beachfront, to be exact. Well, before their deaths they established a charitable trust mandated to spend so many millions annually in the Hawaiian Islands benefiting the indigenous population there, with the other half coming here to the Philippines."

"So you travel between one place and the other?" he asked.

"Yes, it's so tiring . . . but I have a suggestion, it's almost lunch time, why don't you join me?" She smiled, whisking the young priest smoothly up the silent elevator to the penthouse restaurant, where tuxedoed waiters did everything but wipe their chins. Fr. Brendan, although enjoying his meal, nevertheless was again experiencing conflicting emotions. The food was delicious and tasted even better than back in the states, but he felt a little guilty sitting in the lap of luxury while so many of his own parishioners lived in squatter shacks. Questions started giving him indigestion.

Thinking like a member of a religious order, who had taken a vow of poverty, and who, when travelling would always stay with other religious or families to save expenses, he ventured, "Where do you stay when you're here in Manila?"

Judy smiled, "At the Shangri-La nearby."

"I've heard of that hotel. They say it's very . . . er . . . nice."

"Oh, it's adequate for my needs." Judy looked out the window. Some sparrows congregated on the ledge chirping and pecking.

Before he could stop himself, Fr. Brendan said, "If you don't mind me asking, how much does it cost per night to stay at such a nice place?"

Judy had no qualms answering, "Three hundred sixty-five dollars." Fr. Brendan knew that was more than an average Filipino's monthly wages.

"Wow! So I suppose you try to get your work done fast here so you can get back home quick and not spend too much . . ."

"Oh no," Judy said, "I keep the same room there all year round. It's much easier that way, since then I don't have to constantly make reservations. I can even leave some of my things here."

In his head, the priest tried to calculate how much money that would amount to yearly. The offices, employees and everything else added up to some big operation.

"How many street children centers do you operate?" he asked, changing the subject while shifting in his seat.

"Two," Judy answered, "One here in Makati and one up north in Baguio City."

Fr. Brendan stopped chewing his steak. Even though he was new in the country, he knew that the police regularly rousted street kids out of the Makati business district so as not to give the wrong impression to visiting foreign investors. Many of them ended up in his barrio. And he had taken one trip to Baguio, the tranquil, flower-strewn city of the pines, transformed by the American presence into perhaps the only cool (temperaturewise) resort in the Philippines. All the old administrators and military bigwigs from Taft on down fled up there to spend the hottest months from March through May. Again, as far as he knew, there were relatively few street urchins plying the streets of that place of privilege. All this expenditure—he thought—for only two little shelters! And they were located in places where there was little need for them.

He pressed on, even though he knew that she knew what he was thinking. "And how many kids do you take care of?"

"At last count—you know how difficult it is to reach an actual number—they don't like to be cooped up . . . at last count, there were about eighteen in Baguio with another twenty or so here in Manila."

He wanted to say, "All this . . . this . . . for less than forty kids when there are sixty thousand wandering the streets of Manila, sleeping out of doors, scavenging for crumbs, sniffing glue to keep from feeling the hunger pangs . . ." But instead, he clutched the fancy color brochures she'd given him more tightly, quickly thanked her for the visit and the meal and made an excuse to leave. She did not insist that he stay longer.

The elevator ride down was a long one. The rarified air in the penthouse restaurant had made him somewhat dizzy. Exiting the elevator and the front doors, he looked down at his ratty, muddy sandals, and then he breathed deeply, trying to absorb his reaction to lunch. Then he began to laugh to himself. But seeing that this startled the security guards, he went out into the parking lot. Almost immediately, a pack of street children, boys and girls, ranging in age from about six to fourteen, flocked toward him, flitting and hopping around him.

"Hey Joe!" they giggled.

"That's Father Joe, to you kids!"

A beefy guard approached with a menacing baton. The little group tensed for flight.

"It's OK," said Fr. Brendan, motioning to the guard that no help was necessary. The man grumbled then returned to his post.

"You got money, Joe?" said the oldest, a girl dressed in shorts and a T-shirt that read: "Just do it."

"Not all you need," he said, not without sympathy, then out of curiosity he asked her, "What's your name?"

Shy, she hid her smile, putting her hand in front of her mouth in the typical Filipino way, and answered, "Millie."

"Do you kids stay in a shelter around here?"

Millie said, "*Opo* (yes, sir) for a while, but it's like a prison . . ."

"Who takes care of your friends here?" asked the priest.

"I do," Millie said, placing a maternal hand on the greasy head of a little boy, who couldn't be more than six years old.

"And who takes care of you?" he asked incredulously.

When no answer came, he gave them the few coins he had. They wanted more and he felt guilty for saving the paper money to pay his way out of the parking lot. Watching them run off, he saw Millie take the money from the younger ones then run over to a shadowy figure standing under a mango tree across the street. The girl gave the money to the man, received something in return, and then ran smiling back to her smaller companions. Then, all the kids flitted away, disappearing to who knows where. It was Oliver Twist all over again—with street urchins forced to work for a Filipino Fagin. Even in the twentieth century adults were still enslaving children to collect alms. The priest had even heard of some of these unscrupulous organizations blinding children or cutting off their arms and legs so as to make them even more pitiable and thus more profitable. Although full from the abundant luncheon, Fr. Brendan drove back to the parish with a hollow feeling inside.

That afternoon, with the help of Lita, the secretary of Transfiguration Parish, he began cleaning out three storage rooms in the basement of the church. He contracted local plumbers, painters and begged bamboo beds from a local manufacturer. Enlisting the aid of his parishioners, as well as a couple of the nearby religious communities and convents, one month later, the Transfiguration Street Children's Home was officially opened. A week after that, there were seven residents—Millie and her flock—just in time for the Cardinal Sin's official blessing. Now, Fr. Brendan had enough inspirational photos for a brochure of his own.

Over the next couple years, all went pretty well, what with donations from his relatives abroad supplementing those funds obtained from the locals. But MS. Lyons experience also proved true for Fr. Brendan—a lot of the kids simply could not be kept inside an institution. After a life so wild and free, any home, no matter how safe and loving, was still constructed of four walls. Also, there were rules to be followed . . . and school and studies . . . The day Millie flew the coup along with the two older boys saddened Brendan deeply but did not weaken his resolve to keep helping others like them. Even though he searched in vain for her, he found many others in need. Along with the accompanying head and heartaches, there were several success stories—of kids rescued from underpasses and oversights. Some of these actually went on to finish elementary school, high school and even college. Most, however, entered St. Joseph Tech, a vocational institute Fr. Brendan founded three years later with the help of the Richard and Rosamond Harris Foundation.

The Jesuit of Orchards

During his novitiate, John spent a lot of time tending the orchards. The Novice Master, thinking that, at least his charge was making himself useful, allowed him a lot of time among the lemons, oranges and avocados on the property. John pruned in spring, watered in summer and harvested in the fall. There was always fresh fruit on the refectory table. Since there was no obvious reason to send him away after one year, John was allowed to profess. He took the religious name of Ignatius, after the revered founder of their order. In the following years, during the various phases of their long Jesuit formation, where further studies prepared most of his confreres to be professors in their worldwide network of universities, Ignatius's academic performance was merely adequate. But since he had chosen to be a brother and not a priest, his superiors gave their reluctant blessing. Brother Ignatius was then sent to one of the Jesuit communities in a supporting role—to care for the maintenance of the house and grounds. This he did quietly with little fanfare, happy to work with his hands and to be able to spend so much time outside under the sun. Inside the house, when his confreres lunched or supped, he didn't mind waiting upon them. While doing so, he paid little attention to their boisterous, intellectual talk, mostly about how the Church needed to be updated. Some were pushing hard to change the curriculum of their universities. Occasionally, as a joke, one would ask Brother Ignatius's opinion on something they considered beyond him. If he answered at all, he would say something obscure, always referring to something biblical or from the world of nature. For example, when asked about some dissenting theologian, he would answer ironically, "Wheat and weeds grow side by side in the fields . . ."

When cornered about his thoughts on the Vatican's "repressive" tactics, pressuring some of the more radical Jesuits to live their fourth vow of allegiance to the pope, he would look at them gravely and say, "Let us pray to the Master of the harvest to send out workers into his vineyard . . ." A couple of them, both renowned authors of very thick books, full of footnotes, somehow felt insulted by his brief answers. How could such a simpleton presume to know anything, they ranted. The consciences of a few, however, were pricked—sensing in the brother's words a distinct warning from God. But the majority, without consciously choosing to do so, came to dislike him more and more. As the radical sixties became the slovenly seventies, many of these left the community, protesting that they could be more faithful without the faith. The great and powerful Jesuits lost a third of their order, going from thirty-six thousand members worldwide to just twenty-four thousand in a few short years. Those who survived those trying times looked upon Brother Ignatius as an anachronism, out of step with the times. But after asking him for more coffee, they forgot about him altogether.

Another irritant for them was the fact that, when he wasn't outside in the gardens, their confrere seemed to be always in the chapel. On the rare occasions when they would enter the chapel themselves, inevitably they found him kneeling before the tabernacle. The Mass, which they mouthed as rapidly as possible seemed to be the center of his whole day. He arrived hours beforehand to prepare the sacristy and himself, and then stayed a good long while afterward to place everything in good order and to give thanks. Not a few of them considered him to be out of his mind. Invariably, after a few years in each assignment, his mere presence rankled so much—and no one could name anything in particular—that an accumulation of general complaints would cause his transfer. Some maintained that Brother Ignatius was a harmless simpleton, while others avowed that he was the very epitome of the stereotypical Jesuit, complicated and crafty underneath. One superior accused him of mind reading while another, an irascible professor who wrote lengthy books about God's love, said he had no mind at all. Not a few opined that he should never have been allowed to make his perpetual vows. All his detractors, sooner or later, however, ended up contradicting themselves, since they were accusing him of contradictory things. Over the years, a succession of superiors sent him on to other houses, glad to be rid of the man. After the election of Pope John Paul II he was sent up to their university in the Northwest, where he was assigned as a lowly house porter.

There, Brother Ignatius answered the door and the phone of the Jesuit residence for nearly three decades. He took messages, passing them on to his confreres who were all professors and administrators. Inside the rambling house, he swept, vacuumed, dusted and cooked—all with a humble smile.

Outside, he planted fruit trees all around the property—mostly apple, pear, peach, and cherry trees. Irradiating outward from the Jesuit residence, over the next couple years, trees began to appear everywhere, spilling over onto the adjacent college campus. Some of his confreres even began to take notice, accusing him of "planting without permission." One even said he saw the brother digging a hole in the dark.

"It's getting out of hand," one priest-professor complained, "There are so many trees, there's hardly any open space left in the quadrangle. And the birds! It's like Alfred Hitchcock all over again! Whole flocks of them come to roost in the branches to eat the fruit, creating quite a mess. The grounds-keepers have had just about enough . . . But since he seems to have ingratiated himself with them, they have yet to file an official protest."

When one of the Jesuit professors wrote a best seller questioning the divinity of Christ, he received a hand-written letter—signed by Brother Ignatius—pleading with him to take the book off the market. To add insult to injury, the professor kept finding copies of his book in trash-bins all around campus—even in the library and inside their own residence. He suspected Brother Ignatius but had no proof. Another professor, who openly advocated any number of shocking and immoral theories regarding human sexuality, once opened his door to find the brother on his knees, praying the rosary, with tears streaming down his cheeks. When asked what he wanted, the impertinent brother remained silent and would not respond. After the famous professor slammed the door in his face, it is said that the infamous brother remained outside for several hours, refusing to leave. The professor, purportedly shaken by the experience, verbalized his complaint—using multisyllabic words dripping in sarcasm—to the Jesuit Provincial. There was much talk about assigning Brother Ignatius to yet another house but it seemed no other community would accept him. Moreover, having heard rumors about him, no other Jesuit province in the country wanted him. Since he had already made final vows, they were stuck with him. He was told he was "obstinate and proud" and warned never to disturb his brother Jesuits or interfere with their valuable work again. To this, Brother Ignatius only smiled in his inscrutable way and said, "Sufficient to the day is the evil thereof . . ."

Although the superior thought he knew the intended meaning of this statement, he let it pass. Nevertheless, he did punish Brother Ignatius by forbidding him to leave the residence grounds.

This drastic action had unforeseen consequences.

Normally, countless students came to the door with questions for their professors about their courses, with excuses for one thing or another, or with special requests. Although they were usually rebuffed, Brother Ignatius always had a kind word for them, walking them out to the front porch, to point out his favorite trees. "You see how tall and straight and green they are," he would say, "Not to worry, in the future, they will bear much fruit." The students, usually discouraged by their problems and browbeaten by their professors—after talking with Brother Ignatius—always went away feeling more hopeful. The word spread. Many undergrads started coming to him for advice about their various difficulties, from family tensions to girlfriend-boyfriend dramas. "The Brother" always listened to them, giving them his full and undivided attention. He always made time for them, early, late and on weekends. Usually, after telling him their troubles, he would bring them into the little house chapel. Since there was never anyone inside, they could pray unmolested. Then his students would go on to graduate, get married and have families—several even entered the seminary to study for the priesthood. None of them ever forgot the taste of the apple or pear Brother Ignatius gave them as they walked out the door, their personal burden lightened.

When the confreres came to know of this "pastoral" activity, they clamped down. "This is why we hire and pay professional psychologists as counselors. Imagine these students coming right into our own house!" they said, indignant at this breach of their inner sanctum.

Brother Ignatius's only response was, "In the springtime, if the rains don't come, one must water the young plants or they will wither and die . . ."

Now used to his mysterious little sayings, they warned him sternly never to allow students in the house again. That's when the phone calls began. Once the student body learned that they were no longer welcome inside the Jesuit residence, they began to telephone the Brother because they knew he answered all incoming calls. The professors, although many times absent-minded, thinking great thoughts beyond the understanding of mere mortals, at first did not notice an increase in busy signals. But when they finally did become aware of the situation, they complained to the superior who ordered Brother Ignatius not to speak to any students on the phone. That's when the enterprising scholastics began writing Brother Ignatius letters, sending him notes, asking for prayers and advice. These missives all had to be answered by hand, and this meant his spending even more time in the chapel asking for answers. Before dawn and late into night, his confreres always found Ignatius in the same position, on his knees either before the tabernacle or before the Blessed Virgin. Against their will, they were extremely curious about the fact that they saw him writing. They laughed at him: "Brother, what are you working on—your doctoral thesis?"

To this, the brother replied mildly, "When the branches are laden with fruit, they bend almost to the ground . . ."

While, in years past, they would tolerate him, now he was becoming unbearable. Why write so many letters? What did he possibly have to say anyway? What fools would read his simple words? Why, the man had never written a book in his life! He was wasting his time on these lovelorn, brokenhearted teens with their broken families and broken dreams. Only the worst cases came to him anyway. The best and the brightest did their course work then disappeared like they were supposed to after graduation. Brother Ignatius's ever-growing flock, on the other hand, after their graduations, kept coming back to visit him in later years, introducing him to their wives and children. The children giggled, pulling his gray beard. His confreres found him altogether too much for them. That old man, for yes, he was indeed becoming elderly—thin but still quite spry— would meet these families every Sunday afternoon under the trees. He had always been a thorn in his confreres' clerical sides but now they thought he was flaunting his popularity right in front of their eyes. And no doubt, he would continue to do so until his death, which could not come too soon, as far as they were concerned.

They joked about burying him under one of his precious fruit trees. Which one would it be, they joked—the apple for teacher's pet, the peach for the fuzz under his chin, the pear for his bodily shape, or the cherry for the color of his nose! Yet that is precisely what happened. On the morning of the feast of the Assumption, they discovered Brother Ignatius in the chapel—still on his knees—but hunched over, and with a smile on his face. He was dead. The funeral services, celebrated in the university chapel were packed to the rafters with weeping students and alumni. If that wasn't enough, afterward, the crowd around his grave in the little Jesuit graveyard behind the Jesuit residence, refused to disperse until late into the night.

And so it was that Brother Ignatius's body was laid to rest under one of the old apple trees he himself had planted, in the far corner of the community's cemetery. In the spring it would blossom, raining white buds like visible grace down upon his simple, flat gravestone. In the fall, the arching bright red apples were picked by visitors like relics. At first, it was the occasional student. After a while, several appeared daily. Much to the chagrin of his confreres, soon a virtual pilgrimage of students, and even some faculty and alumni began spending long moments there every day. They were obviously praying. Some would even kneel down, tucking notes in besides the gravestone. Brother Ignatius's brother Jesuits did their academic best to ignore this phenomenon, that is, until the day the bishop visited. In answer to their questions, his Excellency responded, "I am not here as your local bishop or as a representative of the Vatican but on a personal "pilgrimage" with a simple request." The priest-professors looked at each other in disbelief.

The bishop stated, "Due to the immense number of letters the Chancery has received lately about heavenly favors received, in my capacity as local ordinary of the diocese, I have decided—if your religious community is not interested in doing so—to go ahead and open Brother Ignatius's cause of canonization in Rome." The superior and all the confreres gathered around him absolutely dumbfounded. Seeing that there was no audible response, the bishop continued, "Therefore, reverend Fathers, I am officially asking your community to cooperate in the necessary investigation into Brother Ignatius's heroic virtues. All his letters and correspondence will be required. We have already collected originals and copies of hundreds of letters in his own hand—of those he counseled over the years—besides the ones he wrote to me personally." With this comment, there was an involuntary but collective gasp. The bishop continued, "Yes, in case you do not remember—I myself was a student here at the university, before entering the diocesan seminary. Brother Ignatius was instrumental in helping me through a very difficult discernment process. If not for him, I'm quite sure I would not be here now. We need to study all the letters sent to him—and so we expect you to make them available to us forthwith—before anything might be lost. I will take it as a personal favor if you cooperate fully . . ."

The superior, very much shocked by the bishop's testimony, but realizing the man wanted the brother's collected correspondence placed in his hands immediately, ran up into the dusty attic, hoping that they had not yet thrown it all away. After bumping around in the dark for a long while with a flashlight, he finally located a cardboard box stuffed with Brother Ignatius's few personal effects. Inside were his old Jesuit cassock and sash, a crucifix, a rosary, a leather-bound diary, a pen and several thick bundles of letters all neatly dated and bound with string. Huffing and puffing, the superior hurriedly hoisted the box downstairs to the foyer. But the bishop was nowhere to be seen. A circle of his bug-eyed confreres, their jaws still dragging on the carpet, all pointed to the chapel. Opening the door—they found the bishop himself lighting a fresh tabernacle candle, the old one having been allowed to expire. They all entered, looking around as if they had never seen the place before.

"Is this his kneeler?" the bishop asked reverently.

That successor of the apostles knelt there all afternoon, in exactly the same place Brother Ignatius graced for so many years, opening the bundles of letters and reading them one by one.

That evening, when the bishop finally came out of the chapel, the superior made a half-hearted attempt at offering him dinner, but his Excellency said he was too excited to eat—and that he had lots of' work to do. "I will have to put all of the letters in chronological order, both these few and the great number we've already reviewed— as soon as possible. His diary will, no doubt, be a best seller."

Cavalry of Woe

S arah felt the interior urge once again to act upon her inspirations. For years, from early childhood through the long years of the two great pontiffs, she felt the calling to enter the cloister. Now the voice was pulling her heart, squeezing it alternately with delight and a sense of urgency. "Now is the day of salvation."

Having been in contact with the Carmelites for two years after college, she informed her parents—who were less than pleased—and entered, body and soul, as a postulant on the Solemnity of the Assumption when the Blessed Virgin Mary entered body and soul into heaven. Carmel of the Desert was far from the city, a low quadrangle ensconced among the huge boulders and cactus. It was solid like an interior castle should be. The chapel bell tower rose above all, ready to sound the hours or the alarm whichever came first. Pray—said the mother Abbess Maria—not only because your lives depend on it, dear sisters, but because the fate of the world depends on it.

That was exactly what Sarah felt, the deep longing to pray, to be united with her spouse and so to implore him to wrest the world away from the brink of disaster.

In the years after the attack on New York and Washington, and the wars in Afghanistan and Iraq, the terrorist threat increased. Suicide bombers began blowing themselves and hundreds of innocents up in most of the bigger cities throughout the lower fifty States. This had the effect of a spiritual renewal across the land. The churches were full and there were many conversions. At the very same time, side by side with a growing militarization in the name of defense, came the ever-more militant persecution of religion in general and Christianity in particular. Wasn't traditional religion, with its absolute truth and its perceived intolerance, responsible for the crisis? Beginning with the main enemy, because she is the Bride of the Bridegroom, the Church was hounded and harassed everywhere and at every opportunity. At first, the enemies of the faith, atheists, ACLU lawyers, abortionists, and the radical political arm sought to hamper her influence through a deluge of lawsuits. The courts approved many anti-Catholic measures specifically designed to destroy her. Because the protestant and evangelical denominations were infinitely divided, and so, much less a threat—having absorbed the majority of the material world's ways—the government was not so concerned with them. Priests were accused and convicted on flimsy evidence in many cases. The bishops, running scared, paid off anyone at the slightest hint of scandal, but without demanding any evidence. Huge settlements forced dioceses to sell off church properties, including parishes and schools. Legislatures struck down any law in favor of religious freedom, issuing many that they knowingly opposed Church teachings. The few priests and nuns still faithful to Rome, that is, still loyal to the Holy Father, had their phones tapped, their internet sites monitored and were insulted and spat upon on in the streets.

The result of this more open persecution was the opposite of what the enemies of God imagined. Throngs of young men and women were inspired to become priests and religious themselves. The haters of the truth forgot the basic truth that, historically, the Church has always done well in hard times. Saints don't live comfortable lives, but rather, are born to give their lives, disregarding the cost, even martyrdom.

After almost three years, making her first vows, Sarah was given the name, Sister Mary John of the Apocalypse—unusual, but with great meaning for her life and for the times. Absorbed in the daily rhythm of prayer, many times she fell into what her spiritual director termed deep contemplation or even ecstasies, prayer so absorbing she was unaware of her surroundings. The other sisters could not help noticing something different; most thought it an affectation, the result of youthful enthusiasm. Some were jealous. To cure her of such fantasies, she was put to work in the kitchen among the pots and pans, thinking that this would keep her feet and senses on the ground. But even there, she would suddenly get a faraway look in her eyes, and breathing deeply, would enter a state where it seemed she hardly breathed at all. Wise and experienced, her spiritual director, Father Thomas, a doubter by inclination, nevertheless felt something authentic about this particular young woman. Her humility, despite the sufferings incurred because of her experiences, was the first sign of authenticity—like a mantle protecting her from prideful vainglory. She accepted the most menial tasks and the meanest rebukes with joy. Under obedience, and with the permission of the mother abbess, the priest ordered Sister Mary John of the Apocalypse to write down her visions and locutions in a small notebook. Mortified by this command, nevertheless, she obeyed, albeit with obvious reluctance and pain. After a month or so, Father Thomas requested to read what she had written. His eyes were opened. The contents, written in a firm but graceful hand, were purported visions of what was soon to come upon the world, along with the constant request by the Lord and the Holy Virgin to pray more and to do penance. Indeed, the prayer of Love from the heart of the Church—the essence of the Carmelite charism—was now the only thing that could stay the hand of God's justice and mitigate the terrible trials to come.

It seemed that the terrorists would eventually succeed in bringing two "dirty" nuclear bombs into the country, detonating them in San Francisco and New York. Hundreds of thousands would sicken and die from the resulting radiation poisoning. The backlash would be fierce and fast. The Congress and the Senate would pass a declaration of War against any country harboring Al Queda and the other terrorist organizations. Diplomatic ties were severed with several Muslim countries in the Middle East, in Africa and in Asia. Those nations of Europe who were hesitant to act for fear of reprisals from their own large militant Muslim populations, were kept from acting, thus distancing themselves from the United States. The President ordered the first nuclear strikes on the area between Afghanistan and Pakistan, followed by Iraq, Iran, Sudan, Somalia, and North Korea. The global reaction galvanized the whole world against America. Economic sanctions and embargos against their main benefactor were put into place, whereupon the USA immediately pulled out of the United Nations. The Holy Father called for a reasonable, measured response, one that included negotiation of peace through diplomacy. He called upon the whole Church to pray urgently for reconciliation. Later, seeing the drama and the danger, he called upon every man, woman and child of goodwill to do penance and repent, so as to avoid the end.

Sister Mary John's visions became ever more frequent and vivid, almost daily occurrences. She saw visions of battles, a cavalry of woe, and of eternal life. She stated that the many modernist theologians and atheist scoffers who proclaimed the nonexistence of hell would be speechless when they arrived there. And still she prayed, sweating and moaning in obvious pain, offering every interior trial and physical suffering for the salvation of a prodigal world. The reason for her agonies became known on the first Friday of Lent, where bloody wounds appeared on her hands, feet and side. Bloody points, produced by an invisible crown of thorns, ringed her head, seeping red through her veil and dripping down into her eyes. She seemed to be suffering the Passion of her Spouse in all its tremendous agony.

Although Father Thomas felt inclined to believe all these manifestations real, he was obliged to report them to the local bishop who ordered a complete battery of physical and psychological tests. Bishop Carl Waters visited on Good Friday, and witnessed everything for himself but still did not believe. He ordered the nuns, under pain of canonical censure to keep things quiet. Yet somehow, word got out—a holy nun was seeing visions of the end of the world and was suffering the torments of the Passion. Soon, hundreds of pilgrims jammed the winding dirt track leading up to the desert monastery. They banged on the door, and when refused admittance to the cloister to see "the Saint," many remained on the property, camping out, even on the coldest desert nights. The majority had either lost loved ones in the attacks or were sick themselves from the fallout. Being so far out in the middle of nowhere, and away from the deadly winds, Carmel in the Desert became an oasis that many saw as being preserved by Providence. The Bishop, enraged at the notoriety the tiny community was generating, clamped down, hard and fast. Father Thomas was interrogated as an instigator, and threatened to have his faculties taken away, whereby he would no longer be able to say Mass or perform his duties as a priest.

The mother abbess was pressured to do something and quickly, especially since the national and international news media had sniffed out the site, and were giving dramatic and distorted, almost hourly reports. Her response was the same as her response to everything—to pray and to ask the sisters to pray, instructing them that when they were tired of praying, they should pray some more.

After Easter, although transported by unknown joys, Sister Mary John of the Apocalypse was now bed-ridden and appeared to be nearing her own personal end. Daily, Father Thomas brought her Holy Communion—the only thing she could keep down. This strengthened her. The other sisters gave up doubting her, and began loving her as much as they could, with countless signs of charity and affection.

Near the end of that dreadful year, the Holy Father himself visited the White House in Washington DC, in the hopes of brokering peace. Afterward he made an unexpected, unannounced flight out to the West Coast. On the heavily guarded limousine ride out to the high desert that very night, he was accompanied by the Cardinal from California and the local Bishop.

Bishop Waters spent the whole time informing him about their stringent efforts to clamp down on fanatical nuns and the foolish faithful who believed in them. They tried to dissuade him from such a visit, since it would be impossible to keep it secret from the Press, but the Holy Father firmly yet politely overruled them. During the three-hour drive, the pope, who himself seemed to be absorbed in prayer, only occasionally opened his eyes to look up through the limo's roof window at the stars above. After some time, he surprised his two companions by asking them to pray the rosary with him. Neither had a set of the beads on him so they borrowed a rosary from the driver and the pope's bodyguard. Arriving at the monastery gates, the crowds of campers outside the compound stirred but did not realize who was in the limo. Once inside the walls, the Holy Father insisted on ringing the bell himself. Immediately, the heavy door swung open revealing several faces underlit by the oil lamps they carried in their hands. Mother Abbess Maria genuflected and kissed the Pontiff's ring. He asked her to take him—first to the chapel and then to Sister Mary John of the Apocalypse's cell. He knelt in the dark chapel for a long time—almost a full hour—while the Cardinal and the Bishop fidgeted in the back pew. It was already well past midnight when he emerged. Entering Sister Mary John's cell alone, another two hours passed. When he finally did come out, closing the door gently behind him, he looked tired but serene. He even managed to smile at the Cardinal; before asking the man to please leave him alone for a moment with the mother abbess. The Holy Father asked her for water.

Returning with a glass of water, he walked with the mother abbess Maria out into the enclosed garden under the moonlight. The two of them whispered together, speaking of many things. In the darkest hour before the dawn, he said, "She is right. The Sun is about to rise. We must be on our way." Then the pope bade all the kneeling sisters' farewell with his blessing, got into the limousine with his four companions and returned to the city, and his flight back to Rome. He felt an interior urge to act on her inspirations.

A Conspiracy of Twelve

Father Jim knew his first assignment would be a trial by fire. With the bishop's hands still hot on his head, he was sent off to Saint Philomena's to labor for two years under the infamous Monsignor Carl F. Robeson. Saint Philomena was the saint of impossible cases—even so, she had her hands full with the good Monsignor. As pastor, the one who had built the parish, and one of the best fund-raisers in the diocese, the bishop did not dare transfer him. Even though it was forty years past Vatican II, the man himself was still seen as a sort of finishing school for the newly ordained. If the young men could survive "the Robeson"—as he came to be known—then there was a better than average chance they might survive their futures. Eleven, thus far, had survived, leaving for their second assignments with their collective tails between their legs, chastened if not well trained.

The Robeson ran a tight ship, a fact that caused pride to swell in his heart, if he had one. Upon arrival, the new cleric would stand before him at attention, and receive the rules of the rectory as well as his list of daily duties. If performed with punctilious piety over the succeeding two years, said assistant would then be passed on to the next pastor already whipped into some kind of shape. Indeed, most pastors, receiving the beaten young men, with their hang-dog expressions, remembering their own encounters with the dreaded Monsignor, welcomed them like soldiers returning from the trenches. Survival was the key word, and Father Jim knew it.

The strict schedule would be ruthlessly maintained. If any assistant complained he would be taken down a few pegs, at first privately, and then again publicly in the following Sunday's sermon. Monsignor Robeson believed in what he termed "teaching moments."

Father Jim was assigned the 6:00 a.m. Mass seven days a week. No day off. God forbid if he forgot to set his alarm clock. Even coffee was forbidden to wake-up. The Robeson's nearly deaf, spinster sister, "The Robesister"—as she came to be known in diocesan lore—forbade any incursion into her realm, even by her brother and especially not in the middle of the night or early morning. Snacks, indeed, any in-between munching was verboten. Father Jim, after an evening's Bible class or after the youth group on Saturday nights, often longed for something to eat. He was, after all, young with a healthy appetite. The first week, he got caught bringing some potato chips upstairs into his tiny garret on the third floor. It was strategically located above the pastor's suite. The Robeson liked to be able to hear the footfalls of his fledgling charges. There was no way to avoid making the floorboards creak. Some few had gone to great lengths to master the problem, pouring talcum powder in the cracks, laying down lumber on top of the existing floor to walk upon. All these efforts proved in vain, for everyone got caught sooner or later—trying to stay out late. There was always the rub. The Robeson refused to give his assistants their own keys to the rectory. There was a ten o'clock curfew, and if they came home after that, then they would have to make other arrangements—like sleep on the sidewalk or in their cars. These drastic measures—a remnant of a bygone era—were deemed necessary for the maintenance of order. Getting to bed late meant running the risk of waking up late for Mass, and that simply wouldn't do. Legend had it that Monsignor caught one hapless fellow climbing up the drainpipe after midnight. The creative types tried other forms of ingress and egress but these were always foiled. But leaving the cellar door ajar, or a window unlocked were the usual things. Everyone knew full well that Monsignor Robeson never gave his assistants keys to his kingdom. "You will all jolly well have to be in the house on time," he would snort. "If we find a door unlocked after curfew there will be consequences." The unfortunate offender would be given his walking papers and sent away. He meant, into exile—usually to the furthest and poorest parish in the extensive diocese. Yet to the young man who received such a harsh sentence, it might actually seem a reprieve.

The Robeson considered two years of this basic training ideal. The first year took the spirit out of them; the second ingrained into their memories, and indeed, into their very souls the seriousness of their life's task. Many, arriving with a sense of humor were able, by sheer willpower, to maintain a certain grim sarcasm throughout the first twelve months, but invariably, as surely as fall turns to winter, they would surrender their smiles halfway through the second year. He often wondered what would become of the Church, if such was the state of the new clergy. This is why he kept a knowing, albeit wary eye on all the newly ordained, choosing his next assistant. Each choice was, after all, just one more in a long line, neither the first nor the last. Nevertheless, Monsignor felt uneasy about the latest one—number twelve—a certain Reverend James Cartwright. The fellow bowed and scraped well enough, but there was a glint in his eye that did not bode well.

Monsignor Robeson noted the first sign of trouble on a Monday, after a very busy Sunday. The young priest Father Jim, was expected to uncrumple and iron flat all the dollar bills that had been placed in the offertory baskets, so they would stack neatly into hundreds for deposit in the bank. He was unable to complete this sacred ritual because he got a phone call just before dinner. He informed his boss that an elderly and long-time member of the parish, now residing in a nursing home, was near death's door. Then, without apologies, grabbing the Holy Oils, he left the pile of crumpled bills where they were, causing The Robeson to raise a disapproving eyebrow. There would be time—he thought—yes, he would bide his time before responding. Number Twelve was very respectful, punctual and seemed well prepared for his homilies and catechism classes, but there was just something about his manner that did not fit. Perhaps it was the way he related to people. A nervous affable cleric was the norm but not a smiling, confident one. "Oh no, that would never do," he thought. He resolved to do something about this just as soon as a suitable "teaching moment" presented itself.

The very next day, young Father Jim received another sick call, but this time at nine in the evening. Monsignor watched him go out the door, thinking that people always had the nerve to call at the most inconvenient hours. He was also thinking that curfew was only an hour away. Would the young man be able to beat the clock? Or would he be left out in the darkness, wailing and grinding his teeth. Fr. Jim drove to the hospital, not the nearby one, but the one all the way across town, which was technically in another parish territory. He spent three and a half hours there with the family, talking and praying with them until the moment arrived to take their dear mother off her respirator, the only' thing keeping her brain-dead body alive. Returning to the rectory as fast as he could, Father Jim found everything dark and locked up tight. It was past one in the morning. He automatically reached in his pocket for a key, but found only his car keys. "That's right"—he smiled grimly—"the old man's number one rule is—no keys!" How could anyone think that such a rule made life simpler, he thought. It was a hot summer night and his clerical shirt was soaked. He didn't want to sleep in the car, and his priest friends all lived in faraway parishes. He was left with no alternative but to ring the doorbell, come what may. Otherwise he would have to risk the drainpipe or even go to a motel. No, that wouldn't work, since he had left his credit card and cash in his room. Screwing up all his courage, he pressed the buzzer which could be heard ringing loudly inside the silent rectory. The noise sent electric shock waves through his heart. Monsignor Robeson would already be in bed, fast asleep, as would The Robesister. Both would be awakened and definitely not pleased. Surely, one or the other—perhaps both—would come to the door and give him what for. He might even be sent away. A strange thrill of hope leaped in his heart. But what could he possibly say to them? What excuse could he use?

Then all of a sudden, Father Jim started feeling angry. "How about the truth! Hey, wait a darned minute! Am I not an ordained priest out on official Church business, tending to the flock placed in my care? Why should I be punished *for* that?"

He knew he had to calm himself down. He had to think. Standing there under the lamplight, awaiting his doom, he breathed heavily. Minutes passed and neither nemesis arrived at the front door. He rang the buzzer a second and longer time. It was inconceivable that his two keepers did not hear it. The injustice of the situation struck him again and he decided to throw all caution to the wind. If he was going to hell in a hand-basket, then he might as well go all the way, so he pressed the bell again. "Third time's the charm," he said aloud. It rang and rang but still, even after nearly a full minute no one came to the door to berate him.

That's when the thought occurred to him that there might really be something wrong inside. The Robesister's deafness could well keep her in blissful somnolence unaware of the bell—but by any stretch of the imagination—the Robeson himself should have responded, grumbling down the stairs from the second floor. Perhaps the man was incapacitated? Maybe he was in need of the Last Rites himself? Perhaps he had had a heart attack and was—at that very moment—lying helplessly on the floor, clutching his chest. That would certainly justify everything he was about to do. Father Jim ran down to the corner pay phone, dredging up change from his pocket. He dialed a local number first. A cryptic conversation ensued and ended with: "Tonight's the night. Pass the word." Then he inserted another dime and a quarter into the pay phone and calmly dialed the three digit emergency number. "Please send an ambulance to St. Philomena's Rectory as soon as possible . . ."

Within ten minutes, not only had an ambulance arrived but also a long red truck from the local firehouse—both with sirens blaring and red lights flashing. Even with this incredible din, no lights appeared in the rectory upstairs. This confirmed his worst fears. Both paramedics and firemen tried the bell themselves, but with the same result. Pounding on the thick oak front door, and shouting at the top of their lungs-—"Open up! Fire department! Paramedics!"—Two burly firemen took out a sort of battering ram reserved for just such situations. With several resounding "BOOMS" the door crashed inwards—right off its hinges. The whole lot of them rushed up the stairs, and finding the Robeson's door similarly bolted, used the same very effective technique again. The last crunch of the battering ram sent the door flying into splinters. Father Jim half expected to see Monsignor lying on the floor, passed out. The uniformed men filed in but stopped short seeing Monsignor Carl F. Robeson coming out of his bathroom, straightening his robe. Dumbfounded, both paramedics and firemen stared at the man, wondering why he had not responded to their shouts. Father Jim pushed past them to his side, saying, "Are you all right, Monsignor? When you didn't answer the door, we thought you had had a heart attack . . . or something." He voice trailed off feebly. Under the Monsignors darkened gaze, he unconsciously backed away slowly. That's when the Robesister, enshrouded in her formless grey housecoat, arrived to add to the confusion by shouting several unintelligible things in German.

The Robeson quieted his sibling with a severe glance, sending her back to her own room. Then, quivering with suppressed rage and speaking in a low voice, he pronounced each word as if it were a knife he was sharpening: "What is the meaning of disturbing my peace? You gentlemen—directing his withering gaze at the firemen and paramedics—may consider yourselves thanked and withdraw. Your superiors will hear from me in the morning. And as for you, Father James, you know perfectly well that I never answer the door after ten at night! Why, in heaven's name then, did you allow them to break down—not one but two—of my doors?"

Father Jim took a deep breath and said, "Because you didn't give me a key, Monsignor."

The Robeson checked his assistant's expression for the slightest hint of sarcasm or mockery, but to his dismay, found none.

He called the bishop the following morning, instructing his old seminary classmate to transfer his young assistant to the farthest and most rural end of the diocese. After packing his few possessions, Father Jim drove downtown to O'Grady's Irish Pub. Upon entering, he smiled to see eleven of his brother priests waiting for him, glasses in hand. Seeing the twelfth member of their conspiracy, they cheered.

Some Distant Heaven

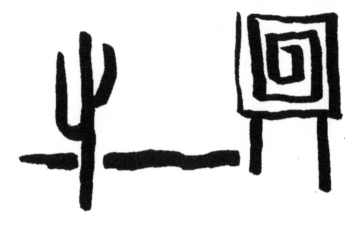

I saw the bus waiting out in the parking lot, blazing like a silver bullet in the high desert heat. Emblazoned on its side was the moniker Hellman Express. After the final blessing, the faithful exhaled out of Our Lady of Fatima, moving like a segmented insect with many legs across the black asphalt, climbing up the steps and into the door gratefully. Being the last to approach—for I was chaplain of this little excursion—a wave of guilt enveloped me like the cold conditioned air. How could we be fervently praying one minute and then, the next, running off to a casino? A lesser thought zoomed past like traffic on the nearby freeway: How many of those present neglected the offertory basket for the poor to save money for the slot machines?

As if reading my mind, one octogenarian smiled at me and said, "Don't worry, Padre, after a few hours in Sin City, we'll all be a lot poorer!" With that I stepped up into the bus, looking for an open seat. Running the gamut of grinning parishioners, I saw that the only available seat was at the back next to the on-board restrooms. The last tour I had been on to Lourdes left the front seat—with a view—for the priest. When the bus doors closed, the driver pulled slowly out of the parking lot, steering with one hand while holding a microphone in the other: "Just sit back and relax folks—next stop, nonstop fun . . ." This statement provoked some nervous laughter. Feeling encouraged, the man, whose nametag read "Bubba" said, "That's right, Las Vegas, Nevada, seven deadly sins, one convenient location."

I could have sworn I saw the driver look pointedly back at me in the rear-view mirror. Although only his eyes were visible, he seemed to be smirking. I wondered if his baseball cap—the California Angels—hid two small horns protruding from his forehead just above the hairline. Weary from a long morning, after having celebrated three Masses consecutively, I now wondered why I had agreed to go on this trip at all. The pastor had suggested it as a fund-raiser for the elderly, those slow moving fun-seekers who filled the pews on a typical Sunday morning.

The fifty-passenger cruiser sailed almost silently under the pale-blue desert sky. Soothing music wafted down from hidden speakers, calming nerves and sending several into dreamland. Just like my sermons, I mused.

Despite the fact that few seemed to be paying attention, every now and then the driver interjected slogans: "What happens in Vegas, stays in Vegas," he laughed, a little too loudly I thought. "Sinatra, the Chairman of the Board, sang of New York as the city that never sleeps, but he was wrong, wasn't he?" Again, I could have sworn that the man looked back at me in the rear-view mirror, somehow challenging me with his eyes. This time he winked at me, switching on the video monitors spaced at four row intervals above the seats. A movie started—one most of them surely had all already seen. But that didn't stop those who were still awake from staring blankly upwards. In real life, the star had been married so many times she had rice marks on her face. One particular scene would have made a tomato blush. I wanted to cover the screens and guard their collective eyes. They all watched television at home, all day every day, so watching TV while zooming along through traffic was a novelty. When the movie was over, another one just like it began. The thought occurred to me that, perhaps, I could get the group in the back of the bus to pray the rosary together, but the roar of the engine and the noise from the movie drowned us out in the back.

The five-hour trip across the desert was designed to make the passage as painless as possible, with everything orchestrated to make time disappear. Remembering the only time I had ever been to Las Vegas, it occurred to me that this was purposeful and somehow sinister. A clock is the one thing you will never see there. Why? Because seeing a clock reminds people about how much time has passed, how much time is passing, and even worse, how they are spending their time—these oldsters who have so little of it left. The idea was to spend—first time and then money. The more time you spend in a casino the more money you lose. All the passengers had been given a twenty-five-dollar complimentary betting card by the El Mirage Casino and a voucher for the free buffet. The bus ride too was free. It seemed all too easy, like a Faustian contract with the devil. Bubba kept laughing and staring back into the rear-view mirror. Scanning the rows of graying heads, it seemed to me that he was scrutinizing the face of each passenger. Most would end up pouring substantial sums of cash down the drain that afternoon but would justify their actions by saying that they were merely enjoying themselves.

When the second movie ended, the youngest among them, an usher named Joe, who was sixty-four years old, stood up to stretch and then began a stand-up routine: "I'm so old, my back goes out more than I do . . ." General laughter.

A man across the aisle chimed in: "You're so old every time you suck in your gut, your ankles swell . . ." A few guffaws.

"I'm not afraid of death, I just don't want to be there when it happens . . ." he said, straightening an imaginary tie, doing his best Rodney Dangerfield impression.

That got the biggest reaction but I didn't laugh. It dawned on me that the real purpose of this bus was to put some distance between them and death. Surely, the cheery atmosphere contrasted sharply with their day-to-day lives.

They were speeding toward the epitome of excitement, a break in the monotonous routine of aches, pains, doctors, and hassles with the insurance companies and funerals of friends. In Las Vegas, with a minimum of effort, one could forget. And there would be fatty foods against their doctor's orders—all the things they were not supposed to eat.

Rivers of free alcohol, too, would flow through the desert like a new Colorado. And no one could legally complain about them smoking cigarettes. Everything in Vegas was allowed. There was a consensus that this was the way things were meant to be.

Arriving at the doors of the El Mirage, Bubba picked up the microphone again and snickered, "Don't do anything I wouldn't do!" Their laughter smelled of conspiracy. I felt an interior urge to warn them, but it was too late. "Be back on time or you all will turn into pumpkins or worse!" he grinned. A strange euphoria overtook them, as fifty passengers simultaneously fought to be the first ones off the bus and in through the plate glass doors. Like lemmings—I thought—as one elbowing entity, they rushed inside to nearest slot machines, pulling coins from pockets and purses as they went. Their right arms twitched involuntarily, as they sucked in the smoky air. Suddenly I found myself standing all alone outside the bus.

Bubba smiled knowingly at me, "Don't worry, Padre, they're just blowing off a little steam—spending their children's inheritance." The man's eyes seemed to blaze, reflecting the red neon lights of the entrance. More unwelcome thoughts invaded my mind. This was a trap. We were here forever. This was the gateway to the inferno. Bubba spoke as if he knew them well: "After all, Padre, their ungrateful progeny, who live in such garden spots as Bakersfield and Fresno, all have televisions of their own and no longer need their elderly parents anymore. As you well know, the new generation abandoned him long ago, and so has no qualms about abandoning old Mom and Dad. Some of their children actually have the nerve to complain that their parents are never home. They're all in for a rude awakening one day, aren't they? When the last will and testament is read, more than a few will be left out in the cold, gnashing and grinding their teeth."

Bubba then closed the door and drove off until the time he would return to pick us up.

I experienced a sudden chill despite the desert temperatures, like one who passes through a ghost in a haunted house. It suddenly occurred to me that my parishioner's pilgrimage to Las Vegas was, in reality, not only a diversion from dull routine but was actually a form of revenge—like Bubba said—first of all on their unthinking, selfish children, and secondly—on God himself—their children for not visiting, and God for allowing them to get old. It was God who, according to a worldly way of thinking, forced them to endure the indignities of adult diapers. My head swirled, entering the Casino. Could they actually be laboring under a false sense of injured justice—that the Almighty was treating them unfairly? Conscious of being the only one in Las Vegas wearing a clerical collar, I fully expected to see Dante's warning hung over the betting tables: "Abandon hope all ye who enter here."

The further I walked into the dim confines, the more I realized how ineffectual my preaching had been. Another boring Sunday sermon about loving one another and saying one's prayers—all these time-tested devotions to save one's soul suddenly seemed to pale next to the "real" life of star-studded glitz. What was so great about being good? But then, what was I thinking?

Wandering around the floor, I saw my parishioners laughing and joking, or intently frowning, with some erupting in glee or frustration depending on their winning or losing. An urge to find and pull the fire alarm came over me. I wanted to yell, "Save yourselves! Get out while you still can! Run for your lives!" I recognized three old ladies as the ones who prayed the rosary before Mass on Saturdays. They were standing near each other, but oblivious to each other's presence. Their glasses reflected the spinning numbers of the slots, so that it looked like their own eyes were revolving, turning sevens, lemons and cherries. Management knew they would just keep trying. Red lights were everywhere. Some of my choir members stood round the poker table. One lady, who always asked for rent money at the end of the month was feeding the dollar slots and swearing loudly. I suddenly saw them all with a strange clarity—all of us in danger of eternal perdition but not caring.

With a further shock, I realized that the games they were playing were no longer mechanical or even electronic as in the past but were now entirely computerized. That meant it was even harder to win. Both winning and losing were preprogrammed. The probability of being struck by lightning was greater than beating the odds. The fact that the bettors knew this but still continued to bet seemed incomprehensible. I looked up and around, with the feeling I was being watched. Cameras pivoted overhead. It occurred to me that they knew I was a spy. Searching, there was nowhere to hide. Soon guards would come to take me away. Stumbling into the men's room, with mahogany walls and marble floors, I turned the gold water tap and splashed cold water on my face, hoping all these visions would disappear. Looking up into the mirror opposite me, my eyes were red and my breathing labored. Going back out onto the crowded betting floor, I searched in vain for some out of the way chair to sit down and pray. That was the craziest thought of all. The prayer police might come. There was only the bar. Sitting down on an empty stool at the end, the bartender who strongly resembled our bus driver approached, smiling, "What's your poison, Padre?" When I ordered a Coke, he laughed. After a few minutes a young woman with bleached blonde hair, wearing a tight red dress took the seat next to mine. She whispered the line from the book of Genesis: "It's not good for Man to be alone." I stared at her. She looked at me and then at the bartender and this time, they both laughed.

Recognizing a set up, I hurriedly left the bar, stumbling forward, toward where I expected the front doors to be. But there was only another row of slot machines glowing in the dark. One of the ladies there turned and yelled, "It's not time to leave yet, Father!" I stared at her for an instant and then practically ran in the opposite direction. Finally spotting the entrance, I exited, spewed out the glass doors like Jonah out of the whale's stomach. Once outside, almost gasping for breath, after a while I felt a little better. Perching myself on the edge of the sidewalk, out of the way of the incoming crowd, I sat down to wait for the bus, however long it might take to arrive. Several buses identical to ours pulled up right in front of me, spewing out more and more people. None of them seemed to notice me sitting there, like I had become—without knowing it—one of the invisible ranks of homeless. I don't know how long I waited there. Finally, our bus appeared magically in front of the Casino. The doors opened right in front of me with a hiss.

The Thing with Feathers

The doorbell rang at seven in the morning. Fr. Lawrence grumbled a bit since he was hoping to finish Lauds without interruption. But interruptions, he'd come to learn by hard experience, were the stuff of life. Phone calls and doorbells were the one constant in his busy days. And each portended a crisis, either in full bloom or nearing its crescendo. It seemed that people only came to an exhausted priest when all other avenues, including 911 and soothsayers had already been exhausted. "Now, Padre, work a miracle!" In most cases, what the good padre offered appeared too little too late.

To most, his seemingly feeble spiritual advice hardly registered on the Richter scale of their chaotic lives. The priest's failure to comfort or resolve a problem was somehow interpreted as God's failure to be "Johnny on the Spot," that is, to give instant satisfaction. With this somber thought in mind, Fr. Lawrence descended the long staircase, and opened the front door to find Mrs. Martin standing there, clutching her cane and her Bible. In their neighborhood, she needed both for survival.

"What's wrong, Teresa?" he asked, genuinely surprised to see her at that hour of the day. She was one of the pillars of the African American community whose numbers both in the neighborhood and the parish were dwindling because of age and economic attrition. Most of his elderly parishioners doggedly persevered, staying in the neighborhood while the younger members gradually moved out, looking for better jobs and housing elsewhere. Fr. Lawrence believed African Americans to be the most faithful of all believers, enduring slavery, years of prejudice within the society and unfortunately, even within the Church herself. Teresa Martin once shared with him how she, her daughter Pat and all the other black Catholics had to sit in the last pews, allowing the whites to receive communion first. Add that to decades of different priest-pastors passing by like so many sorrowful mysteries and you've surely earned the right to gripe, at least a little. But Teresa Martin was not one to complain. She was a doer, putting her substantial faith into daily practice, helping Brother's Ricardo's social center distribute food and clothing to the new immigrant families inundating the neighborhood. Out in the greater community, she protested regularly, praying the rosary across the street from the local abortion clinic.

Now Mrs. Martin looked genuinely distressed. "Well, I've come to ask a question. Is it true that Jesus didn't really rise from the dead?"

Fr. Lawrence wasn't expecting such a theological question this early in the morning, at least not from her. The first thing that came to his mind was that one of the many Protestant evangelical fundamentalist sects sprouting up on every block had knocked on her door.

"Why do you ask that?"

"I could hardly sleep last night . . ."

"Come into the chapel, my dear," encouraged the priest, "We can talk there." At that hour, he knew it would be quite empty except, of course, for the Presence in the tabernacle.

They went in and despite the onset of arthritis; Teresa genuflected reverently before taking a seat.

He waited until she was ready. Then she began: "Father, last night in the Bible study, Father Louis said that it didn't really matter if Jesus rose from the dead. That the important thing was that we feel Him rising in our hearts. That sounds nice and everything, but for some reason it really bothered me . . . because, well, a lot of times I don't feel nothing."

Keeping a poker face, Fr. Lawrence grimaced interiorly. The other priest in the parish, although older than him by fifteen years, was full of some very radical theological ideas, remnants of the 1960s. Up until that moment, he had considered Fr. Louis's opinions pretty harmless, thinking that normal people would not pay him too much attention. At that moment, however, it struck him, like a blow to the stomach, how much he actually disliked his brother priest. The commandment was not "Thou shalt like one another" but "Thou shalt love one another," a demand infinitely more costly. He always hated a lack of charity in others because he was so often guilty of the same sin himself. Over the past couple years, his pastor, the Very Reverend Louis Zenone had said many, what he considered imprudent things, but mostly different versions of the same thing—in general, that everything the Church taught in bygone years was bunk, while more specifically, that all the miracles of Jesus either never really happened or could be explained away quite easily. According to Fr. Louis, there were perfectly logical natural explanations for every supernatural one of them—despite the ample scriptural evidence. Because, after all, as Father Louis put it, the first believing community wrote the Sacred Scriptures in order to make a point, that Jesus was not only human but divine and the "so-called" miracle stories underlined divinity. His real point, however, was that we, rational, modern-day Christians don't need all that "hocus pocus" to believe that Jesus was really only "a good man."

Fr. Lawrence winced as Mrs. Martin went on: "He said the miracle of the loaves and fishes never happened. The real miracle was that the people learned how to share what they carried with them and that the only thing Jesus multiplied in his public ministry was enemies. He said Lazarus didn't really get raised from the dead but was having some kind of out of body experience . . ."

"You have your faith, hang on to it," said Fr. Lawrence, getting hot under the clerical collar. He was about to go on when she began to weep.

"You see, it's my daughter. You know Pat's situation. If it's true what he said and Jesus didn't really rise and all his miracles were just made up—then she don't have no hope . . ."

The priest thought of Teresa's adult daughter, Pat—transparently beautiful but also bedridden for as long as he'd known her. The two, mother and daughter bravely faced each new day—with humility connected to holiness by a sense of humor.

"Forgive me, Father, for I have sinned. I want to strangle a priest . . ." Mrs. Martin whispered, as if in the confessional.

"Present company excluded, I hope." Smiled Father Lawrence. If this was a sin, then certainly he was guilty of the same thing a thousand times over, he thought. She chuckled and then listened to his calm, consoling reply, explaining how he would speak to his coworker in the fields of the Lord about the matter. After praying for a minute together, she said, "You won't forget to bring Pat communion on First Friday, Father?"

"I'll be there with church bells on."

"Now that I'd like to see . . .," said Teresa, struggling to kneel. Fr. Lawrence left her there, alone before the tabernacle. He knew that a moment of quiet prayer worked wonders, more than any words of his.

When Mrs. Martin finally came out of the chapel, he said, "Don't you have a home to go to, woman? Why don't you go teach that parrot of yours some new words?" Teresa and Pat had a talking parrot named Bertie.

Despite being in the chapel she couldn't help but laugh, relishing the final word, "Why don't you teach that parrot of yours some basic catechism?" Then it was his turn to laugh.

Fr. Louis was hard to figure out and even harder to pin down. What was the root of his radical rebellion? ' Was he merely a refugee from the Sixties? Fr. Lawrence often wondered if it was frustration over his foiled ambitions. The man had always wanted to be a published and quoted theologian but never made a dent, despite his doctorate. At dinner, Fr. Lawrence spoke to him, raising Teresa Martin's concerns.

"That woman is a plague, an infestation, a menace . . .," said Father Louis, stuffing his formidable mouth with spaghetti.

"She's a faithful daughter of the Church," Fr. Lawrence countered. He tried not to sound angry, deliberately modulating the tone of his voice.

"She's the worst kind of fool—a Catholic fundamentalist! She repeats words like that damned parrot of hers!"

Fr. Lawrence thought of Teresa's quip earlier but didn't want to sound silly defending a talking bird so he switched gears, asking, "What are you trying to do in that Bible class of yours, anyway?"

"Proclaim the truth!"

"The truth according to who?"

"To whom?"

Annoyed at the petty correction, Fr. Lawrence said: "Your famous International Jesus Seminar—in all its wisdom—has decided that the Church, all the popes and the teaching authority of the Magisterium—after two thousand years of Living Tradition, being guided by the Spirit—are wrong. Imagine saying that the Lord never really gave us the Our Father, that we made it up?"

"There was a need in the first Christian communities for structured prayer, especially after the whole glossolalia mess at Corinth with everybody speaking in tongues . . ."

"Paul taught them about love, friend, and at this moment I'm not feeling very inclined to be either patient or kind to you. Love bears all things but this time, Father, you . . ."

Fr. Zenone interrupted him, still chewing, "The correct translation is . . ."

"Go to hell!" fumed the younger priest, immediately regretting what he said.

"You still believe in that? Hell was an invention of the medieval church to keep rebellious peasants in line . . ." The man went on for quite some time about the institutional Church oppressing the truly prophetic voices—meaning himself—with threats of excommunication, eternal damnation and so on. After the current saintly pope was mentioned on a par with Lucifer, who after all, did not exist, Fr. Lawrence suddenly lost his appetite and, not being able to think of anything else to say, blurted out, "What would your own sweet sister say—she who, after your mother's death raised you and taught you your prayers? I wonder what she would say about all your heretical theories."

"My older sister—muttered Fr. Louis—through no fault of her own, is an uneducated woman—of the staunch Italian matronly variety—who has prayed the rosary every day every one of her sixty-four years. But give me just twenty uninterrupted minutes with her now and I would make her see the light."

Fr. Lawrence got up from the table, hurriedly blessed himself, and then left the room to go prepare for the evening Mass an hour later. Why did the Lord send the disciples out two by two, he wondered? Teresa and Pat were united by the bonds of peace and love, but he and his own brother priest were light years apart. He felt like a hypocritical Pharisee for professing love for the God he cannot see while hating the brother he can see.

All the usual suspects were there at the Mass, singing like off-key angels. He gave a bread and butter homily on the supernatural virtue of Hope, saying, "Where there's life there's hope and where there's hope there's life." Catchy but a little phony he thought. After the final blessing, upon returning to the sacristy, he found Teresa Martin waiting for him. He said, "Now, you're not still upset about what . . ." He stopped himself, always hating priests who preached at people outside Mass and who spoke before listening. They were worse than the affably nervous types, and he knew plenty of them too.

"Pat's getting worse," she said, a quiver in her voice.

"Give me five minutes . . ."

"How about four and a half?"

They drove the three blocks together in silence with the Viaticum on the seat between them. Neither one wanted to think of the inevitable, that Pat had been deteriorating for a long time. No matter how long they might be expecting it, Pat's death would still be a terrible shock. Fr. Lawrence hated funerals more than anything else he had to do, especially if forced to celebrate them for people he loved.

The Martin home was a typical whitewashed bungalow fronted by a postage stamp lawn, raucously edged by an explosion of budding roses. No dog outside, thank God—only an obnoxious parrot inside, thought Fr. Lawrence. Teresa opened the metal door to let him in first. All the houses in South Central had unbreakable, bulletproof deterrents for thieves. Bars on the windows reinforced the siege mentality. It was odd how, in order to protect their homes, people had become prisoners behind bars. Teresa turned on the living room light then ushered him into Pat's room. It took a minute for Fr. Lawrence's eyes to adjust to the comparative dark. There she lay, exactly in the same position, and in the same place for as long as he had known her. She had once been a young, brilliant medical student, at a time when Martin Luther King was still dreaming his dream. Then came the Multiple Sclerosis and the slow slide into paralysis. It was going on fifteen years like this. Yet he marveled at how, every time, she seemed genuinely happy to see him, asking how he was, as if all was perfectly well with herself. Only this time she had to work harder at it. Her cheeks were dark hollows beneath her sunken eyes. Twisted lips barely covered her yellowing teeth.

Noticing the open book on the nightstand next to a lit candle, Fr. Lawrence said, "So you've been reading our favorite poet again?"

"No, Father, I got her all memorized." Then she recited: "Hope is the thing with feathers that perches in the soul, and sings the song

without the words, and never stops at all . . . *Isn't that marvelous? It reminds me of Bertie."*

The priest looked for the large green and yellow parrot perched in his corner cage. "Say hello to Father, Bertie!" she coaxed. Right on cue, the bird squawked, "Beautiful day!" That was all it ever said. "Beautiful day!" Pat painstakingly taught him that one phrase. On his very first visit, years before, when asked about Bertie's limited vocabulary, Pat's reply had been, "I need to be reminded of that, Father, that every day is a beautiful day."

Teresa left the room so her daughter could have privacy to confess. Father Lawrence felt ashamed, listening to her sins that seemed somehow better than his virtues. He gave her absolution followed by the anointing. With some difficulty, she managed to swallow Holy Communion. Viaticum, holy bread for the journey, he thought. "She who eats my body and drinks my blood will have eternal life within her." The two sat in companionable silence for some minutes together. The priest didn't feel like cheering her up because he realized he was the one who actually needed it. She lay there, eyes closed, breathing shallowly, half-grimacing, and half-smiling, her pain transformed into some private ecstasy of gratitude. When she finally did open her eyes, she said, "I'm almost finished here, Father. Will you take care of Mama when I'm gone?" He wanted to say something but none of his stock replies surfaced.

"Not that I'll be far away . . ." she added, with obvious effort. Then putting a bony, trembling hand on his, she whispered, "I'm ready, but she's not."

"Are you afraid?" he asked.

"No, Father, I can't wait to have a brand-new resurrected body."

After a few minutes she drifted off into sleep. He said goodbye, bending down to kiss her brow, hating himself for noticing the stink of the bedsores.

Three days later, Pat fell asleep and never woke again. At the funeral, there were very few people present. Some wept but the ones who knew her best did not. At the graveside, the wind blew dry autumn leaves into the hole next to the casket. And Fr. Lawrence found that he could not parrot even one more consoling maxim.

Perhaps for that reason, the image of Bertie kept coming into his head, forcing him to smile. "It's a beautiful day . . ." he began, "to enter heaven . . ." Then, remembering the lines from Pat's poem, he went on to give arguably the best homily of his life.

Later that afternoon, in the rectory, Father Louis Zenone received a long-distance phone call from Italy. He talked a full hour, his Italian rising and falling in volume and intensity. No, it was not the Vatican calling to censure him, but his sister to inform him that she had "stage four" cancer. Overhearing half the conversation, Father Lawrence felt more pity for the brother than for the sister, wondering how the man would be able to face her death without the comfort of old beliefs. Quite naturally, and without thinking, he said a silent prayer to Pat for a miracle.

The Autumn Poets

The prospect of playing nursemaid to three octogenarian Italian missionaries for the entire summer rankled. I had just endured the torture of an entire scholastic year in our Roman seminary. Imagine having to study Latin, Greek, and Hebrew—all at the same time and all in Italian. On top of that came the hard realization that most Americans are blissfully ignorant of, how much other countries hate the USA. Being the only representative of the Stars and Stripes, the depth of this antipathy—especially from professional do-gooders—amazed me. I understood that they thought America to be a mixture of Hollywood and the CIA, but couldn't they see any good there? One Brazilian seminarian, steeped in radical "liberation" theology, approached me shortly after my arrival, and said, "I am prepared to hate you."

I responded, "Well, at least let me give you a few good reasons to hate me first."

That little exchange set the tone for the following scholastic year, with me being the object of my confreres' constant mean-spiritedness. The twenty-five other students, all from Europe, Latin America or Africa bridled at the very sight of me. At Thanksgiving, for instance, upon returning from class I was greeted with scribbled signs on the message board pointing to photocopied articles about the various tragedies endured by the native North Americans. I had become personally responsible for Wounded Knee. It didn't seem to matter that I was a vowed member of the same community they were, dedicated to the same ideals. In addition, the first Gulf War made me the object of everyone's political frustrations. The part that rankled most, however, were the false smiles shrouding outright hypocrisy. By year's end I found myself weary, to the point of questioning—for the first time—my calling. Did God really want me to put up with such hostility for the rest of my life? After all, I was not being persecuted for being a Christian, but rather, for being born in a certain geographical area of the planet. If this was how it was in the green wood—I wondered—how would it be in later years when the wood was dry?

But my attitude had always been, put respective noses and shoulders to grindstones and wheels, and carry one's cross to the bitter end. And indeed, it was a very bitter experience. The finale was that I had eleven final exams in the month of June—all in Italian—each one covering the entire course-load for the year.

The first of July found me shell-shocked, on a train heading north to the little town of Aretto on the picturesque Lago di Garda. Even though I just wanted to get away altogether, I was glad not to have to go through my companions' vitriolic reaction to the Fourth of July. My religious community there had a house for elderly confreres, those still ambulatory, but still in need of some supervision and medical help. The house was chosen for the same reason the Austrian Emperor Franz Josef had spent time there, the same reason sanatoriums were built there for sufferers of tuberculosis—the warm winds swirling down the valley from Trento were healthy. Lemons could even be grown on the steep inclines of the nearby villages. Despite a sour feeling in the pit of my stomach, I was determined to make lemonade with my summer. At the back of my mind, however, lurked the very real possibility that, after yet another negative, prison-like experience—this time with the oldsters—like a coward I would pack my bags and retreat to the land of the free and the home of the brave.

I arrived at the train station by late afternoon. No one was waiting for me, so I hoisted my backpack onto my slumping shoulders and, asking directions in my halting Italian, eventually found my way to our tree-lined compound. The first surprise was that the superior did not immediately express his disdain for my nationality, but just the opposite. Fr. Oliver had even worked in the States for some years and still corresponded with some close friends in Michigan, after many intervening years in the African missions. He showed me to my room, gave me a copy of the community schedule, and bade me welcome. After evening prayer, dinner was quiet, not because of imposed silence but because each of the thirty or so elderly missionaries were concentrating so hard on the pasta placed before them. The secondo *piato*, if possible, received an even more intense attention. Only with the *insalata mista* at the end of the meal did some conversation finally sprout. I surmised that these guys had done some serious starving in their day back on the Dark Continent and were decidedly making up for lost time.

Since I was not eating at Fr. Oliver's table, there was no chance to speak with him. The five greybeards at my table hardly noticed me, or asked me anything. One eventually looked up, eyeing me as possible competition for the one large green apple that sat on top of a bowl of pears. He grabbed it like a frog would lasso a dragonfly with its tongue. His eyes mirrored his delight. It was going to be a very long summer indeed. After dinner everyone obediently trooped up a wheel chair incline into a TV room for the evening news. On the small screen, big Italian politicians yelled at each other across long tables in ornately carved rooms down in Rome somewhere. The old missionaries stared listlessly ahead, hanging on every word, all hoping to catch some international news, something about their beloved, Uganda, Sudan or Ethiopia. On the rare occasions when this did happen, their eyes lit up and for a few moments they would visibly resurrect, talking excitedly, or even breaking into the local dialect and laughing at some joke only a tribal chieftain might appreciate. Then they would slide back into what could only be described as a general malaise. They were just so many fish out water. Imagine joining the seminary when you were eleven or twelve, going through a rigorous formation, then spending fifty or sixty years in another land, then being sent home to a place you never really knew. All the people they loved and served so faithfully were far, far away. I felt sorry for the old guys because, in a way, I could relate—I too felt far away from home, living amongst strangers.

The next morning, I began my official duties, changing the diaper of the oldest—Padre Fabio, ninety-seven years old. After that fiasco, it was a potpourri of cleaning, lemon picking, and helping to prepare the midday *pranzo*. What did I know of pasta? But it didn't matter much since the cook was a Filipino. At least we spoke English while chopping the onions and garlic. The former made me cry while the latter was abundant enough to keep any number of vampires at bay.

After lunch, one fellow dressed in a tattered black cassock approached me and in a mysterious way asked me to come upstairs into the TV room so he could "show me *qualcosa importante*." I followed him with feigned docility. That was my problem, at that time in my life, I was rather proud of my humility. He stood in front of the recliner I had sat in the previous night, and said, "You see this chair?"

"*Si*," I answered truthfully. A pregnant pause followed. He then continued with great seriousness, "You see this *sgabello* (footrest)?"

I saw no point in denying the obvious. "Yes, indeed, there it is in all its glory." My sarcasm, I saw, was wasted on him.

With a flourish, the old geezer got to the point: "This is my chair and my footrest. This is where I sit when I watch the news" He looked at me significantly. Romanita was the Italian art of saying what you wanted to say without ever actually saying it. He was really telling me that he had a cousin named Guido from Sicily who would happily cut off my thumbs if I ever took his place again.

Seeing that it would not be good to argue the point, I decided, discretion being the better part of valor, to let the old coot have his way. So with a flourish of my own, I confessed mournfully, "You are right, dear Father, I have sinned against heaven and against you . . ." Not expecting even such feigned humility from today's crop of seminarians, he was taken aback, and frowned significantly, as if contemplating a great Gospel truth. Before he could begin a speech of the whacko variety, one that I wanted to avoid at all costs, I high-tailed it out of there. The only thing worse than listening to so many sermons in Italian was having to hear one outside of Mass. In the space of one short year, having had occasion to live with so many priests, I was beginning to understand anticlericalism very well. How could I be contemplating entering a state of life I was beginning to abhor? It was then that I realized that the place was not merely for the aged and infirmed but also for the mentally ill. It was a species of loony bin for guys who, for one reason or another, had "lost it" in the hinterlands of the missions. Constant pressure, wars, uncertainty, wholesale genocides, persecutions, famines, torture had obviously broken more than a few minds. This thought bothered me because I was right there in their midst, one of them, surely moving along the same path in life.

My free time came after lunch when the whole wild bunch sped off to make their horizontal devotions to Santa Siesta, a custom I quickly adapted to. When in Rome, especially during the hottest part of the blistering summer afternoons, it was best to take a snooze. Their cacophony of snores was enough to wake the dead but not me. I shut my door and dreamed peacefully, before my afternoon duties began. After a few days, I became a fixture around the place, noticed by neither man nor beast. The "normal" brothers seemed to be comparatively few, while the lunatics abounded. Yet feeling sorry for fish out of water lasts only so long. Such a cranky, grumpy group I could never have imagined. I spent most of my energies just trying to stay out of their way. When one ordered me to do something I either obeyed immediately without comment or spent the rest of the day avoiding that particular inmate. But one of the things you find about crazy people, be they men of God or not, is that they—much like elephants—don't forget. It's not that they have all kinds of odd ideas—they only have one—and usually it's all consuming. For Father Giuseppe it was the proliferation of weeds in the garden. For Fratello Alessandro it was the position of the fan. For another it was his chair and footrest. For another it was the lone green apple. It was almost as if clinging to that one simple idea could moor them to reality.

If all this sounds too pessimistic, that was pretty much how I felt at the time. The dark cloud would lift during prayers when I saw the obvious love and devotion these screwballs had for God. They clung to Him, hoping that He would come rescue them from themselves. The afternoon rosary too, oddly enough, was an almost mystical experience, with all eyes raised to heaven. Voices cracking with love for the Blessed Virgin. I prayed right along with them, like there was no tomorrow.

Then one day we got the news. The Italian government, amid all their fruitless arguing down in Rome had decided that all the ancient buildings on the peninsula—which was just about all of them—needed updating. In their great wisdom, they mandated that every single construction from Roman times to the present needed a new electrical system, to come up to European Community standards. Electricians across the land were delighted. The old missionaries' home was slated for renovation during the month of August. Drastic measures would have to be undertaken. We would all be shipped out to our other houses throughout Italy for the duration of the messy work. Fr. Oliver informed me that I would accompany three confreres to our community in the city of Trento, some thirty kilometers, up the valley. I wondered what sort of disaster this portended.

It would have been a pleasant ride, past quaint villages and vineyards, with castles perched precariously on the mountainsides, had it not been for a deepening sense of doom descending upon me. I would be in charge, the one responsible—practically left alone with all three. Our Trento house was modern and spacious with a great view of the town and valley below. The superior, a relatively young missionary, recently returned from Togo, welcomed us. Two more stood by, eyeballing us like we were the Black Plague popping in for the weekend. Pointing north, he said, "That's where the barbarians came from. The Nazis too." Pointing south, he added pointedly, "And that's where the American bombers came from."

"Kaboom!" I said.

The superior did not smile, "As the Germans retreated, your country bombed this valley. You destroyed many churches and killed many innocent people."

Before I could stop myself, I blurted out, "Well, if it hadn't been for us, pal, you'd all be speaking German right now, wouldn't you?" That little endearing comment would have been better left unsaid. Coldly, he handed me a copy of the house schedule and warned me, "Keep a close eye on those three. As you see, we live on a cliff. It's a long drop, should one fall."

I was tempted to either push him over or jump over the side myself. One thing I noticed, however, that evening, despite the emphasis on punctuality, was that there were usually only five of us present at evening prayer in the chapel—myself, the three oldsters' and one ninety-six-year-old brother named Gianni. The superior and the two younger missionaries were conspicuously absent. Since everybody except me was pretty much deaf, the recitation of the psalms became something of a tower of babble. If I wasn't stifling laughter, I was once again impressed by the obvious devotion and love with which they were being prayed. After that, it was time for dinner. My guys, although never having been in that house before, because it was a new one, instinctively knew in which direction the refectory lay. The superior and his two minions were, however, punctually present for dinner. A cursory prayer opened the general discussion dominated by these wise youngsters.

It was all about America. What a surprise. They had never-been there but they knew all about it. Then followed an extended diatribe about modern-day seminarians. Then came the lack of virtues of American seminarians in particular. Everyone knew—they said—God hated America and consequently, all it was good for was to send money to the missions, not to offer missionaries itself. Now I knew why the three oldsters concentrated so hard on eating their vittles—perhaps chewing would drown out the inane conversation of the superiors. As one of the inferiors, I concentrated on the *faggioli*, loudly slurping my soup, imitating my three charges who seemed oblivious to everything else. Except for opening my mouth to shovel food inside I kept my big trap shut. Besides, I really didn't want them all to hate me on the very first day, like my Brazilian classmate.

To distract myself, I took a long, hard look at my three ancient sons, sitting directly across the table from me. There was Bonfanti, that was his last name. He was a big fellow, eighty-five years old, bald and with a long, white beard. His elephantine legs required wrapping daily to keep down the swelling. What I appreciated about him was that he only spoke to express his gratitude for some small kindness rendered. It was embarrassing but the guy was always thanking me. Pretty soon, I found myself thanking him for his thanking me, wondering why I never noticed such a noble fellow back in the big house of Lago di Garda.

Next to him sat Egidio, ninety years young, with Alzheimer's. I spent a significant amount of my time keeping the outside doors locked, wandering around the big house looking for him, and occasionally peering over the cliff just to make sure he hadn't accidentally made the leap of faith. He was really quite pleasant, with rare moments of poignant clarity, where his eyes teared up and you just knew that he knew what was happening to him.

Last but not least, there was Pietro. He was eighty-eight, about the same weight in pounds, a wisp of a man with a white goatee. He wore thick black-rimmed glasses and had quite an eye for detail. Dressed in a frayed black sport coat, with rosary beads in hand, he paced the corridor from morning until evening. He was always already up and dressed when I entered his cell to wake him. I began to doubt if he ever slept. He spoke little but always had a point. The first thing I ever heard him say—after our first meal in the refectory together with the Superior and his two cohorts—was a surprise. He had spent the entire meal, looking down at his plate, eating with an almost religious fervor. Afterward he approached me and, staring up into my eyes, motioned for me to lean closer. He whispered with a wink, "*Stupidaggini*! They're saying such stupid things! Don't pay them any mind!" That was the beginning of our budding friendship. He understood very well which way the wind was blowing, even if it looked like the slightest breeze might lift him up and carry him away.

Every three days, I had to help him trim his beard, shaving his concave cheeks on either side of his missionary beard. I said, "*Facciamo la barba*," which, translated, literally means "Let's make the beard." To which he replied, gently correcting my Italian, "No, dear brother, the beard is already made, as you can see. Let's trim it instead."

I laughed, he laughed, we both laughed as if this was the funniest thing we had ever heard. In that house, any attempt at humor was like light entering a tomb. I managed not to slit his throat. He showed his appreciation for this fact with more jokes and, little by little—over the next days—by revealing to me the secret of his life.

The next day, after wrapping Bonfanti's legs and corralling Egidio for the evening, I went to check on Pietro. He was not in his room but in the chapel. Seeing me, he made a reverent sign of the cross, tried his best to genuflect without falling over, and then followed me out and down the hall to his room. Laying out his pajamas, I asked him if he slept well at night.

He shook his balding head and answered, "No, *caro fratello*, the memory of my sins keeps me awake."

That surprised me. How could such a holy man of obviously deep prayer be worried about faults confessed long ago? I asked him about this. He replied, "I joined the order when I was twenty-one years old. I was sinning badly then and knew that if I didn't go away I would be lost. Alas, fifty-five years in the Sudan did not manage to convert me. I am still sinning each and every day. I can't stop, only for brief moments during prayer, that's why I have to pray constantly. Even then . . ."

I didn't know what to say. If this was the case for him, then what was the state of my own soul? He seemed to read my mind, and not for the last time that summer, said gently, "Do not fear, *carissimo*, when we're lost, Our Lady helps us find the way." With that, he laid himself down on top of the blankets, without putting on his pajamas. Closing his eyes, he sighed, "Morning will come soon enough. *Buona notte . . .*"

The hot summer days passed quickly, falling into something of a routine. After, lunch, while my Tridentine trio rested, I would walk down into the *centro historico* of Trento, walking the streets until it was time to climb the hill again to prepare an espresso for my guys. I visited the Cathedral where the great Council of Trent took place, as well as all the other churches. Walking along the river, I brooded over my future. It wasn't that I was doubting God's call but mostly my ability to respond. The superior and his companion with the superior attitude made me feel that the future was bleak while the three old inferiors made me feel that a future might just be possible after all.

Then came the fateful day when I lost Egidio. Brother Gianni, the ninety-six-year-old member of the local community, leaving for the plaza to spend the morning with the pigeons in the piazza, accidentally left the door open. Before I knew it, Egidio was gone. Neither Bonfanti nor Pietro saw him leave. The young superior began yelling at me in Italian, gesticulating wildly like the crazed conductor of a provincial orchestra. I didn't respond but shot out the door to begin the search. First, I covered the grounds, then the nearby streets, before proceeding methodically downhill, asking everyone if they had seen an old man wandering by. Anything could have happened to him. He could have been hit by a car or a bus, and it would all be my fault. In the midst of my panic, I suddenly thought of Pietro's words, "Don't be afraid, when you're lost, Our Lady will help you find the way." This thought calmed me enough so that I managed to pray an Ave. An image of Pietro in the chapel appeared clearly in my mind. Don't ask me how, but I knew that—at that exact moment—the little man of God was praying for both Egidio and me.

I continued the search, fighting off despair. Reaching the town center, in the great open space next to the Cathedral, I spotted Brother

Gianni. He was laughing loudly, the way deaf men do. A group of old men resembling pigeons, all younger than he was, looked up at him like he was a statue in the town square. A lifetime of building churches and schools in Africa, added to a mountain family's robust constitution, made his arms still ripple with muscles. He recognized me, and, after explaining my plight, mobilized the troops, sending his disciples, each in a different direction, like so many slow-moving good shepherds seeking the lost sheep.

Seeing a male *Carabinieri* chatting up a female *Carabinieri*, I asked them for help but they just looked at me with cultivated disdain, the fruit of many years of official lethargy. Frustrated, I pushed the huge wooden door of the cathedral open, taking a moment to allow my eyes to adjust to the dimness. Approaching the altar of the Virgin, I knelt down, closed my eyes, and breathed deeply. After a few moments, someone tapped me on the shoulder. It was Egidio, smiling down on me, his face side-lit by a sea of candles. "It's time for lunch," he said. Not knowing whether to kill him or kiss him I took him by the elbow and led him outside into the square. Brother Gianni and his gang were resting on their benches, having already given up the search. Seeing us, they laughed, tipped their hats and discussed whose poor wife would provide the pasta for their midday ritual.

Egidio and I made our way slowly back through the town, and up the long incline to our house. The young superior greeted us, red-faced, and fuming. We walked right past him into the refectory, where Bonfanti and Pietro were already doing yeoman's work on some lasagna. To be expected, the Superior's main topic of conversation was that morning's little drama. We four sat silent throughout. After the last course, I motioned to Pietro, "You look like a goat with that salad stuck on your beard."

He smiled, "I'm saving it for a midafternoon snack."

Winking at me, he smiled conspiratorially and said, "*Stupidaggini!*"

The summer ended with our return to the renovated house at Lago de Garda. Fr. Oliver thanked me for my service. My three brothers each kissed both my cheeks in the Italian way. Egidio seemed to realize—deep down, somewhere—that I was bidding him farewell. Tears streamed down his ruddy cheeks. "Don't wander off, buddy!" I said. Bonfanti nodded at me seriously, balancing precariously on his swollen legs. "I thank God for you," he said, over and over again. Finally, Pietro came close and whispered in my ear, "Remember my poor soul in your prayers, *carissimo*."

I didn't have to ask him for his prayers, because I knew that they were already mine.

Wrinkles in the Road

After his first traumatic year of college in California, Luke faced the long, cross-country trek back home to the East Coast—alone. Three thousand miles, no matter the beautiful scenery, was still a journey to be reckoned with. Travelling west, the previous year to begin studies, he had felt lonely and quite naive. The whole year also proved to be a lonesome experience, not because he was from back East—everyone in California seemed to be from somewhere else—but because he was the only actual painter in the very avant-garde art school he was attending. He painted highly detailed, representational paintings, that is, that were not abstract. They were not super-realistic but you could recognize real objects, scenes, people and places. This fact alone made him the object of much highbrow artistic scorn. Every two weeks at the faculty-student critiques he would be verbally torn limb from limb.

This made him angry, and he knew himself well enough to know that when someone pushed him, he usually did not back down. His small, even beautiful, portraits and landscapes were visible slaps in the face of the abstract majority who seemed to adore the ugly and meaningless.

He knew he was a problem for them yet there was no way they could kick him out, since there were no actual grades given in that institution, only "satisfactory" or "unsatisfactory." As long as one submitted work to the biweekly jury, that was enough to obtain a pass. The prevalent theory was that it was pretty hard to grade art.

Luke knew that, deep down, his problem was not with his creative colleagues but was much more elemental than paint and canvas. It was a crisis of faith in the Creator. Two years previous, his earthly father had died, leaving his mother and brothers and sisters alone, so he was angry with the Almighty Father. If God had allowed that to happen, in effect, abandoning him, then, like his companion atheist artists, he would jolly well ignore him as well. He knew in his heart, however, that this was superficial reasoning based upon a profound wound. On Sunday mornings he would go religiously to his-empty studio, trying to fill his colorless spiritual life with vermilion green, cobalt blue and alizarin crimson. Yet no matter how hard he tried to ignore it, every time he passed the local parish church in town, he felt pulled in that direction. It was, he realized later, an urge to come home.

Now that he was faced with the actual journey home, he felt torn. He wanted to go badly but he didn't want a trip that, no doubt, would afford plenty of time for reflection. After a long year he didn't want to think too much about his life, that his father would not be there upon his arrival. And his mother would greet him with questions in her eyes: Why did you have to choose a school so far away? Don't you see you are needed here? But another less emotional reason to go home pressed upon him—the fact that he had no money. He would have to work hard all summer to make ends meet during the school year. In some ways he was indeed the stereotypical starving artist. If the typical hangdog "Look at me, I'm a misunderstood genius, I just cut off my ear" expression was missing from his clean-shaven face, nevertheless, his bank account spoke of the garret. In fact, all he had to make the journey was sixty-nine dollars and forty-one cents. By 1975, gas alone had risen to the unheard of sum of almost seventy-three cents a gallon. And his tiny two-seater British sports car—a beat-up 1971 monkey-brown Triumph TR-6—might easily require emergency maintenance along the way. He soon realized that in order to make the trip at all, he would be forced to take on a passenger, one who could share the economic burden. He placed an index card advertisement on the student bulletin board reading: "Passenger to New Jersey wanted, split gas and expenses." His first name, dorm room and phone number were written clearly on the bottom of the card. His dad had always said that he had the hands of a doctor or an artist. It was something of a disappointment that the latter emerged, and the proof was good penmanship.

The next day, a knock on the door came early. A young man named Walter introduced himself. Walter, it seemed, needed a ride to the Windy City of Chicago, which, if he wasn't mistaken, could be on the way to the Garden State. Arrangements were made to leave at dawn the following day. Walter willingly agreed to share the cost of gas, oil, and any minor repairs besides shouldering some of the driving duties. He was familiar with a stick shift since his father, who lived in a wealthy suburb had a green MGB GT roadster in the garage.

Luke hurriedly boxed up his studio and room, placed everything in student storage, and almost without realizing it, prayed that all would go well. The journey had to be made, since his low-paying, minimum wage job painting houses started within a week and would not wait. At least it was painting, he mused.

The next morning before six, Walter helped load everything into the tiny trunk and into the miniscule space behind the two passenger seats. Then they roared off north, up I-5.

With an overnight stop in Sacramento at a friend's house, the following morning they headed west on I-80 across the California line into Nevada where they stopped for lunch in Reno. Luke was alarmed by the fact that the little car was really sucking gas. Perhaps it needed a tune-up. Or maybe it was just the extra weight of a second passenger. Whatever the cause, they had to keep moving. He worried, hoping against hope to be able to make it all the way across the nation on such a small budget. After wolfing down a burger, fries and shake, Walter insisted on entering a nearby Casino. Luke followed him, thinking the worst, that his traveling companion would lose all the money he would be contributing for gas.

Walter boasted that he was a natural born gambler, even though he was all of nineteen years old. He went straight for the craps tables and picked up the dice like they were paintbrushes ready to render his life's masterpiece. Not able to stomach this scene, Luke cautioned his blonde-haired, bug-eyed passenger not to lose too much, even setting a time limit. "Twenty minutes, Walter, no more! After that, I leave, with you or without you." He swallowed hard, realizing that Walter paid him no heed as he rolled the spotted cubes. Luke retreated to one of the one-armed bandits. All of a sudden he felt that old feeling, even worse than in his lonely studio back at school. He longed for a familiar face, a friend and not just some forced acquaintance like Walter, but someone who would know him and see things the same way he did—like his dad. He took out a single quarter and launching another half-hearted prayer into the stratosphere, slipped it into the slot machine. Pulling the lever, he started when the machine lit up and bells sounded. Quarters started pouring out the bottom into the metal tray. The jackpot drew several people who commented on his good luck. He looked at the machine as if it just appeared before his eyes and spoken to him. A scantily clad waitress with an empty tray asked him if he wanted a drink or anything else. The negative reply sent her away, rolling her eyes at the innocence of youth. Luke, blinking in disbelief at the pile of coins, began scooping them up, filling his sweatshirt and pants' pockets. A weather-beaten, chain-smoking lady nearby handed him a large, empty paper cup.

"Put the coins in this, honey, then bring it over to the cashier who'll change it into paper money." Luke looked at her through the cloud of smoke, recognizing something real in her voice. Eyeing him, not unkindly, she added, "And if you want my advice—and you want to keep some of your winnings, get out of here PDQ."

He thanked her as if she was the angel sent to warn Lot of the danger of owning property in Sodom. Then, he returned to the craps table where Walter seemed obviously intent on losing everything. Luke took his high-rolling friend by the elbow and literally dragged him out to the car. Despite his companion's protests, he knew he was doing the right thing. Surely, if even one more minute were spent inside, they would lose everything and hence, never make it to their final destination. He did not tell Walter about his own winnings. Driving over the next several hours, with the mountains turning to desert, he thought about winning at the casino. Something had made three red cherries pop up on the machine when he least expected it and least deserved it. As the miles flew by, he wondered if his half-formed prayers had actually been heard. If they were careful, now they had enough gas money to go at least as far as Chicago, but not enough for a cheap hotel along the way. But then again, he had not prayed for that.

Hitting the Bonneville Salt Flats around nine that evening they reached speeds of over one hundred miles an hour, a velocity which the little six-cylinder was quite capable of. But not wanting to tackle the looming Rockies in the dark they pulled off into some small town in the foothills, parking near a postage stamp sized park and made themselves as comfortable as possible. Luke was exhausted, having done all the driving thus far. He still had a hard time trusting anyone else behind the wheel of his little brown baby. Although he never had the funds to get her fixed up properly, she was, nevertheless, his first automobile love. But he knew, however, that at some point on the long trip, he would be forced to let Walter drive.

Breaking their morning fast with peanut butter and jelly sandwiches, they faced the mountains ahead. Climbing steadily, they decided to take what looked like a short cut on the map. And as it so often happens, although there was some pretty dramatic scenery, it ended up taking twice as long.

The winding two-lane road whipped them through the canyons out into unexpected valleys. At times, the road dropped off precipitously into deep gorges to the left and right. After many hours of nerve-wracking concentration, they eventually emerged near Estes Park, north of Boulder, Colorado. At dusk, Luke, this time with an intentional prayer, handed the keys to his companion. Walter got in, revved the engine, ground the gears noisily and pulled out onto the two-lane highway that would take them back up to Interstate 80. And this would lead them straight, as the crow flies, to the City of Big Shoulders. After a couple of hours, Luke allowed himself to relax a little, since, to all appearances, Walter seemed to be a competent and responsible driver. Exhaustion dropped him like a rock into the depths of a troublesome dream. He was on a road, driving away from something horrible, a darkness that followed the little car like a predator. But his uneasy dreams synchronized with the sound of the vehicle hugging the asphalt. Awaking suddenly, as if someone had just shaken him, he looked ahead to see the headlights illumine the black night. Evidently he had slept a long while. But something was wrong. The car seemed somehow unstable, almost like they were weaving from one side of the empty road to the other. Luke glanced quickly over at Walter. There was his companion, nodding, with his blonde hair hanging down in front of his closed eyes. He realized, to his horror, that Walter was asleep at the wheel. He did not yell for fear of startling him, but grabbed the steering wheel, calling his name. Walter made some effort to open his eyes and after a second or two, came to his senses.

"Pull over, you idiot!" Luke yelled angrily. Fear pumped adrenaline through his veins, removing any vestige of tiredness. The instinct for survival—pure animal desire to keep on living—took over. Once parked on the side of the road, he continued to yell at Walter who was now fully awake, and offering a lame apology.

Luke grabbed the keys and got into the driver's seat and started the engine, ready to leave Walter on the side of the road if he didn't get in fast enough. The two of them drove on in complete silence until dawn. They stopped for breakfast and, although conversation picked up again, Luke made no more attempts at sharing driving duties. He just kept stopping for coffee. This is when Walter informed him that he had no money left to pay for his own meals or for his share of the gas. Reno had indeed been cruel. Luke was sorely tempted to lose his temper once again but said only, "Better hit the road if we're going to be in Chicago by tomorrow afternoon."

Walter, without further ado, or apologies, settled himself into the narrow passenger seat, and fell fast asleep. Miles of cornfields soothed the savage beast in Luke and pretty soon, despite being so tired, he began humming to himself, every song he could remember. Walter, snoring away on the passenger side, didn't even notice. It struck him that, after such a close call on the road, he was simply happy to be alive. Certainly, if he had not awakened at that precise moment, they would have died in a car crash out in the middle of nowhere. He half-remembered someone shaking his shoulder, but it could not have been Walter.

As the scenery flew by, he felt like he was in a continually trans-forming landscape painting, with Thomas Hart Benton of Kansas giving way to Grant Wood in Iowa. Finally, crossing the mist-en-shrouded Mississippi River at dawn, the land of Lincoln opened up before them.

Walter's dad had just divorced Walter's mother to live with a blonde floozy named Karen in a big house in River Forest, one of the oldest and wealthiest suburbs just west of the city. Walter seemed glad just to have somewhere to go for the summer. But there was no welcoming hug and barely a smile, so Luke couldn't help feeling sorry for the guy. Even if he was the worst driver in the world, any son deserved a better welcome home than that, especially after his first year away at school.

That evening, the four of them—Luke, Walter, the Dad and Karen the floozy—went out to Maywood Park where Walter's father owned part a racehorse. Which part was never determined. Karen eyed Luke, making him feel uncomfortable. He couldn't help notic-ing the black roots of her bleached-blonde hair. Jersey was still nine hundred miles distant.

Walter's father ordered them all drinks and then asked Luke—not Walter—to place a bet for him. Seeing the look on his companion's face, Luke tried to refuse, saying he didn't know how, but the father insisted, explaining everything step by step. Walter pretended to be watching the parading horses entering the track. A hundred dollars was to be put down on Washer Woman in the FIFTH to WIN.

Taking the money in hand, and getting up hesitantly, Walter said to Luke, "Hey, I'll go with you. I need to stretch my legs after being crammed into that tin can of yours all week." His dad simply ignored him, being far too busy putting the squeeze on his much younger girlfriend.

"She likes you," Walter said nonchalantly.

"What?" Luke responded, surprised.

"Yeah, Little Miss Peroxide. You had better lock the guest room tonight . . ."

Before asking what this odd statement meant, they arrived at the bettor's window. A bleary-eyed fat man behind the grill took their money without saying thank you, and handed Luke a little stub receipt. "Don't lose that" said Walter, "When we win, you'll need it to come back and collect the dough."

Luke said, "What do you mean, when we win?"

"Oh yes, I forgot to tell you—dear Dad knows some people here. Washer Woman is not his horse but she does belong to a good pal of his, so he has inside info on who's going to do what and, most importantly, in what order they're going to finish."

"You mean to tell me the race is fixed?" Luke said, his voice rising.

"Keep it down to a dull roar, babe-in-the-woods! Do you want to spoil a good thing?" Walter pulled Luke out of the lines of the betting public and led him back to his father's table where he duly handed over the receipt. After the race, with hardly a hint of joy, the father sent Luke back to pick up twelve, crisp one hundred dollar bills. Puffing a big stogie, he handed a hundred-dollar bill to Walter, one to Luke and three to the floozy. Despite qualms of conscience, Luke accepted it and thanked him, since this now meant he would be able to make it home to Jersey at last. Walter simply looked bemused. When the floozy touched Luke's foot with hers under the table, he jumped, spilling his rum and coke. After that, they all drove back to the big dark house and called it a day.

At six the next morning, Luke tapped on Walter's bedroom door. Bleary-eyed, Walter opened it a crack. Luke explained that he was getting an early start, adding, "Thanks for everything. Sorry, I yelled at you back in Colorado. See you in September, back at school . . ."

"I'm not sure I'll be going back," Walter said, yawning.

"Why not?"

"Dad wants me to stay and work for him," said Walter, not looking him in the eye.

"What will you be doing?" asked Luke.

"Don't ask . . ."

Luke heard a giggle behind the half-closed door. Walter looked him straight in the eye and said, "Oh, well, what did you expect? She said your door was locked . . ."

Luke stared at Walter for a long moment, and then waved goodbye.

Back on the interstate again, Luke drove hard across Indiana, Ohio, and Pennsylvania. But after slipping through the Delaware Water Gap around sunset, he took several back roads home. Finally, pulling in the driveway of his family home, he got out of the car, stretched and looked up at the stars. Going up onto the front porch, he rang the bell, half-expecting his dad to open the door with a smile.

Weeds Triumphant

T he metal door had been ripped from its hinges. Brother Ricardo stood barely breathing, leaning on his white, red-tipped cane, trying to take in the enormity of my description. "Are all the toys gone?"

Since he had lost all sight in one eye and was almost 75 percent blind in the other, he relied greatly on his volunteers' sight. As a deacon, during the six months of service before my priestly ordination, I was at his beck and call, his driver and faithful guide.

"We'd better call the police," he groaned.

Our big annual Christmas Eve toy giveaway was three days away. The poor kids from the neighborhood got a few toys to bring a little joy into their lives. Brother couldn't see them but he could certainly tell when the kids were smiling. The mothers, many of who were pushing baby carriages, had signed up weeks in advance. All would be in line before dawn on Christmas Eve but now—because of the robbery—we would have nothing to give them.

The cops shook their heads, as if to say, nothing could surprise them in South Central Los Angeles, even this. Murders by the truck-load, violent assaults, robberies, and general mayhem were all par for the course. But this—stealing little kids' toys just before Christmas—was too much.

I spent most of my time assisting Brother Ricardo in the St Michael's Social Outreach, where we helped more than six hundred families a month. Most were very poor, and not receiving any type of government aid. At least that was what they told us. One of my jobs, besides shadowing Brother, was to check out the new appli-cant's stories, to see if they were indeed telling the truth. Sadly, more times than not, they were lying. Instead of seven kids they had three. "No husband" meant they had a drunken, abusive, live-in boyfriend. Birth certificates could be easily faked and presented to any num-ber of do-gooder church aid organizations. It seemed the more fraud I uncovered the more cynical I became, to the point of not trust-ing anyone I had to interview. I began to assume, from the start, they were all lying. After a while I realized what a blessing it was for Brother to be almost blind. He had to accept a lot on faith and most people on their word, whether in Spanish or English.

The policeman who wrote up the report said they would do their best, which, unfortunately, meant precisely nothing. Under siege as they were, what could they do, anyway? All those toys, mostly donations from richer parishes in the San Gabriel Valley would be long gone, bartered for a pittance at swap meets or traded into few tiny vials of crack cocaine.

Brother Ricardo sat down on a folding metal chair in his little office, looking pretty dispirited. "What are we going to do?" he kept repeating. I wondered if it was a rhetorical question. I didn't answer, not knowing what to say. Working with the poor day after day often left me speechless. Unlike the romantic picture of them many people have, I found them to be often neither noble nor selfless, but just like everybody else, greedy and grabbing. I told myself that they were just trying to survive, and that if God loved them, so I should at least try to. After all, He never commanded us to like them. For example, one day that week, after handing a woman a bag of free groceries—service with a smile—she complained: "I don't like this kind of cereal. Don't you have any Cocoa Crisps back there."

"Sorry, ma'am," I grimaced, trying my darnest to reverence the presence of the Deity in this irritable, bothersome old windbag.

"Well this whole grained crap gives me gas!"

"I'm truly sorry to hear that . . ."

"You're damn right you're sorry. All you people do is say 'sorry,' but you're not sorry at all. Someday you'll be sorry, I can tell you that!" she ranted.

I murmured, "Have a blessed day, ma'am." I knew that if she would not leave I would have to forcibly show her the door or, in the worst case scenario, call the cops. Seeing that I was not about to search the shelves for something we didn't have stocked, she frowned at me, grabbed the two bags of food and hefted her considerable bulk up off the plastic chair, tottering for a moment. I leapt to catch her elbow to steady her. If she happened to fall, she would sue us for sure. Almost disappointed at my quick response, she summarized my period of service thus far, "You'll be sorry all right."

Brother Ricardo came out of his office, announcing, "Let us call the newspapers."

The *Times* was notoriously anti-Catholic and never printed anything that made it appear the Church did anything other than scandalize others. I thought about his idea as it formed in the air like a cloud between us.

"I doubt if they'd help us," If it was a story about how some fallen priest stole the toys to pad his retirement fund or, better yet, to pay off some secret mistress, then it would make the front page. I called the city desk anyway.

Brother Ricardo and the other volunteers began the onerous clean up, making an inventory of what we didn't have. The Santa suit I was supposed to wear hung like a scarecrow on its hanger behind the office door.

After lunch, a stringer for the *Times*, obviously doing his apprenticeship, dropped in, leaving his car parked out front.

"Is my car safe out there?" he asked, putting a role of new film in his camera.

"You'd better bring it inside," I deadpanned.

He noted my sarcasm, being so full of it himself.

The stringer extricated a small pocket notebook from his shirt pocket and began scribbling down my slightly dramatized version of the events.

I began with something I was pretty sure the reporter was unfamiliar with—the truth.

"We had over three thousand toys piled in the backroom, all donated by people who want these poor kids to have a nice Christmas. The thieves left only the broken ones . . ." After scribbling furiously for a few moments, the man disappeared, obviously worried about two hooded youths who walked by his car three times during the space of our short interview. I had little hope but tried to sound cheerful when Brother Ricardo asked me how it went.

"Super-duper," I said.

The next day, with just two days left before Christmas Eve, there was a front-page article by the boy journalist entitled. "Broken Toys, Stolen Dreams." Reading it aloud to Brother at the breakfast table, it opened his blind eyes: "A well-organized band of thieves stole not only a roomful of toys but the dreams of hundreds of poor inner-city kids . . . The St. Michael Christmas Toy Campaign, run by Brother Ricardo Stradapiedi, with help from a cohort of dauntless volunteers, were all prepared to . . . when . . ."

There was a picture of Brother with his cane and dark glasses standing in a room conspicuously empty of toys. His expression was perfect—a mix of despair and chagrin, with still an infinitesimal, almost unidentifiable trace of hope lingering on the edges of his mouth.

That afternoon, we did our stoic best to stave off the disaster that was ready to arrive in just forty-eight short hours. We called several other shelters and nonprofit organizations but there was no help to be had for the helpers. But just before we were about to close up for the day, there was a phone call. I answered it, ready to tell whoever it was that we were closed.

"Hello, my name is Colleen McDonald from Channel Four Action News," said, a well-modulated professional voice, cheerful yet compassionate.

I almost said, "Yeah, sure, and if we have Prince Albert in a can, let him out . . ."

The extremely pleasant female voice continued unabated, "We saw the article in the *Times* this morning and would like to come down to your Center tomorrow for an interview. It would make a good human interest story . . ." She ended, waiting for my response.

I still thought it was some sort of joke, "Come one, come all . . ." She ended by saying that she herself would come down first thing in the morning. Hanging up, I added, "Yeah, I'll believe that when I see it" Brother Ricardo smiled when I told him the news. Good news was a rarity in our neighborhood, and had to be savored before it inevitably turned sour.

Sure enough, the next morning, as we were removing the myriad locks and chains from the metal gate and door, a white van with a satellite dish on top pulled up to the curb like a knight's steed. The lady anchor herself pulled up behind it in a separate car. She was well dressed and seemed genuinely shocked at what had happened. Her perfect hair and smile stood out like diamonds in the dirt. She trained the camera on herself, on Ricardo, then on me for a few sound bites. Before disappearing like Glenda the Good Witch of the North, she asked for our address. We gave it to her along with whatever thanks we could muster. Most of the volunteers, not speaking any English, didn't understand exactly what was happening. They had disappeared into the back, thinking perhaps the well-groomed *Gringa* was from immigration. After her departure they stared out the front window, thankful to have escaped another raid.

Brother explained to them what was happening. They were disappointed. One less story to tell the grandkids. In fact, they didn't seem too perturbed about the situation in general. Their lives were already so full of thorns a few more made little difference. Besides, they guessed that the kindly Ricardo would no doubt give them whatever unbroken toys remained from the heist. I always suspected that this was why they volunteered to begin with. Once, I caught a couple of them carrying food out with them or hiding bags of clothing behind the Dumpster. With Brother's poor eyesight, they thought they would never get caught. But I kept an eagle eye out for the sneaky and dishonest. I warned them that God sees everything, but as time passed, I kept discovering more evidence of our smiling helpers' dishonesty. One day, driving by one volunteer's house I saw she was having a yard sale, full of stuff that she had pilfered from our Center. Brother didn't want to cut her loose, saying: "Weeds among the wheat, that's our life."

My response, was, "The weeds seem to be winning."

On the evening news that night, Colleen McDonald did a credible job pulling at the hardened heartstrings of the greater metropolitan area. Then, at the end, she actually made an impassioned personal plea. When the camera swung back to the whole studio, the other anchor, the sportscaster and even the weather-person were misty-eyed. Then our address flashed across the screen, asking the world for donations of toys. They were asking for a miracle.

The next morning by six, several cars and pickups were already parked out in front of the Center. They were people who had seen the broadcast the evening before—and were kindly bringing toys to replace those that had been stolen. Each one had arisen before dawn, risking the freeway traffic, and then overcoming their fears of venturing into the war zone of South Central. Most seemed embarrassed by our attempts at gratitude. And no one wanted a receipt for tax purposes. Now, I was surprised to find myself misty-eyed. I know Brother was very moved because he kept taking his dark glasses off to wipe them. His dark, sunken sockets were like watery wells. Our volunteers duly carried the replacement toys inside, all day long. Brother and I welcomed all the donors, incredulously thanking this nonstop parade of generous souls. By the end of the day we had collected several hundred toys. Brother's tanned face split into a big grin.

I hated to be a killjoy but I had to tell him the truth: "Brother, the good news is that we got a lot of donations today. But the bad news is, unfortunately, it's still not enough. At last count . . . let me see . . . There are seven hundred thirty-four toys plus a few odds and ends, Christmas decorations and the like . . ."

He pressed his lips together, removing the fixed smile that had taken possession of his face. "Even if we give only one toy to each child, at least half the kids will get nothing. *Niente!*"

"No, it's not going to be enough . . . You're right . . ." he sighed. The volunteers chattered cheerily in the backroom inspecting the new cache. Some were placing the nicest toys off to the side to be absconded with later.

"Well brother, we did our best . . ." I said.

"That's all the good Lord asks of us . . ." he said. "But what are we going to do? We have to be ready by dawn, tomorrow morning. Tomorrow's Christmas Eve. They'll all be lined up early, ready for Santa."

"Santa will be there because I'll be there," I snorted. "Maybe we can make some signs. Christmas means sharing! Share your toys with your brother and sister! One per *familia!*"

"That'll never work. There'll only be one policeman assigned as security too. There will be a riot." The brother was back to looking like his old self, worried as hell.

We needed the presence of law enforcement because in past years some unruly holiday fun-seekers had gotten greedy, and were not content with the toys they had been given. One black lady thought that the Latinos were being given more than the African Americans were. We separated them with difficulty.

"Maybe we should just forget the whole thing this year . . . Use the donations for next year." I suggested, half-hoping he would buy it.

With a voice of infinite sadness, brother said, "But this is why we're here—to help them . . . I know it's not much but it's something, even for one day . . ."

I could see the headlines in heaven: St Michael's Cancels Christmas.

We closed up and went to say Vespers together in the parish church across the street, thanking God for those kind souls who had responded to the televised appeal. After dinner, I returned to our store front to make sure all was locked up tight, tempted to even spend the night there—since thieves often returned to the scene of the crime. If they knew we had replaced some of the toys, they might come back. In fact, this is what I resolved to do, wrapping a blanket around myself, hunkering down next to the little nuclear space heater in the back office. About eleven PM I heard voices out front.

"Uh-oh," I thought. "Trouble! This is the time when the bad boys come out . . ." I ran to the phone ready to call the cops. Then there was a knock on the front door. I hesitated. Robbers rarely knocked and even less often used the front door. Perhaps they were simply being polite before they did their dirty work. I opened the metal door slowly, peering out into the dark. "Dam it! Someone stole the light bulb again!" I thought. Two hulking figures stood silhouetted against the street lamps. Their whispers stopped when they heard the front door hinges creak.

"Who is it?" I asked, afraid and irritated at the same time. I always got cranky when frightened. And believe me, at night there were plenty of scary things out there wielding guns and knives.

"Sir, we have come with a donation," One of the dark figures responded. I turned on an interior light that allowed me to see them better. At first, I thought they were cops or maybe highway patrol since they appeared to be wearing uniforms. Opening the door, the speaker approached and extended a big ham of a hand for me to shake, saying, "Sergeant Charles Webb, United States Marine Corp." The other soldier introduced himself too. I stammered out my name, almost saluting them both.

"We saw the news and the unit captain decided to send your kids some toys." He turned left oblique, pointing to a big trailer truck parked halfway down the block. "Permission to unload them, Sir?"

"By all means," I said. "In the old days the cavalry would ride to the rescue on horses, today they come in eighteen wheelers," I yelped joyfully.

"Yes, Sir," they both responded. I directed them around the back into the alley and up close to the back door, which had been boarded over. With a hammer, I knocked off the plywood and helped my two new friends empty the long trailer. It took us a couple hours, trip after trip, stacking everything neatly inside. There were all the latest toys, many of them heavily advertised on the boob tube. The kids would want these and no others. Plus, there was a big supply of sports equipment: bats, baseballs, gloves, soccer balls, footballs, basket balls. We were having a ball all right, right up until we finished emptying the big trailer. Then, the two marines said goodbye, driving off into the night. I breathed a deep sigh of gratitude, feeling my belief in the goodness of human nature being restored. Not everybody was a thief or an ingrate.

I was so excited I couldn't sleep. Walking around the big back room, I stared at the mountain of toys that had miraculously appeared. Just three days before, we faced certain disaster but now there was new hope. I couldn't wait to tell Brother. In fact, I didn't have long to wait. Around four in the morning I heard the tap of his cane on the sidewalk outside, followed by the rattle of keys, outside. He was coming to get things ready—that is—to somehow explain to the people already lining up outside why we would not have enough for them this year. I opened the door. He cocked his head, listening intently. He could always tell when someone was smiling. I said, "Brother, don't go telling them any lies . . . that Santa doesn't have enough toys . . ." But he didn't catch my meaning.

"But we must tell them . . . They will be so disappointed, but we owe it to them to tell them the truth . . ."

Guiding him by the arm into the backroom I turned on the light. His face looked confused by the sudden brightness, barely discerning a swirl of colors where yesterday there had only been dirty white walls. I told him the good news. He hugged me and promptly bumped into a pile of Barbies, knocking them all to the floor.

"Alleluia!" he shouted, "Now, hurry up and get dressed, Santa!"

All through the morning, one by one, the waiting parents ushered their kids into the decorated front room to meet Santa. And Santa did his best to greet the throng in both English and Spanish, believe me. The fat guy gave away toy after toy, two to each child. Most left happy and smiling, thanking us. Admittedly, Santa expected the kids to be grateful, but several of the boys, not getting the latest electronic video games, grumbled. One actually pulled on my fake beard, something Santa did not appreciate in the least. By the end of the day, I was not only exhausted but was getting more than a little fed up with such blatant ungratefulness. You would hand a brand-new, beautiful toy to some wide-eyed whelp and he would sneer, "This isn't what I wanted." Then both mother and child would stomp out, more dissatisfied customers.

"Better than a lump of coal, kid," I muttered more than once under my breath. To be fair, sometimes the mother would apologize for her spoiled progeny, but more times than not, the long line of mothers would complain about the long wait. The off-duty police officer, acting as our security guard actually had to break up two fistfights. So much for the Christmas spirit, I thought. In the end, the weeds appeared to be triumphing over the wheat once again. The last few families in line, however—those newly arrived immigrants, who had not signed up, and who were not yet spoiled by the system—hugged their gifts happily, with smiles as wide as Main Street, never expecting to receive such blessings. Throughout the whole long day, blind Brother Ricardo kept smiling too, imagining the joyful faces of the children.

A Room Called Morning

After several skirmishes, Loretta finally lost the battle. Giving in to her children, she moved in with the Sisters at the Ave Maria Extended Care Facility. That was a fancy name for Nursing Home. Her three offspring had long since moved away to Omaha, Tucson and Fremont respectively. The fact that she could no longer bathe herself, get dressed without help or prepare meals for herself—they felt—necessitated the selling of the only home she had ever known. It had been her childhood home, inherited after her own mother's passing. But the fact that there would be a chapel at Ave Maria eased Loretta's pain. The Presence made it possible for her to be present even there, in that place. Yet Loretta accepted this cross as a promise made long ago, a cross long foreseen, rough perhaps and overweight, but nevertheless, meant to be embraced. "Not my will but Thine be done." That had always been her prayer while digging in her backyard garden, in the cool of the evening, after a long day working the line.

And Loretta's prayers had always been answered by heavier crosses. For she had laboriously excavated an empty place in her heart a long time ago, one longing to be filled. Why should she be surprised if it was being filled with the passion. Once self-surrender became a habit, it was hard to shake. The hardest part was always the initial effort of accepting. After that, the embracing invariably led to deeper union signaled by a peace, deep down, far beneath the tempests raging on the surface. Since her children flew the coup, through years of caring for her alcoholic husband, she persevered, walking only by dark faith, believing yet hardly seeing, hardly hoping but never ever desperate. Her favorite psalms, committed to the safe harbor of memory, expressed her deepest feelings. Moving into the nursing home brought Psalm 69 to mind: "Save me, O God, for the waters have risen to my neck."

So it went, in what she knew would be the final act of her particular Passion play—like "sinking into the mud of the deep" where "the waves overwhelm." She knew that David the psalmist was speaking prophetically of the Christ's final hours on earth. Besides, she thought, a horse race was not won in the first quarter mile but only in the last furlong. The winner of this particular race would wear the crown of roses, made more glorious by the sheer preponderance of thorns.

Loretta knew that there were now states, doctors, nurses and hospitals that would snuff out her life legally, and without a Hippocratic qualm, throwing her old bones away like a useless rag. And they would do so thinking they were doing her a favor, saving her from possible future suffering. How hard it was for the world to understand that it was precisely in suffering that she had consummated her love once her husband had died. Accepting her daily death here below—and being purified by pain like fire in a furnace—she hoped she would not have to endure the necessary purging after death, in order to see her lover face-to-face. She praised God for the faithful sisters left who still defended life, from the first instant of conception in the womb until the last natural gasp.

Loretta did not complain about the fact that Omaha, Tucson, and Fremont—God bless them—rarely visited. They popped in only after visiting Disneyland with her grandkids. Once they had come to age, when she refused to leave their drunken daddy, they walked out the door and never looked back. "It is for you . . . that I have become a stranger to my brothers, an alien to my own mother's sons." If she felt called to leave him, that would be another story, but she didn't; in fact, just the opposite. And now she was apparently alone. The Son of Man, she surmised, was alone His whole life but especially at the end—why shouldn't she share his loneliness? Yet surely, the Holy Virgin was always close, suffering with Him. This assurance, she found, made her willing to suffer for the souls who did not know they were lost. She also prayed a lot for unwed mothers and for the souls suffering in the womb of Purgatory. Over the long years—reading the biographies of the saints—imitating them had become a source of delight, in what she considered her very mediocre, ordinary life. Yet it was the sacrifice of love her beloved demanded of her daily. It seemed that there was always more to give, because love was a deep well, dark but never dry, although it seemed that way at times. In her little room, she could not help weeping for her own sins and those of the world. It was not so much distress as desire that moved her. "I am wearied with all my crying, my throat is parched. My eyes are wasted away from looking for my God."

And now the time had come for her to die an anonymous death, bereft of almost all human consolation. In the eyes of the world she was no one, "weighing less than a breath"—but all would come to light and would be known when the time came. Heaven would take note of her every pain, humiliation and sorrow, until the last breath bridged the final abyss of eternity. That is what she had always been taught to believe as a child by her mother and the belief of a child remains when the mother has gone ahead. Besides the final consummation, her only daily desire was not to give offense to anyone—to be a good example to the nursing home staff. "Let those who hope in you not be put to shame through me."

The major stroke happened on a Friday during Lent. Rushing her to emergency surgery, they stemmed the bleeding hemorrhage by removing a small part of her brain. That was a blessing, because it seemed afterward that they had also removed her ability to worry, leaving only the capacity to live one minute at a time. She jokingly wished she had had such an operation years before. For Loretta, time did not mount up, with the present on top of the past, casting fearful specters toward the future. Rather, the past was safely gone, sliding slowly beyond memory, with nothing to be done about regrets but hand them over to her little Jesuit in Confession. The present was always knocking, with nurses checking blood pressure, swabbing and feeding, bathing, waking and giving medicines. Like the flagellation, it was one lash and one day at a time.

Since she now swallowed with difficulty she had begun aspirating, a prelude to pneumonia. The doctors checked her living will, and did a quick operation, plugging her stomach with a feeding tube so the overworked nurses would no longer have to take the time to feed her by hand. Bed bound, she could hear laughing in the cafeteria down the hall and was tempted to believe it was about her. "When I afflict my soul with fasting they make it a taunt against me." But no, that was foolishness. What was necessary, however, was still more self-giving. Since she had consciously offered her life so often, she trusted that the general intention was still in effect even if she could no longer bring the words to mind so readily.

At times, the drugs they were giving her made everything spin. Morning turned to night and dark to light again, like a top wobbling off balance. Her room was on the eastern side of the long, low building. The sun rose above the olive trees in the garden and entered her room to wake her up. At night, she thought she could almost see Him prostrate in the shadows, sweating blood in order to obey. She realized that this was her Gethsemane and did not want to sleep through the hour like the apostles, overcome as they were by fear and anxiety, so she resolved not to take any more painkillers. She would pretend to swallow them and then spit them out after the nurse left the room. The morning sun would fall fully upon her hospital bed, warming her face and making her arthritic bones ache less. In this way, Loretta was bathed in a luminous glow each morning. This was the time when the chaplain brought the viaticum to her. Although able to receive only the tiniest particle, this "way bread" for the last journey warmed her heart and she felt a tender caress. After swallowing the small host, it felt like the morning was entering inside of her. And each day began like the very first morning in Eden, innocent, when the world was young. It was there that she encountered her Lover in the garden, who spoke long and sweetly to her, as if she were once again a budding young woman. Her heart burst with desire. "In your great love, answer me, O God, with your help that never fails."

She knew she had always been a burden to Him, yet she intuitively understood that her small attempts at honesty could somehow lighten His burden. Moreover, she sensed that He used this willingness of hers—-to be displeasing to herself—like a key to open the closed hearts of many others laboring in the dark. The divine physician performed open-heart surgeries all the time, on people she had never met. And each time she felt Him removing more and more of her own heart, until she wasn't sure there was any light left. There was so much light her eyes could not take it in. Faith and despair danced in the darkness. Yet "even darkness is not dark for you."

Those hours endured like the sun, a thousand years or a day, it was all the same, for she knew she was being prepared for eternity, one morning at a time. Oddly, the nights grew longer but then suddenly shorter. As her breathing became more labored, they performed a tracheotomy, so she could breathe a little easier, like the great Holy Father from Poland. Now, there was one who knew how to live and how to die! Seeing him struggle to speak at his last public appearance at the window overlooking St Peter's Square, she wept for him and for herself. "I looked in vain for compassion, for consolers, not one could I find."

On that last morning, she awoke, with her Jesuit sitting by the bed with two of the sisters leading the Rosary. Their habits almost glowed in the bright morning sunlight. In fact, the three looked almost transparent to her. Looking through them, there was her old familiar room, the same as ever, but what was it, behind and beyond them—the Monet landscape on the wall had suddenly grown bigger and was struggling to escape the prison of its frame. She looked at each of their bright faces, unable to speak, yet trusting that they knew what she was thinking. She was so grateful to them—for this help. One last time, she struggled to sit up and searched for the crucifix on the wall behind them. Her eyes darted almost desperately left and right but for some reason could not find it. Her spirit then was cast down, into a darkening abyss, as if she was being sucked through a black hole in the bed. "As for me, in my poverty and pain, let your help lift me up," she cried aloud.

That's when she saw them—three black, gnarled stumps on short hairy legs, dancing around the bed. Then she knew these three had been allowed to tempt her throughout her life—to discouragement. This was the last temptation, their last chance, and they looked almost desperate, surrounded as they were by ever-growing light. She looked at one bright figure at her side and knew he was her guardian, encouraging her to fight. She breathed deeply and with one giant effort of will, threw the three deformed creatures down, where they slipped and scrambled, searching for a place to hide. When she laughed, they ran away, shrieking. An invisible crowd—the very air itself—cheered her on, and then began to sing.

When the sun rose above her visitors' heads, Loretta smiled at two new approaching figures, coming, not to bid her farewell but welcome. "The poor when they see it will be glad and God-seeking hearts will revive," she thought. These words seemed to take on particular forms, like small luminous clouds, before ascending into the great song now being intoned above and all around her.

With her strength completely spent, and her skin transparent in the streaming light, she closed her eyes and struggled for breath. The priest's mysterious prayer ended with a blessing, "Go in peace." The room groaned, with the walls contracting then expanding, and the ceiling heaving like a womb in the pangs of birth. And suddenly, there she was, standing and gleaming with an interior light, at the very peak of youthful vigor, penetrated by a warmth which sweetly, yet painfully purged her of the last shreds of self. And there before her, were two radiant figures—the king, and next to him, the queen mother—just as they had promised. Resplendent, Loretta bowed low and then was raised on high.

Forest of the Dead

W hen the three friends walked through the seminary doors, they thought they knew what to expect. It was their first trip to Washington DC, the first tentative step toward taking the bigger step in following the call. The weekend stay was not forever but it might possibly reveal to them their future path in life.

They stood there in the entrance, listening to the tall, thin seminarian give a simple orientation: "Meal times are breakfast at 7:30 a.m., lunch at noon. Afternoon recreation is on the lower level in the common room next to the gym. Happy hour starts at five but is only interrupted by dinner at 6:00 p.m." Their guide concluded his little discourse by saying, "Any questions?" David, Joe and Jude looked at each other. Had the seminarian actually winked at them, or was it their collective imagination?

David felt something important was being forgotten: "And the prayer times?"

The seminarian frowned slightly, looked at the three of them as if they had just landed from another planet, "Oh, that," he said. "Don't worry, we are all good Catholics here." Then he rattled off the times for Lauds, Vespers and the celebration of Mass as if he were reading a bus schedule.

The three friends were left standing there with their luggage as the seminarian disappeared down the hallway.

"Perhaps it was something we said?" Joe quipped, raising an eyebrow.

Another seminarian came by, looked at them through his sunglasses and without a word motioned them to follow him upstairs. Their rooms were on the third floor, next to one another, with a beautiful view of the National Shrine of the Immaculate Conception. Its blue mosaic cupola glinted in the setting sun.

After a few minutes, a bell rang. "That must be Vespers," said David. "Hurry or we'll be late." After some trouble finding the chapel, the three companions entered, and automatically looked for a holy water font to bless themselves, but finding it dry, genuflected in unison before kneeling down in the last pew. Two seminarians they had not yet met sat in the half-light rummaging through their breviaries, trying to locate the right pages. Joe, David, and Jude opened their own breviaries, ready for the two seminarians to begin. After some minutes of waiting, and seeing no one else enter the chapel, one of the two seminarians began by reading, not singing the hymn. The other listlessly sighed the antiphons and launched perfunctorily into the psalms. Everything was done as quickly as possible and without any pause for reflection. Dave noticed that the sanctuary light had been allowed to go out. The tabernacle stood in the dark, dusty alcove to the right of a makeshift altar that appeared to be a table garnered from a garage sale.

Asked about this, after their prayer was concluded, the sighing seminarian responded, "Oh, we got rid of the marble altar a long time ago."

"Hey, time's a wasting," chirped the other, pinching his comrade's elbow, "Happy hour's well underway." The three visitors again looked at each other, and then obediently followed the two seminarians downstairs into a crowded common room. All eyes turned to inspect the newcomers. The three felt very strange all of a sudden, almost like they were being inspected. A few furtive comments reached their reddening ears: "Oh look at the tall one . . . His jacket is so Sears and Roebuck . . . Oh, leave them alone, they just got here . . ."

David elbowed Joe who pushed Jude out front. All three, always able to know what their friends were thinking, wanted to beat a hasty retreat, away from that strange scrutiny. But all three hesitated to judge their new acquaintances at first sight. So they mingled, each accepting a frosty mug of beer. The alcohol dulled other warning signs until dinner which was served in a large, wood-paneled refectory upstairs. There, they were seated under the gaze of a gaunt, graying, middle-aged priest who stared at them under half-lidded eyes. Joe leaned toward his friends and whispered, "This guy is giving me the creeps." After a long period of uncomfortable silence, the man began asking them questions, one after another, but not the normal ones like: "Where are you from? How was the train trip down? Where did you do your undergrad studies?" Rather, with the same serpentine look, he asked, "Do you have girlfriends?"

The three were warned interiorly not to speak, and just keep eating. Laughing at some inside joke, the priest, who happened to be the Rector of the seminary, seemed to lose interest in the visitors, writing them off with a half-turn of his somewhat emaciated torso.

The tall seminarian that gave them their initial orientation at the door, suddenly stood up, and introduced the three formally to the thirty or so other seminarians seated at the long wooden tables. At first, he had a hard time getting their attention. It wasn't until the Rector cleared his throat that all quieted down. Again the friends became the object of disquieting looks. If they could believe it—in a seminary setting—they might almost have believed that they were the objects of a growing, collective hunger, as if they themselves were the next course on the menu. No thanksgiving prayer was said, all simply dispersed, perhaps to their rooms, to the common room to continue the happy hour, or to other outside destinations. Since it was exam week, the three imagined that many of the seminarians were going off to study in the campus library a block away.

They ignored the elevator and climbed the stairs up to their rooms, crowding into Joe's room to discuss things so far. They couldn't find words for the growing tension they were all experiencing. None of them wanted to admit the obvious.

"I guess we couldn't see the forest because of the trees," said David, shaking his head, "What do you say, fellas, let's get out of here."

They talked about packing up their things, then and there, and catching the next train back home. But after a long discussion, thought better of it and determined to stick it out until after their scheduled tour of the Catholic University of America the following morning.

A knock on the door silenced them. Jude had the distinct feeling that whoever it was had been standing outside their door, listening to their rather animated conversation before knocking.

It was the sighing psalmist who poked his head in, saying, "You're all invited to a little get together in the TV room. Come on down, we'll be showing a special film, very controversial . . . for mature audiences only . . . But you boys look like you can handle it . . ." With that, he disappeared as quickly as he had mouthed the psalms during Vespers, leaving the three friends with mouths agape.

"Let's go to the Shrine," said Joe.

They left without being seen through a side door. The Basilica of the National Shrine of the Immaculate Conception was open and the warm lights lead them straight into the Blessed Sacrament chapel. There they prayed silently until Jude began the recitation of the rosary. The three felt maternal arms surround them, comforting them, affording new strength. In whispers, they asked for the grace of their future lives. If the Lord was calling them, then He would protect them from all dangers. If God was for them who could be against? Returning to the seminary, they looked up to see someone resembling the Rector looking down at them from his office window. Once inside, suddenly out of nowhere, the tall seminarian approached them asking, "Now, where have you three wandered off to?"

David, all enthused by his first visit to the National Shrine answered, "To the Immaculate Conception."

"Oh . . ." said the tall seminarian, "we call that place the Blue Tit."

The tall seminarian, so very thin, began to shake with laughter, fully expecting them to join in.

"What did you say?" asked David, unable to believe his ears, that a seminarian could be so disrespectful of such a holy place. "You know . . . because the blue mosaic dome is shaped like a big breast complete with nipple on top. Hahaha." The tall seminarian was then joined by the sighing psalmist. Both obviously appreciated their own inside joke. Jude fought off an urge to punch them both in their snotty noses.

Joe said, in a low, menacing tone, "I don't know about you guys but where I'm from, if someone insults your mother, they had better watch out . . ." The implied threat of physical force did not seem to register with the two seminarians who now stood arm in arm.

Jude and David tensed, ready for anything. They knew their friend was quite serious. "So all the other guys are not out studying for exams in the library, are they?" David asked slowly.

"Oh no!" answered the tall one. "They're probably out at the bars by now! But don't worry, they'll be back later tonight to include you all in on some extracurricular activities." The tall seminarian and the sighing psalmist both laughed uproariously again. This time, the three friends were left in no doubt about the winking.

Joe asked incredulously, "And what about the Rector? What does he think of all these goings on?"

The two looked at each other, smirking, but the tall, thin one spoke pointedly: "Believe me, Father Rector's door is always open, if you know what I mean . . ." The two seminarians, after one last meaningful glance, disappeared down the stairs, giggling all the way. David, Joe and Jude did not hesitate any more. They bounded up the stairs, two at a time, grabbed their packed bags and hurried on out the front doors into the dark night They knew not where they would be spending the night, but they dared not look back for fear they would be turned into pillars of salt.

Her Hallowed Mystery

What he always feared was actually happening. In his second year of novitiate—the two-year period of spiritual preparation before first vows—Andrew was left alone in the mission church for a whole week. The two priests and deacon had gone to Guadalajara for the provincial assembly. He was terrified. Still struggling with the language, not yet being a priest, what good could a gringo seminarian possibly do in their absence? Rather, how much harm might come to pass if left on his own. The first night he could hardly sleep. *El Valle de Chalco*, which literally translated, meant "the valley of holes" was cold at night, being in the high plateau region between the sprawling Mexico City and the pristine city of Puebla two hours to the south. In between was this gargantuan place, filling up with squatters—more and more every day—all hoping to scrounge a better life nearer the urban area. There were no paved streets, no electricity—it was pilfered from the main lines near the highway—and little hope. All there was, smack dab in the middle of five hundred thousand poor people, was the little parish of Our Lady of Guadalupe, named after the famous shrine to the North. The people or parishioners—mostly *indios*—hailing from every possible *pueblito* in the country, held her in high regard, as the one who knew them and cared for them in their daily trials—of which there was no lack. The main church, along with twenty-seven chapels or outstations, comprised the mission. In the dry season, tornadoes of dust called *remolinos* roamed the valley, touching down to cover one's hair and clothes, penetrating everything with the finest brown dust. In the rainy season, one could sink up to the knees in mud. The novice Andrew now found himself in charge of this kingdom for the next seven long days. He earnestly prayed to the Blessed Virgin for help, since he knew he was helpless on his own.

The very first night, just after dark, a frantic pounding on the iron door frightened him practically out of his skin. Opening it there stood a short dark-skinned woman, who through her tears endeavored to explain her plight. Something terrible evidently had happened. That's all the young seminarian was able to make out. Andrew put on a coat, grabbed a flashlight and accompanied her through the winding pathways and cinderblock constructions to her ramshackle home where her husband, who was introduced as Jorge, was in serious condition. The day before, after finishing his twelve-hour shift in a factory in the city, a gang of robbers had beaten him bloody, stole his pay, and then for good measure, ran him over in their pickup truck—not once but twice. His right leg was so badly damaged it had had to be amputated. But since the family—wife and eight young children all living in the one cement block room—had no money, after the operation, the hospital refused further treatment. The only thing they could do was take Jorge home and pray. They all wept too, but after the rosary, with even the little ones taking part, everyone calmed down and eventually slept. Andrew returned to the parish in the pitch-blackness with rocks in his hands, ready to launch them at the roaming packs of dogs that ruled the abandoned alleys after nightfall. He made it home safely, exhausted by the ordeal, praying that Jorge would make it through the night.

The following day, catching up on some paper work in the parish office, there came another insistent knock on the door. "O Lord," he moaned, "not another tragedy!" He wondered how the poor managed, but then he knew the answer—one day at a time, by the grace of God. What money shielded the rich from, the poor were at the mercy of.

This time it was an *indio* couple, both dressed in their bright traditional ponchos. Most probably, they came from the base of one of the two volcanoes on the southern horizon, *El Popo* or *La Mujer Dormida* (The Sleeping Woman). Although they spoke little Spanish, they tried to explain the problem to him in their own indigenous dialect that, no doubt, had changed little from the time of Cortez. And Andrew, with his broken Spanish, somehow managed to understand. As was the case with the previous emergency, they wanted him to accompany them home, but he didn't quite understand why. He obediently followed the couple through the streets, which, after a morning downpour had become pools of rank water, through piles of garbage and debris, to their little hut, which consisted of pieced together plywood, mud and bricks. The ceiling was very low. And since there were no windows, it was dark inside. A small fire smoked in a grate below a blackened iron pot. Andrew smelled beans, the caviar of the poor.

In the middle of the room was a sort of platform, obviously serving as a bed. On top of this, under a heavy woolen serape blanket lay a little girl, apparently asleep. The worried parents pointed to the bundled form, gesticulating, imploring Andrew's help, or rather, God's help through him. He looked at them and then approached the little girl, gulping, and desperately imploring the divine assistance. She appeared to be about two years old and was not moving. But what could he do? His faith was much weaker than theirs? How foolish they must be to ask him, of all people, to pray for them. He touched the child's forehead which felt as cold as ice. Wooden crosses in a nearby potter's field revealed the fact that infant mortality was only too common in that valley.

"Have you taken her to a doctor?" Andrew asked the parents. They nodded but tried to explain that the doctor had sent them home, saying there was nothing further he could do. Andrew closed his eyes and wondered if they had been turned away for lack of funds. Then, he said to himself in English, "Lord, at least give me the strength to believe what I cannot feel!"

He called the two of them closer attempting to explain once again that he did not know what he was doing. Nevertheless, he led them in praying the Pater, three Aves to the Morenita, Our Lady of Guadalupe, and one Glory Be. Then he mouthed some halfhearted platitudes before returning to the parish. He expected to hear from them soon, informing him of the death of their beloved daughter. Along with two assistants from the youth group, he spent the following day painting a mural on the wall behind the main altar. It showed Our Lady resplendent, giving instructions to Juan Diego, telling him to go to the bishop. God's mother wanted a church constructed on Tepeyac hill. Of course, Bishop Zumaraga didn't believe the poor *indio* and sent him away, demanding more proof. Juan Diego, hoping to avoid another encounter with the mysterious lady, went home by another route. But she intercepted him, ordering him to pick the roses flowering on the crest of the hill. Then she gave him the roses to wrap in his *tilma*. These were to be the sign for the doubting bishop, since roses could never be grown during winter. Upon opening his *tilma*, the roses fell out on to the floor, thereby revealing a perfectly painted image of the Woman Clothed with the Sun. What the conquistadores could not accomplish by the sword was done in a few months by heaven. Over the next couple years, seven million Aztecs and Mayans converted to the faith, not by the sword but because of love. The woman was dark like them, but more importantly, she was revealed as a mother who loved them. What more did they need? While painting this lively scene, Andrew contemplated the great faith of such people, the same faith that had sustained them up to the present day. The man who had lost his leg was the spitting image of Juan Diego. In the little indigenous couple flowed his blood as well as his simple belief.

A second day passed without news about the little sick girl. But on the third day, there was another knock on the office door, but this time early in the morning, as the sun was rising. It was the mother and the father again. Bowing and smiling, they chattered excitedly in their own dialect, practically dragging him out the door, all the way back to their ramshackle hovel. The tears in their eyes told him the little girl had finally died. The way the two of them kept crying out and looking up to heaven, he figured this was the way they expressed grief in their particular indigenous culture. Bowing down to enter the low doorway, it took a moment to adjust his eyes to the dim scene before him. There was the cooking fire beneath the ever-present pot of beans, like the eternal flame of hope. And there, in the center of the cramped space, was the raised platform bed. But it was empty. Even though he had been preparing himself for the worst, his heart sank when he saw that the little girl was not there. Perhaps they had already buried her, he thought, and without a funeral. Looking at them for an explanation, neither one said a word, but in response, both simply pointed to the dark corner of the room.

"Oh no," he thought, "Her body is over there."

He peered into the blackness and then suddenly heard a noise. If he didn't know better, he could have sworn it was laughing. Then, all of a sudden, emerging from the dark sprang the little girl, curly-headed, smiling, and bubbling with glee. She clutched a worn-out, homemade doll in her arms. She ran right up to him and showed him the pathetic, dirty rag as if it were the most beautiful thing in the world. Andrew picked the little girl up, hugged her and began to ball like a baby himself. Tears of joy, like her parent's, rolled freely down his cheeks. The three adults smiled and chuckled at her antics for some time, praising heaven for hearing their cry, and thanking the Mother of God for not being like the sleeping mountain, La Mujer Dormida. Andrew returned to the parish for the remaining three days of his week alone, before the return of his confreres. Savoring the experience, he found that he no longer felt afraid. And the painting too was almost finished. His two fourteen-year-old assistants were painstakingly putting the final details on the flowers growing at the feet of the beautiful, dark-skinned lady.

Three months later, the day before he was to return to the States, for the period of immediate spiritual preparation before his first religious profession of vows, the pastor, asked him to lead the early morning procession of the Rosary to one of the little far-flung chapels dedicated to the Virgin. Consequently he rose while it was still dark, found a group of faithful already gathered outside in the muddy street and began intoning the familiar prayers. The crowd, growing as the procession advanced, responded, carrying lit candles. They stopped in front of certain houses to mediate on the dolorous mysteries. The diminutive *indio* couple emerged from their humble home carrying their sleeping daughter. Both prayed with great fervor, flanking their *padrecito* who was carrying the statue of Our Lady Guadalupe.

The last stop before reaching the chapel was at Jorge's house, the poor fellow who had lost his leg. The man emerged, balancing his weight on two crutches. Accompanying the procession along with his wife and children—his bandaged stump swinging along with the incense thurible—he seemed to gain strength with every step.

This Humble Tourist

When the phone rang at 11:33 p.m., I hesitated answering, because I knew who it was—an old friend with an even older problem. Wishing that I had an answering machine, and feeling guilty about such a thought, I picked up the receiver, forcing a smile on the eighth ring. There was the familiar sound of breathing and the voice, unmistakable yet unintelligible for almost anyone but me. For some reason, I had always been able to understand Doug's torturously slow and distorted speech patterns. Of course, one realized that he was laboring mightily, struggling to communicate his meaning. Yet over the phone, without being able to visualize the context, deciphering his message was at times a challenge.

On this particular occasion, however, I knew exactly what he was saying because I had heard him echo the same refrain many times before. The "hello" was a groan that ended in an extended sigh. I took a deep breath and asked the million-dollar question: "OK, Doug, what's her name?"

Half laughing, half-choking, with a tremendous effort he managed to say, "Elizabeth."

"Doug, Doug . . ." I began with soothing tones. The next question followed automatically, "How old is she? I hope you're not robbing the cradle again, buddy."

"Eightteeeeeeen," he sighed, waiting for my reaction.

"A freshman, uh? Well, at least, she can vote, buy alcohol, and join the army," I said cheerfully. My attempt at lightheartedness silenced him altogether, as I knew it would. For this is what he wanted—that I run the gamut of expected inquiry.

"So where did you meet this one?"

"In the cafeteria . . ." The University of Colorado where Doug was getting his Master's Degree in Social Work had a large, well-supplied snack bar.

"Ah, I figured you might be parking your super-scooter there for more than the French fries." His electric wheelchair was capable of light-speed.

An attempted laugh meant the conversation was right on schedule. Discussing Doug's latest infatuation always made him feel better, as if words made such a relationship more of a possibility. For him, talking about a girl, even ten years younger, somehow placated his feelings and longings. I felt guilty for encouraging him even in a left-handed sort of way by playing the devil's advocate.

The moment to introduce a strong dose of reality arrived. "Dougie boy, if I've said it once I've said it a thousand times, you know what your problem is . . ."

Indeed, knowing what I was going to say—having heard it so many times before—he finished my thought, "I keep falling in love."

"You got to stop doing that, big guy."

"I can't help falling in love again."

"Yeah, you and Elvis. You've got to control yourself. Stop being so damned charming."

"Can't help it."

"I know, I know, you're irresistible." And he was, in his own way. Seeing Doug, seated in his wheelchair, staring longingly at an unreachable food counter invariably attracted nice, well-meaning, even charitable, young coeds to help. They were always coming to his aid. But before they knew it, they were sitting by his side at a table, amazed that they could understand his Cerebral Palsy drawl. Then, about midsemester, one would be chosen. She would be the ONE he would fall out of his battery-powered wheelchair over. This time, it just happened to be Elizabeth.

Usually Doug's love interest hailed from the university parish, the after-Mass-free-coffee-and-doughnut-student-crowd or the Bible-study group. So this new girl was something of a novelty.

"You don't want me to fall in love," he accused me, as I knew he would.

"It's not that, Doug, it's just that I don't want you to get hurt again—like all the other times."

"You don't think a girl could fall for someone like . . . mmmeee . . ." his voice trailed off sadly.

"How could they not love you, Doug, my friend? Everybody loves you! All the girls love you . . ."

"But not in that way . . ." Another deep but not unexpected groan punctuated the conversation. We both realized it was time for the wrap-up.

"Doug, all I'm suggesting is—why don't you look for someone you have more in common with . . ." I always felt terrible saying this.

Doug could walk with great difficulty with the aid of a walker. He was even something of a world traveler. On campus, he always managed to make friends with students who lived in parts of the country he had never visited before. So just before summer break, he would plan his itinerary. The man had it down to a science—planes, trains, buses, automobiles, even hot air balloons. He even came to visit me once at the seminary I was attending in New Jersey. Warning him repeatedly of an impossibly steep stairway, he came anyway, hauling himself laboriously up, step by step, to the guestroom. I had warned him, half-hoping to dissuade him from coming to visit me at all, since it was a busy summer, but if there was one thing I learned about Doug was that he had a will of iron. His body was twisted by the disease but the man was unstoppable once he set his mind to something. To a great degree, he was a shining example of how to overcome a debilitating handicap through grace and sheer determination. And Doug was smart too. All kinds of well-meaning people made the mistake of thinking, that just because he talked funny, he was stupid. Just read the term papers he painstakingly typed out on his old Smith Corona—using nothing but a pencil gripped between his teeth. In his own way, I suppose, he was like the famous Stephen Hawking, but without the Nobel Prize or gargantuan ego.

His voice brought me back to the matter at hand: "You mean—I should look for a handicapped girl."

With all my heart I wanted to say, "No," but ended up answering, "Yes, that's exactly what I mean." Dead silence. This time, I could tell he was really depressed, and with each episode, he sank lower. Of course, living alone didn't help. But it would be much worse at his folk's farm just outside of town, with his younger brother stricken by Multiple Sclerosis. Imagine having only two sons like that—the first deprived of oxygen to the brain at birth and the second deteriorating daily. The aging parents, patient as could be, would love both of them until death, whoever died first. Besides, Doug did not want to live at home. With some help from the city, he occupied a ground-floor one-bedroom apartment near campus that was accessible to public transportation. I gave him many a ride, however, because, believe me, Dougie-boy maintained a busy social calendar. First, I would load him in the front seat followed by his chair or walker in my miniscule hatchback. Then I would drive him wherever even as he drove me crazy.

Suddenly, the lightning bolt of inspiration struck. "Doug, as you know," I began, wondering at the words pouring out of my mouth, "I have to drive back to the seminary in Jersey next week—

why don't you come with me. Goretti—the exchange student from China is coming. She wants to see the country before she heads home to Hong Kong."

I don't know why I offered, but true to form, the man did not hesitate. "OKAY!" he whooped.

"No, really, Doug, I want you to take your time, think it over . . ." I said the words purposefully, knowing full well what I was getting into. Four to five days in a cramped compact car, with potty breaks, gas stops, photo opportunities, and more.

"Goretti?" he asked.

"You remember her, from the Saint Thomas Study group two years ago . . . Hey! Don't get any ideas!" I warned, "What happened to Elizabeth, all of a sudden? Goretti only wants to see the sights between the Rockies and the East Coast, nothing more. There will be no falling in love for you on this trip, is that clear?" He laughed, then hung up, relatively mollified. It was my turn to shake my head.

"Oh well," I thought, "Everybody needs something to look forward to. At least, the trip took his mind off his problems . . ."

We packed up and left the following Wednesday—midweek to traverse the middle of the country. It was a tight fit, with all my luggage and Doug's wheelchair crammed in the back. Luckily, Goretti traveled light. She had just finished her engineering degree and was ready to see roads and bridges. On top of that, she had what is often described as a bubbly personality, so she was always breaking out into song. She coaxed the two of us to warble along with her across the Great Plains. We stopped every couple of hours to give our limbs a stretch and our strained voices a rest. We ate only at the greasiest spoons. Both my passengers were tickled pink by the goofiest things. Doug hung his head out the window to imitate the cows we passed, "MMMmmmoooOOOHHH!" Goretti, for her part, innocently waved at all the truckers passing us. As for me, seeing the two of them enjoying themselves so much, I spent my time watching the road ahead, listening to the two of them make noise. Wherever we stopped, small groups of curious locals would stare at us like we had just landed from another planet. I was a little afraid some overzealous state trooper would arrest us for just having too much fun.

"This land is your land, this land is my land . . ."

Thus, Doug, Goretti and their driver sang our way across the miles. When we weren't singing we were talking, each in our own way—English, Cantonese, and, of course, Douglese. Amazingly again, like three misplaced apostles on the day of Pentecost, we all seemed to understand each other just fine.

The first night we stayed at the home of an elderly couple in Kansas City, Kansas. Doug had made their acquaintance at a conference on campus that winter, promising to come visit. Presto! "Here we are!" Not just one but three stooges. The next morning, after thanking them, and finding ourselves on I-70 once again, I quipped, "We made those nice folks twice glad—glad to see us come and glad to see us go!" Doug thought that was pretty funny.

The next stop was Cincinnati, Ohio, where Doug knew an unsuspecting undergraduate and his family. Then followed the long, hilly trek across Pennsylvania. Goretti sang on unabated but I could tell Doug was tiring, so I resolved to push on until we reached our destination in northern New Jersey.

After a particularly exhausting day for all three of us, we slipped through the Delaware Water Gap, arriving just in time for dinner. We ate, drank, and joked with my sister and her family over Bar-B-Q in the back yard. My two-year-old niece took a particular liking to Doug because he let her use his walker. The two of them—she with her baby talk and he with his own brand of banter—seemed to understand each other perfectly. The very next day we hit New York City for a play. We were the happiest people at *Les Miserables*. The day after that it was the city of Brotherly Love, Philadelphia, where Doug kept making cracks about the Liberty Bell.

The Italians have a saying, "After three days, the guest, like the fish, begins to stink." So on the third day, it was time to load my two companions up and take them to their respective planes and trains. My very patient brother-in-law drove us to Newark International Airport where we bid fond adieu to Goretti, who was heading back to Boulder for a few days before returning to Hong Kong where she planned on working for her father's engineering firm. A few short years later, after the city would be handed over to China by the

British, she would choose to stay, convinced that 1.3 billion communists needed cheering up.

Doug, we brought to Newark's downtown Union Station. While my brother-in-law parked, I waited in line to buy Doug's ticket to Washington, DC, which was the next stop on his summer agenda. Finally extricating myself from the line, I could see Doug take off for the narrow escalator that led to the train platforms above.

"Hey, Doug, wait up!" I yelled. But either he did not hear me or was ignoring my plea in order to prove his independence. As I struggled with his luggage, my fears were suddenly realized. Entering the narrow escalator with his walker, the thing seemed to swallow him whole, whisking him upward beyond my reach. Three other travelers ensconced themselves between us before I could jump on to the rotating metal steps myself. Another call to Doug, to "be careful at the top," went unheeded. I could see him above me, moving inexorably toward the summit. Doug, the fearless explorer, was showing me that he didn't need my help. Not for the last time did I remember that his was a will of iron. This time, literally, there was no stopping him—from being spewed out at the top of the escalator onto the platform which lay between two sets of busy train tracks. I made one last futile effort to squeeze by the three people on the escalator in front of me, but it was no use. Disaster ensued.

The whole scene seemed to unfold before me in slow motion. I shouted, seeing what was happening, but my words were unintelligible, just like Doug's cry of alarm when he realized his danger. Popping him out the end of the rapidly moving steps, he shot out on to the crowded platform just as his Metroliner was pulling in from New York. Falling into a heap of arms and legs at the feet of two old black ladies, the crowd gasped, thinking his inertia would throw him over the edge of the platform in front of the oncoming train. Startled by the noise and clatter, and alarmed by the drama of my friend's crash, the two well-meaning, church-going African American matriarchs began to scream, flapping their arms in terror. As Doug's forward motion stopped, they saw me run up, and assuming me to be my brother's keeper, vented their fears upon me. There, in front of the conductor, who had just exited the Metroliner, calling "All aboard!" and the rushing crowd, the two old ladies scolded me like I was their wayward nineteen-year-old nephew.

"What kind of fool are you! Why weren't you watching him?! Couldn't you see he was falling?! Don't you see that this poor boy needs help?" It was useless to argue, since I could see that, once again, even without trying, Doug had gotten women to feel sorry for him. Their verbal diatribe petered out as they climbed onto the waiting train. Having done their good deed for the day, they never looked back. If they had, they would have witnessed my exasperated effort at getting Doug back up on his feet again.

"Why are they yelling at me?" I glared at Doug. "They should be yelling at you—for not waiting for me, for going up that escalator ahead of me . . ." With the two ladies gone, my own nervous adrenaline ground to a halt. Picking up both the walker and my friend, I had to admit that neither one seemed the worse for wear. He actually had the nerve to mimic the two defenders, "Yeah, what kind of fffooolll are you?"

"You're impossible!" I said, grim-faced.

"Terrible!" he countered.

"Pig-headed!" I shouted quite serious but starting to calm down.

"Last call! All aboard, Washington DC!" called the conductor, eyeing first us and then his pocket watch with a frown.

There we stood, the last people left on the platform. I hurriedly pushed him inside the compartment entrance along with his luggage. There was no time to say much, because the train had begun to pull away, so I yelled, "Doug?"

"What?"

"You make me twice glad!"

As the train pulled away, I could hear him shout back, "Glad to see you come and glad to see you go!"

As the train picked up speed—even above the engine noise and clanking wheels—I thought I heard him add, "I'll call you . . ."

Catching my breath, I smiled, knowing that he was not lying. And although I might hesitate, I knew I would surely answer that call.

Upon a Daily Street

After the ten o'clock Mass on Palm Sunday morning, the family stopped at Kim's minimarket on Fifty-Second Street across the park. The Passion of the Lord had been proclaimed and meditated upon. All cried out "Hosanna!" and just a few short minutes later, "Crucify him!" The three daughters, two young teens plus their baby sister picked out candy and, to their mother's chagrin, managed to persuade their *Papi* to pay for it. Going outside again, all headed for the aging Ford minivan. Four-year-old Erica's mother strapped her into her back-seat car seat first before her two older sisters climbed into the back next to her and buckled up. Both father and mother saw the young black man pass behind them, between them and the store. What they saw too late, however, was a late 1960s model Chevrolet swerve around the corner in front of them, unrolling the passenger side windows, while rapidly gaining speed. The barrels of two guns emerged and were aimed at the African American teen, who, hearing the screech of their wheels, sensed trouble and began running toward the side alley. Several bullets strafed the red minivan, shattering the windows. Living in South Central Los Angeles, it was an all too common an experience. The whole family instinctively ducked down—all except Erica who was already strapped into her car seat.

Even as the Chevy pealed away, the father rose from his crouching position to check on his youngest, inside the van. To his shock, the little girl's face was covered with blood. He undid the buckle and, pulling her thin body from the seat, held her close to his heart in a vain attempt to stay the bleeding. Erica had been hit in the head, just behind the temple. Realizing what happened, her mother and sisters screamed, while her father ran with her in his arms into the minimarket for help. The Korean owner didn't have to know Spanish to recognize the gravity of the situation. Having been robbed on numerous occasions, he was well-versed at calling 911. The police and the paramedics arrived quickly, rushing the little girl off to the emergency room of County USC Hospital, a fifteen-minute freeway ride away. The mother rode in the ambulance with her oldest daughter Janet, while one paramedic radioed the hospital, telling the emergency room staff what to expect. The other paramedic tried desperately to staunch the blood which continued to flow from the wound. Erica's short black hair was now bright red, as was her best Sunday dress. The father, accompanied by the middle daughter, Dorothy, followed in the minivan.

Finally arriving at the hospital, Erica was removed to a side room to be prepped for immediate surgery. This was unusual, since on the mean streets of Los Angeles, the victims usually had to get in line for emergency room help. The body bags of the poor with no insurance piled up in the morgue. In their parish area alone, the previous January saw eleven murders, all gang-related, only one of which was reported by the mainstream English language media. The *LA Times* gave them a one-inch blurb. Regarding Erica, the English language TV stations reported nothing at all—it was news deemed too depressing for their clientele. The Spanish language channels, however, soon got wind of it-and rushed to the hospital. "*La pequena Erica*" was soon the subject of constant reports and updates. Both parents as well as the two teenage daughters, Janet and Dorothy, were interviewed. For their Hispanic viewers, it was another tragic tale of what happens to poor immigrants whose American dream had turned into a nightmare.

Their parish priest, Father Philip got the call and rushed to the hospital, waiting with the family for the outcome of the six-hour long surgery. In the Post-Op room, he anointed Erica and soon discovered that their worst fears were realized—that there was nothing to be done. Despite the evidence, he encouraged the weeping family to have faith. After all, it was Holy Week. Erica's heart was still beating so she was not put on a ventilator. The priest visited several times, encouraging her parents and sisters to stay with her in shifts so the others could get some much-needed rest. The whole parish, urged by Father Philip, invoked the Almighty day and night. Over the next three days, the little girl battled valiantly, clinging to life, until—on Holy Thursday—her brainwaves flat-lined. But Erica kept breathing. By Thursday evening, when the parish celebrated the Last Supper, Erica was finally put on a ventilator. The Spanish language television channels reported this news, and the whole barrio waited in suspense. The child's family sweat blood that night in their own garden of Gethsemane.

At nine the morning of Good Friday—the day of the Crucifixion—it was mutually decided to take Erica off the ventilator. After a few tense moments, she quietly died. By noon, her death certificate had been signed and her body was released to the mortuary where it would be prepared for burial. At three that afternoon, the faithful gathered to follow the Way of the Cross, which was being dramatically reenacted by the youth group outside in the parking lot. They had practiced every day for a month. It was a full production, complete with costumes, dialogue, live music and lots of ketchup to simulate blood. The parking lot of the church was jammed with both the curious and the devout alike, and many commented on the fact that the young man portraying the martyred Messiah did a masterful job. But everyone agreed that the two young women—Janet and Dorothy—playing the Sorrowful Mother and Mary Magdalene, respectively—were truly inspired. Gazing up at the bleeding body hanging lifeless on the Cross, they wept. Many in the audience, not knowing they were little Erica's sisters, wondered how the two young actresses were able to summon so many real tears. Easter Sunday seemed to be just another beautiful spring day in sunny southern California.

On Easter Monday, the day after the Resurrection, Erica's funeral Mass was celebrated in a packed church. Her parents and sisters stood in the front pew, peacefully resigned. Fr. Philip gave a brief but heartfelt sermon. The television cameras were nowhere to be seen.

Each Beloved Hour

On the day of the big fire the alarm buzzed on the night-stand as usual—five in the morning. Fr. Fred reached over, tapped the ten-minute delay, and then groaned. Just a few more minutes. He'd stayed up late the night before again. Not doing anything in particular. He just couldn't sleep. And for how many nights now? Though tired most of the time, there were times when he just couldn't bring himself to go to bed. At the same time, his body craved sleep. He knew he was sleep deprived and was suffering the clinically chronicled effects.

He was forty-seven, twenty-five pounds overweight, with a graying, balding head and a forced, friendly demeanor. A smile of sorts arched habitually over a sagging chin. Whenever any well-meaning parishioner sent photos of their baptisms and weddings, he promptly tore them up.

Father Fred's own father had died three years before, after six years of paralysis due to a series of strokes. At the funeral, from the pulpit—preaching in the presence of his own deceased dad's corpus—the priest noticed his mother looking none too well. Two weeks afterward, a doctor sent her home with an aspirin. A month after that, she was diagnosed with cancer. It was a long year watching her melt away before his very eyes.

Monthly, during his mother's chemotherapy, he attempted to describe his own slow death to his well-meaning spiritual director. The kindly old Jesuit listened and said feeling depressed was all quite natural. But he always left Fred wondering what was so natural about a priest not wanting to live anymore? Although he recognized that his intentions were not pure like those of St Paul, he often wished the race were already run.

He felt like an open wound that if touched would recoil and then strike out in unexpected ways. Sometimes he would get angry for no apparent reason but mostly he would just stay locked up in his room alone. It seemed more charitable not to reveal the true state of affairs to his bishop, to his parishioners, and certainly not to his family. His few friends drifted away one by one. He hoped to spare them all.

There was one brother priest, however, whom he would call occasionally, usually late at night—Father Joe, a transplant from New Jersey who spoke with an accent and wrote articles on Social Justice for the local diocesan newspaper. Fred phoned Joe the night of his mother's death. Joe invited him over for lunch the following day. After a meal of Memphis Bar-B-Q, they talked the whole afternoon. And Fred felt a little better, that is, until he returned to his own empty rectory. The long weeks passed slowly by, like heavy-laden barges down the Big Muddy.

The parish secretary, Fred knew, resented his intrusion on her turf. She was a fixture long before his transfer to St Joseph's two years previous, and she let him know in countless little ways that she would be there to see him off. A series of well-planted comments, thrown like poisoned seeds into the eager ears of like-minded parishioners, ensured the gossip mill its grist. "He's antisocial . . . He drinks too much . . . He sleeps too much . . . He doesn't sleep at all . . . He's always in his room . . . What does he do up there all day . . . . His sermons are too long . . . His homilies are too short . . ." Most of these people were still emotionally attached to the revered Monsignor O'Fallon who had been more an indulgent grandfather than a watchful father. It was he who had built St. Joseph's thirty years before. Out of misguided loyalty, his faithful followers wrote regularly to the Bishop, complaining about his successor. Father Fred believed them capable of murmuring against Jesus Himself, that is, if the Son of God were to have the extreme misfortune of being assigned there. When preaching on Sundays, he could see them checking their watches.

Father Fred could not help but think about all these people who didn't like him. Praying for enemies took on a new meaning. The worst part was that he found it so hard to pray. He still believed, but even the devils did as much. God was surely present everywhere yet seemingly nowhere to be found. After all, hadn't he given up everything to serve? Well not exactly everything—to assuage his deepening depression, his drinking was getting worse.

On the day of the fire, he awoke, struggled out of bed, showered, and prayed his breviary like always. After this, he went downstairs and put on a pot of strong coffee. The phone rang. Since it was only seven-ten AM he didn't pick it up. But what if someone was dying in the hospital, needing the Last Rites? He finally answered it but whoever it was hung up without a word. He ate some cereal with a cut-up banana. It was a quiet morning, so he worked on the books together with the secretary. Even though he knew she disliked him, he found himself depending more and more on her to do things. She looked at him knowingly. Many parishioners openly voiced their opinion that she was the real pastor of the parish. At midmorning, he went out to buy some cleaning supplies. He tried to say the Rosary while driving, even though he cursed a reckless driver who cut him off. A counseling case appeared just after lunch. He advised patience, the only thing he knew he lacked. Afterward, he went into the church to clear spent candles and sit for a few minutes before going off to the adjoining parish for the monthly deanery meeting. Fr. Joe was not there. The other priests all laughed and seemed to genuinely enjoy each other's company. He tried to join in and to smile as much as possible. No one was the wiser when he left early, pleading pastoral duties.

Once home again, he went up to his room and put on some music. But even Mozart didn't help calm his nerves. He wrote a six word outline for his Sunday sermon in the dust on his desk: "Perfect loves drives out all fear." For dinner, he wolfed down a piece of cold pizza left over from the night before. Then he answered the phone because the secretary had mercifully gone home. He then went over to the church hall to make an appearance at the prayer group's weekly meeting, staying only a couple minutes. As he walked over to the church, it started to snow, an unusual occurrence in those parts. Entering by the side door, he found it completely dark except for the little red candle flickering beside the Tabernacle. For a while, he stood staring up at the barely illuminated cross from which hung the tortured body. Then he went over to the side altar, knelt down and lit a candle to the Blessed Virgin. Maybe that's where it started. No one could ever quite figure out how the fire started. He did remember exiting the church by way of the sacristy side door, and didn't notice anything unusual. Returning to the rectory, he didn't see the large stained glass windows beginning to glow in the northern transept. Once inside the rectory, he opened the bottle of Chivas Regal his brother had given him for his birthday, poured two fingers worth over the rocks and drank it. That's when he heard cries and a growing commotion outside. Someone was banging on the rectory door, shouting. Jarred from his lethargy, he jumped to his feet and knocked over the bottle of whiskey. Opening the door, a man from the prayer group, yelled, "The Church is on fire!" Stunned, he just stared at him. The man smelled the whiskey on his breath while lunging past him for the phone sitting on the hall table.

It wasn't until the fire trucks arrived that the priest realized that his attempt to drag the cold stiff garden hose across the parking lot would do little good. And even though no one had seen him enter or leave the Church that evening, he readily confessed the fact to the first fireman he met. With that information, the police seated him in the back of a locked squad car. The faces of the prayer group reflected the leaping, orange conflagration in their widening, horrified eyes. They had been praying for the fire of the Holy Spirit to descend and renew the face of the earth, but never expected this. Shaking their heads, they saw the patrol car taking their pastor away.

The chief interrogator at police headquarters wanted to know why he did it. Waiving his right to a lawyer, Fr. Fred repeatedly said that he didn't do anything. Another officer pressed him about other arson cases, fires smoldering in mostly Protestant churches throughout the South. Despite the lack of witnesses or other evidence, charges were quickly filed and the shocking story filled the local newspapers. Most of his parishioners felt betrayed, believing what was plainly presented in black and white. In the evening news, their ex-pastor, Monsignor O'Fallon waxed poetic about his beautiful church, beautiful no more. At the news conference the next morning, flanked by a gaggle of attorneys, the bishop looked grave.

Father Fred used his only phone call, not to call an attorney but to call Father Joe. It was Father Joe who obtained legal expertise, and who, in turn, tried to get the Judge to consider a psychiatric exam before trial. Wasn't it obvious the man was severely depressed? But the Judge, being a good Baptist, up for reelection in the anti-Catholic Bible Belt, overruled the motion, thinking that an arsonist priest must be made an example of. The testimony of the firemen hurt the most. Fr. Joe and a couple of the faithful testified on his behalf. But several more recounted his odd behavior of late. His fate was sealed by the prayer group's testimony. An empty bottle of whiskey found in the rectory had Fred's fingerprints all over it. After a short trial, Father Fred was sentenced to four years in federal prison near Belleville, Illinois, just a few miles away from the Shrine dedicated to Our Lady of the Snows.

Once a month, like clockwork, Father Joe made the drive out to visit prisoner no. 67534. The Bishop never visited him but did write one letter, advising Father Fred to consider leaving the priesthood. The prisoner should not offer Mass or hear confessions either. Doing so would incur canonical censure. It was a low security prison for white-collar criminals, so there was television and ping-pong. The time passed slowly, each day a repetition of the previous one. Fred, however, found that he did not mind the routine so much. He found himself beginning to pray at the oddest times, even while sitting on the stainless steel toilet in his cell, but mostly in the middle of the night when the snoring chorus of his fellow inmates raised the roof. Working in the prison's carpenter shop, he never once was tempted to see how the wood would burn. Nevertheless, he often thought about the smoldering pews of St. Joseph's.

Starting with his cellmate, Tom the Embezzler, but without realizing it, he began to have a positive influence on the other prisoners on his block. Several asked him to pray for them and their families. After a few months, they formed a Bible study group.

One night, Tom began breathing rapidly and heavily in the bunk below. Fred recognized it as a heart attack and called the guard, who arrived then disappeared, going for help. For a full three minutes the priest was left alone with his cellmate, who asked for confession. Automatically, reacting as a priest, Fred listened, his ear close to the man's whispering mouth. He then gave the soothing absolution, trusting God to forgive them both. The man in the next cell, however, an ex-con as well as an embittered ex-Catholic, overheard the whole thing, and the next morning, reported the infraction to the Catholic chaplain, who alerted the Bishop who promptly and officially stripped Father Fred of his priestly faculties.

Months passed. In hindsight, always comparing him to the previous pastor, many of St. Joseph's parishioners began to admit that they had never really given Father Fred a fair chance. Many had indeed noted his deepening depression but did nothing about it because priests are supposed to help people in need, not need help themselves. It was his moral failure more than the fire itself that offended them. That much-publicized conflagration, however, did not destroy the whole church—just part of the apse, which was restored to its former glory within the year. Flowers once again festooned the altar of the Virgin. Ironically, several of the worst gossipers lit candles there for Father Fred.

Fr. Joe contacted the more sympathetic parishioners and initiated a "Free Father Fred" campaign. With the help of his media contacts, some awareness of the harshness of Father Fred's punishment was raised. Yet in the South, possible injustices against Catholics don't galvanize public opinion. The Bishop was particularly irked by Father Joe's weekly column in the diocesan paper, which rarely failed to mention the case, and once, even went so far as to suggest that "*w*hat we need in our diocese is a new outpouring of the Spirit—a new Pentecost to spiritually consume all our tepid, lax, mediocre churches . . . So as to start all over again—purified by the fire of faith and the warmth of love."

Despite all the efforts undertaken on his behalf, not to mention his exemplary behavior, Fr. Fred served every hour of his sentence. After four years, he walked out the prison gate, not knowing exactly where to go or what to do. At the precise moment that Fr. Joe's car pulled up, it began to snow.

Two Inland Souls at Sea

Brendan felt called by God as early as the seventh grade. When his English teacher, a Sister of Mercy, known simply by the religions name of Sr. Mary openly wept the day Martin Luther King was shot, he knew he loved her. Although she was impossibly old for a twelve-year-old—she being all of twenty-two—he loved her for who she was but also for what she represented. That is, he wanted to be like her—capable of loving so deeply. Love and pain, words and beauty, even the horror of a weary world. He loved her joyfulness, and began to desire joy also. Throughout that whole year, he walked about in an infatuated daze, always thinking of her, writing her initials on his textbook covers like most boys his age would do their latest crush. But this was a pure love, springing from a holy font. Her bright face filled his waking mind and beckoned to him in his dreams. During the summer after seventh grade, he wrote to her about them, his dreams—of life and the future. He stated, quite seriously, and repeatedly, that he was ready to give himself to God, simply because she had. In a sense, they were love letters, written by the innocent hand of youth. And the good sister received his avowals with good-humored gravity. There was extreme elation whenever a letter would arrive from her. He would savor her encouraging words for days, contemplating an appropriate reply. Once he even told her that he loved her, something he had certainly never even contemplated before. He loved her because she was a contemplative. And she reciprocated in the same transparent way, writing to him about the basics of prayer.

All was well and all manner of things seemed well until, one day, by God's Providence, his blood sister chanced to meet Sr. Mary at a late summer, preschool, spiritual retreat. There, both of his sisters discovered their little brother's secret. Evidently Sr. Mary had let the cat out of the bag, and upon returning home, Brendan's blood sister tortured him unmercifully: "Brendan's writing to a nuuuunn-nnn . . ." And so on and so forth.

So mortified was Brendan at this apparent breach of confidence that he didn't write to Sister Mary again that summer or, indeed, for seventeen long years after that. And to make matters worse, news spread that she was being transferred, to some other school up in North, a world away. Still smarting from his feelings being exposed to public scrutiny, he entered eighth grade. Even with its prospect of graduation and high school ahead, the future held no attractions. Now, he walked around listlessly, hardly speaking or smiling, the very light gone from his eyes. He spoke when spoken to, and occasionally would erupt into fits of uncustomary stubbornness. He was nominated for class president—based mostly upon his former seventh grade enthusiasm—but ran a lackluster campaign promising longer lunch hours. Not surprisingly, he lost the election by a landslide.

With his eighth grade teacher, Sister Andrew, he was polite but noncommittal, never offering his help for any extracurricular activities. When asked for volunteers to wash the convent floors, he looked at the ceiling. He sensed that something had gone wrong with everything. He felt like an inland soul cast adrift at sea. Sr. Mary's name was hardly ever mentioned publicly, or if it was, was followed by a silent pause. No one seemed to know why, least of all Brendan. But once, out on the playground, he punched one member of his class when the bigger boy suggested that she had left religious life altogether.

After an interminable eighth grade year, graduation was followed by high school. Four years of being bused one hour to and fro. He tried football and wrestling to quench his restlessness. During that first year Brendan made friends with, not exactly the wrong crowd, but not the right one either. He would purposely avoid the popular kids, associating instead with those classmates who had few friends if any. It never occurred to him that he was imitating Sr. Mary, quietly doing good by befriending the unlovable. Life went on. And he tried to forget how charitable Sister Mary had always been to him. His new friends got into trouble regularly, mostly for juvenile pranks, but when they were eventually asked to transfer to the public high school, Brendan inexplicably chose to follow them, although he had done nothing wrong. Brendan's mother was worried since he was the first member of the family ever to attend a non-Catholic school. Phillipstown High was a notorious amalgamation of hippie drug users, race rioters, jocks, and red-neck kids bused in from the surrounding countryside.

Once there, and being ineligible to wrestle or play football for one year, Brendan gave up the idea altogether. He joined an experimental program called the Learning Community which allowed him to skip classes if he completed various independent study projects. After a rigorous Catholic school curriculum, this was a breeze. So in effect he spent most of his time either in the library or in the cafeteria, reading and eating doughnuts, whichever came first. The dean of students passed by regularly, searching for truants, but merely looked at him quizzically, as if to say, "Do I know you? Shouldn't you be in class?" The two final years of his secondary education passed by in this way. The only subject he actually liked was art, so despite a tyrannical instructor, somehow it was decided that his adolescent dream of entering the seminary was for the birds. And those had flown away long ago. Memories of Sister Mary appeared less and less frequently in his mind. But each time they did, he wondered about her, how she was, and where she might be, had she forgotten about him altogether.

After graduation from high school he drove cross-country in a 1969 Volkswagen Beetle to California in the hopes of attending art school. With only modest financial means, he worked during the day and painted at night—enough to amass some tuition and a simple portfolio that got him into the California College of Art. He had been accepted only because the art school's board thought him a "primitive." But when he arrived there and steadfastly painted only recognizable objects—an occupation the faculty themselves had abandoned long ago—the "primitive" misnomer began to wear thin. Every two weeks they tore him apart, verbally, in the "critiques" with sharpened tongues honed on the latest artsy trends. He remained calm throughout, however, knowing that the work was good and they were simply jealous because he could paint and they couldn't As the majority of his colleagues waited idly by for the lightning bolt of inspiration to strike, he labored on quietly in the comer of a basement studio, rarely visited by anyone. He participated in a couple group exhibits only because it was required to receive a bachelor's degree. He was regularly rejected for the more prestigious, "judged" shows. The silent loneliness of putting paint on canvas occupied all his attention and became a form of prayer. Without realizing it he was beginning to pray, and to realize that the images he was creating had a life of their own. And some were even beginning to speak to him. His One-Man-Show before graduation, made it clear that the small, detailed oils were speaking to others as well, since he sold several at respectable prices. The President of the art school even bought two, one for a big benefactor and one for his own home.

Now, if he would only die—he mused—they would really be worth something. After graduation, he continued his silent, solitary existence two blocks from the beach in Santa Monica's Main Street district, before it became fashionable. He painted and wrote, built bookshelves to pay the rent, and wondered where life was leading him. He had always felt that life was more than art. It had never been the "be all and end all" that it was for others, even though he was still producing at a prodigious pace. Living alone in a postage stamp size apartment, in the vicinity of a few like-minded artist friends, they shared the ups and downs of their common vocation plus many a frugal meal. When one had no food the others usually provided. This was his first experience of a nonreligious, starving artist community based upon the virtue of human friendship. Yet he felt some interior longing for something more. He thought it was the desire to fall in love—at least to commit to loving someone—but the few girls he dated were either put off by his poverty or by his growing prayerfulness. They would always call him a "good Catholic boy" even though he only went to Church when visiting his mother.

Then one Lent, he read a book by an obscure German mystic on the Passion of Christ, which made his own attempts at passion pale by comparison. He knew something was definitely changing within, that merely human loves were simply not enough. Every time he passed the parish church he felt a pull on his heartstrings, like the silent call emanating from one of his canvases. He began reading books by the famous Trappist monk, Thomas Merton, The Seven Story Mountain and No Man is An Island. He realized that he was already living as a monk—ascending the mountain as a solitary pilgrim—the only thing lacking was true conversion. Two years' hand-to-mouth existence passed, a good preparation—he realized—for a vow of poverty. Since there was a downturn in the economy and paintings were not selling so well, he decided to do something radical and get a real job. So he moved to Colorado, to work for a friend. Perhaps more money would remove all such crazy thoughts from his head.

Perhaps it was the clear air, but along with his move came an ever-deepening desire for purity. Seeing mountains on the horizon, he found himself praying for sight.

The reward of the pure of heart was to see God—everywhere—not just in oil paint. He began to desire only one thing, even though, at that moment, he couldn't guess what it might be.

Then he met a girl who also happened to be an atheist. She did her best to indoctrinate him while at the same time enticing him to marriage. But how, he wondered, could it be possible to contemplate a life together without God? Then, inexplicably, in the midst of everything, he decided to put his shaky belief to the test and return to the fold. He chose Easter Sunday for his reentry into the rarified atmosphere of commitment. He went alone, walking the few blocks penitentially, as if on pilgrimage. His unbelieving girlfriend warned him of the Church's hypocrisy. Upon entering the doors of Sacred Heart Parish, the priest, rankled at seeing such a late arrival—after the Gospel had been proclaimed, and half-way through his homily—pointed an accusing finger at him, thundering: "If you think you are going to receive communion, then you've got another thing coming!"

Brendan turned around and walked out, accepting the embarrassment as the well-deserved justice from God, saying, "OK, Lord, I get the message, loud and clear." He spent the following week hoping that that was that. His girlfriend said it was an ill-advised attempt, one best never repeated.

Yet despite her relief, he felt an interior urging all week, like the pangs of an unexpressed painting coming on: "Go! Don't be afraid! Go, find another parish." The following Sunday, he went up the hill to St Thomas Aquinas, the university chapel. Again, not knowing the Mass schedule he arrived late, but this time he was quickly accosted by a diminutive, obviously Hispanic couple saying the only two words he had learned from childhood, spending Saturday morning watching Speedy Gonzalez cartoons, *"Ariba! Andele!"* The two grabbed him by the elbows, placed a chalice and paten with hosts in his hands and practically shoved him up the main aisle toward a beaming priest, who stood before the altar with arms wide open. The man seemed more than ready to accept not only the Communion offerings but also the prodigal son himself. Brendan wanted to scream, "Don't you know that I am not worthy to come under your roof!"

That's when everything began to change. Although it was very strange, it seemed natural, like finding the right color. First, Confession lead to a weekly prayer group, then Mass on Sunday lead to daily Mass going. Honesty was the best policy with his evermore antsy girlfriend who, although angry, hardly shed a tear at their parting. Evidently, she could handle him leaving her for another woman but not for an invisible God she didn't believe in. It was the best preparation for a vow of chastity. He quit his job with the intention of painting and living off his meager savings for a year while he discerned what to do. By the following Easter, he was painting overtly religious pictures. Then one day, while layering on a Vermilion glaze, he suddenly heard the words, "You will become a priest." Although he thought the voice, whoever it came from, God or his imagination, had gotten a wrong number, the persistence of such a crank call eventually wore down resistance, until, on the following Easter Sunday, he simply said "yes." He informed his friends over coffee and doughnuts afterward that he was ready for whatever God had in mind for him. And he was surprised to see that they were not surprised.

That summer he spent much time walking along the foothills, praying for a confirmation of his decision. At a parish retreat, a religious sister gave a talk about falling in love with God. When she said she was a Sister of Mercy, he suddenly remembered his old, unrequited love for Sister Mary, wondering if the speaker was from the same community. After the talk, he approached her, saying, "I once had a Sister of Mercy as my seventh grade English teacher."

Before he could finish his sentence, she stopped him, saying, "You must mean my friend Mary." Brendan's heart skipped a beat. Mary, not Sister Mary. Had she left the convent? If she could not persevere, then how could he ever hope to?

Noting the look on his face, the sister explained, "Now, she's a Trappistine nun up in Massachusetts. You know, the same order as Thomas Merton, but for women." Brendan could do nothing but stare at her dumbly. The speaker went on, "Even though they aren't allowed to write very often, we've managed to keep in touch over the years. Would you like her address?" Brendan felt the brushstroke of the Master at work.

So after seventeen years in exile, Brendan wrote one more love letter—asking if Sister Mary still remembered him. Exuding pure joy, Sister Mary replied that after their time together, she had felt a deeper call leading her to the silence and solitude of the cloister, but that she had never stopped praying for him.

About the Author

Paul O'Donnell studied painting, graphic art, and creative writing at the California Institute of the Arts, dreaming of writing illustrated books. After exhibiting paintings and illustrations for a few years, he discerned a further call to enter the Catholic priesthood. Thus began the great adventure that would inspire both his writing and his painting. Studying in Canada, the USA, and Rome, he spent several years in foreign missions until his current posting in Los Angeles as pastor of a large multiethnic parish. Also a musician, he has produced six CDs of original songs.

CPSIA information can be obtained
at www.ICGtesting.com
Printed in the USA
FSHW021457110719
59919FS

9 781640 829718